Make Do and Mend in Applewell

Lilac Mills lives on a Welsh mountain with her very patient husband and incredibly sweet dog, where she grows veggies (if the slugs don't get them), bakes (badly) and loves making things out of glitter and glue (a mess, usually). She's been an avid reader ever since she got her hands on a copy of *Noddy Goes to Toytown* when she was five, and she once tried to read everything in her local library starting with A and working her way through the alphabet. She loves long, hot summer days and cold winter ones snuggled in front of the fire, but whatever the weather she's usually writing or thinking about writing, with heartwarming romance and happy-ever-afters always on her mind.

Also by Lilac Mills

A Very Lucky Christmas
Sunshine at Cherry Tree Farm
Summer on the Turquoise Coast
Love in the City by the Sea

Tanglewood Village series

The Tanglewood Tea Shop
The Tanglewood Flower Shop
The Tanglewood Wedding Shop

Island Romance

Sunrise on the Coast
Holiday in the Hills
Sunset on the Square

Applewell Village

Waste Not, Want Not in Applewell
Make Do and Mend in Applewell

LILAC MILLS

Make Do and Mend in Applewell

CANELO

First published in the United Kingdom in 2021 by

Canelo
31 Helen Road
Oxford OX2 0DF
United Kingdom

A CIP catalogue record for this book is available from the British Library.

Print ISBN 978 1 80032 314 8
Ebook ISBN 978 1 80032 313 1

Look for more great books at www.canelo.co

Printed and bound in Great Britain by Clays Ltd, Elcograf S.p.A.

1

Chapter 1

Henry

'I'm sorry, I really am. Believe me, I don't like this any more than you do, but we have to let three salesmen go, and as it's last in first out, regrettably, you are one of them.' Paula from HR steepled her fingers under her chin and gave Henry a sympathetic smile, the kind that was more a compression of the lips than an actual smile. She tilted her head to the side, which was also supposed to portray empathy – as well as to encourage him to say something.

Henry Hargreaves didn't think Paula from HR regretted anything: he was just a number to her, and to the company he worked for. He hoped she'd never find out just how dispensable she herself was, but he suspected she probably would.

'Is there anything you'd like to ask me? Any further information I can give you?' False sympathy oozed from her voice.

'When do I leave, and how much do I get?' He knew he sounded brusque, but this was the second time in six months he'd been in this position, and his mind had gone numb. Redundancy had been the last thing he'd expected when he had been summoned to head office this morning. He'd guessed something was up because he'd been instructed to rearrange all of today's appointments, and the head office of Baldwin Ltd was a three-hour drive there and back. They wouldn't have asked him to attend a meeting at such notice if it wasn't important, but he'd been thinking the reason for it was more along the lines of extending his territory. Andrew Mordant, who covered South West Wales – Henry's area was Mid and West Wales – had tipped him the wink that he was leaving which, as far as Henry was concerned, would open up a whole new area for Henry to move into.

Of course, it would involve considerably more travelling and he hadn't been looking forward to that, but as long as he could return to the bosom of his family in the evening, he would have been prepared to put in the longer hours.

'We are giving you one month's notice but as for any redundancy payment… Unfortunately, you've only been with us for such a short period.' Paula sent him another one of her sympathetic smiles, and Henry suddenly felt like crying. She handed him a letter. 'This is your formal notification. Sorry,' she repeated.

Henry took it dully. He didn't bother reading it – there wasn't any point.

What the hell was he going to say to Lottie?

Dazed, he got to his feet, nodded at the HR manager and staggered outside on wooden legs.

Twice in six months! Once was unfortunate and couldn't be helped. Twice must mean there was something wrong with him. Wasn't he doing his job properly? He'd taken over an established territory, the previous salesman having retired, so it wasn't as though Henry had had to build everything up from scratch. Admittedly, sales hadn't been as good as he'd hoped, but farming was a declining industry, especially animal husbandry.

It was already the middle of November. In a little over a month he'd have no income. At least he'd had a bit of a payout from his previous employer, having worked for them for nearly thirteen years. And he'd been able to get another job fairly quickly, so that money was still sitting in their savings account. But it wasn't going to last forever, though, was it? And what about the extension they were planning on? What about *Christmas*? What a crappy thing to do to someone at this time of year.

Henry needed to go home and start looking for another job immediately. He knew from the last time that there were jobs out there – so maybe it would be for the best if he didn't mention anything to his wife just yet? How much better would it sound if he could say, 'Sorry, Lottie, I've been made redundant again, but don't worry as I've found another job and I'm starting it next week.' Besides, he didn't want to spoil Christmas for her or the children, and he certainly didn't want her fretting about being able to afford to buy Christmas presents.

He got in his car, thankful it was his own vehicle and not a company car, and threw his briefcase in the back, before realising he still had the letter in his hand. Not wanting Lottie to see it, he reached behind, snagged the handle of the briefcase on the back seat and drew it towards him. After stuffing the letter inside, he started the engine and made his slow, steady way home across country.

The familiar sights as he neared home set his teeth on edge. Applewell was a little village two miles from the sea in the depths of West Wales, surrounded by farmland and rolling hills. If the wind was in the right direction, which it nearly always was, you could smell ozone and salt in the air. It was beautiful, but Applewell meant home, and home meant Lottie and having to lie to her by omission.

There was another reason he wasn't looking forward to arriving home this evening, and that was the children. He loved them dearly and he'd lay down his life for them, but dear God they were hard work, and so *noisy*. He was exhausted, defeated and depressed, and not in the mood to be clambered over and shouted at.

It would be teatime in about half an hour and he could picture the scene: Lottie in the kitchen cooking, trying to keep her eye on Morgan, their youngest at two and a half, while Sabrina, ten, and Robin, six, played havoc upstairs. The brother and sister argued continually, and after a day at work he sometimes found it draining.

When he was about a mile or so outside the village, Henry pulled into a small lay-by and wound down the window. The air was chilly, a stiff breeze blowing past the car, and it was starting to get dark, the sky laden with heavy clouds. Cows lowing in a nearby field made him twist in his seat to stare at them through the bars of a metal gate. They were a typical herd of Welsh Blacks, hardy and with shaggy coats, and not easy to see in the encroaching darkness. The one closest to him was busily nosing a pile of hay which the farmer had left to supplement the meagre grass at this time of year. It was so quiet Henry thought he could hear the beast munching.

A robin landed on the gate and chirped noisily, cross with the human intrusion into its territory, before darting away, allowing the silence to descend once more as a steady drizzle began to fall. He breathed in deeply, the air redolent with the scent of winter and a hint of cow, and he tried not to cry as he rested his head back on his seat and closed his eyes, wishing he could stay there forever, despite the increasing chill. An old poem came to mind, something about having the time to stop and stare at cows.

It looked like he was going to have all the time in the world to stop and stare at them before too long, and his stomach turned over.

He'd only just settled into this new job, and now he was going to have to look for another one. The thought of attending interviews, trying to sell himself all over again and persuade a stranger in a suit to employ him, made him feel sick. He didn't mind selling – he was a salesman, for goodness' sake, and good at it – but it was one thing selling a product, and quite another altogether to convince a potential employer you were good enough.

For some reason Henry never did feel good enough. Sales, no matter what the product you were trying to shift, was often a precarious business when it came to the salesman's income. He said *salesman*, but it was just as likely to be a *saleswoman*, and he was the first to admit that women were as good, if not better, at convincing people to buy stuff. Anyway, he was getting sidetracked from what was important, which was that traditionally nearly all sales jobs had a basic salary plus a commission. Therefore what you earned was reflected by what you sold. Henry knew his market inside out, but there were only so many companies out there selling animal feed, and he didn't have the luxury of waiting for a suitable job to come up. Thoughts of having to learn the ins and outs of an entirely different product made him wince. He couldn't imagine trying to sell photocopying paper, for instance, or medical supplies.

He didn't know how long he stayed in the lay-by watching the rain turn to snow on the windscreen and darkness descend outside, but eventually Henry knew he had to make a move. It didn't look as though the snow was sticking, but weather conditions could change fast and he didn't want to get caught out.

Reflexively, he checked his phone, and saw there was a couple of texts from Lottie along the lines of, 'Any idea when you'll be home?' and 'I'll put your tea in the oven, shall I?'

Feeling guilty, he glanced at the clock on the dash. It was now gone six, but he'd be home in ten minutes, so he didn't bother replying.

As he drove through the village, he noticed that the majority of shops had closed for the day, despite the festive lights already shining in most of the window displays, although Sid, who owned the newsagent, would probably keep his shop open for some time yet. And of course the pub didn't shut until late. He was tempted to drop in for a pint but thought about the money which he now couldn't afford to spend, and decided he'd better not. For one thing he had to save the pennies, and, for another, if Lottie smelt alcohol on his breath she'd wonder what he'd been up to. He might go for a pint on a Friday evening or sometimes on a Saturday if the rugby was on, but never during the week, not unless they were on holiday, and he didn't want her becoming suspicious and asking awkward questions.

Their house lay on the outskirts of the village, easily walkable to the shops, but not in the thick of things where parking could become an issue in high summer. Although Applewell wasn't right by the sea, many tourists popped into the village to stock up on supplies, or for a meal at the pub or a bite to eat in Eleri Jones's cafe.

Henry and Lottie's house was on a small hill, with a drive leading up to it and views out towards the west. Unfortunately, it was too far away to catch sight of the sea, but they were within strolling distance of a small valley with a stream running through it which led down to a secluded cove. So far it had escaped the notice of most tourists, so it was almost as though the villagers had their own private beach.

It was one of the many things he loved about Applewell; that, and the way everyone looked out for each other. There was definitely a lot to be said for village life, and if you wanted anything livelier, Aberystwyth was only a half-hour drive away to the north. Although it could hardly be called a metropolis, it was their nearest town and they could get most things there. In an ideal world he might even be able to get a job there, but he wasn't going to hold his breath.

Henry manoeuvred the car up the drive, which was a bit hairy in the icy conditions, and pulled up alongside the house. His heart sank again as he looked at it. Henry loved his house; what he didn't love was the hefty mortgage that went with it. It was a four-bed detached house – the fourth bedroom was tiny – with white rendering and draughty windows. They'd bought it just before they'd got married and had lived in it ever since. It had been too big for just the two of them initially, but with the arrival of first one child, then a second and, to their immense surprise, a third, it now felt slightly claustrophobic. They were planning on extending the kitchen into the garden to create a large, open-plan family room, but it wasn't going to be cheap – though it would be cheaper than moving. And it would be nice if Morgan could have a larger bedroom too, at some point, so they'd also planned on extending the upstairs, to create a new bedroom for themselves, with an en suite. The thought of having his own shower, and not having to vie to use the one in the family bathroom, usually lifted Henry's spirits. But not this evening: all he could think about was how they were going to pay for it.

Once again he considered and dismissed the thought of telling Lottie about his imminent redundancy. He took a deep breath and nodded to himself. He'd soon get another job.

Henry extricated himself from the car, pulling his briefcase with him. It was battered and old, but he didn't think shiny new things went down particularly well with his clientele – unless it was a tractor, or a piece of machinery which could be attached to a tractor. To fit in, he dressed like a farmer: waxed cotton jacket, old jeans, a pair of Wellington boots in the back of his car just in case he had to negotiate muddy, muck-strewn farmyards. He used a pair of old trainers for driving, only changing into his wellies when he got to where he was going. He even kept a flat cap on the parcel shelf for cold or rainy days, and a bobble hat for wintry ones like today. He also drove an older model four-by-four whose paintwork had seen better days. It was dusty and dirty, and that was just the way he liked it.

'Daddy, Daddy, Daddy!' His youngest, Morgan, squealed, the minute he spotted his father walk into the kitchen. The little boy wriggled down from his chair and launched himself across the room, wrapping his arms around his father's legs while trying to jump up and down at the same time, and almost headbutting him in the groin.

Henry grimaced and tried to hold Morgan down before his manhood sustained a serious injury.

Robin, their six-year-old, waved a spoon at him, a gobbet of red sauce splattering the wall next to him. Sabrina, their oldest at ten, merely rolled her eyes. Was it his imagination or were children growing up at a younger and younger age? He hadn't thought ten was when teenage ennui began, but when it came to his daughter it clearly had. She was an interesting mix of child and teenager: one minute she was enjoying being carted around on his back as she played horses with him; the next she was doing the shrug and eye-roll thing, which teenagers everywhere seemed to have perfected.

Shuffling forwards with Morgan still attached to him like a limpet, Henry gave Lottie a quick peck on the cheek. 'It's started to snow,' he said, 'but I don't think it's going to come to much.' He hoped not, because if it did he wouldn't be able to visit the customers who were booked in tomorrow.

All three children had been having their tea, sitting at the cramped kitchen table, and Lottie was rinsing the pans she'd used to make the meal. It had been spaghetti bolognese, by the look of it.

He felt guilty, because if he had been home in time, or at least had answered her text and told her he'd only be a few minutes, Lottie wouldn't have gone ahead and fed the children, and they could all have eaten together as a family.

'Have you had yours?' he asked, and his wife shook her head, a lock of hair coming loose from the scruffy bun on the top of her head, the pencil she'd used to pin it up with wobbling around.

She looked harassed, her cheeks a little pink from the heat of the stove, and she had a spot of paint on her cheek. He wondered what she'd been doing today, and he hoped that whatever it was, she'd had a much better day than he'd had.

'I thought I'd wait and eat with you,' she said, but they both knew that although she might put her plate on the table, she would be jumping up and down throughout the course of her meal to see to one or the other of the children. Sabrina wouldn't be a bother, as she usually disappeared off to her room after she'd eaten, and possibly Robin would occupy himself in the living room without needing his mother constantly. It was Morgan who would demand her attention for one thing or another, from now until he went to bed. Even after he was tucked up under the duvet, he continually called down the stairs, wanting his nightlight on or off, or saying he was feeling thirsty, or needing the toilet. The list of things he required his mother to do was endless.

Henry wrestled Morgan free and plonked him back on his seat. 'Finish your tea,' he instructed, and the little boy obediently picked up his spoon but made no move to dip it into his bowl.

'Feed me, Daddy!' he demanded, but Henry just pushed the bowl closer.

'You're a big boy now; you can feed yourself.'

'But I want you to do it. I'm *not* a big boy.' Morgan thrust his bottom lip out and scowled.

'You're going to have to be. Mummy is busy and Daddy's going for a shower.'

'Read me a story before bed?'

Henry saw a way in. 'Only if you feed yourself, and you eat it all,' he said.

'I want *The Very Hungry Caterpillar.*'

'I bet the very hungry caterpillar would have eaten all *his* tea by now,' Henry pointed out. 'Finish your food, then perhaps Mummy will put some cartoons on TV for you while Mummy and Daddy eat theirs.'

'Yay, cartoons!'

—

When Henry returned to the kitchen after having had a quick shower, he noticed that between the promise of watching TV and his father reading a story to him later, Morgan had discovered that he was in fact a big boy and could feed himself.

Henry always washed off the farmyard grime before he sat down to eat, and although he'd been nowhere near a farmyard today, he didn't want to risk Lottie asking questions. He'd never been very good at pulling the wool over her eyes — he thought back to her surprise thirtieth birthday party, which hadn't been any kind of surprise at all — so he'd have to be ultra-careful if he wanted to appear to be his usual self. *Bloody hell, this is worse than being in MI5*, he thought. *And today's only day one of trying to pretend everything's normal.*

Sabrina finished her meal, pushed her chair back and leapt to her feet. 'I've got homework,' she announced. 'Spellings.' She didn't look pleased about it. Henry didn't think he would be, either — spelling wasn't his strong point. 'And chunking,' she added.

Henry shot Lottie a confused look and mouthed, 'What's chunking?'

Lottie sighed. 'Maths, apparently. Excuse me, young lady, you know the rules. Rinse your plate off and put it in the dishwasher before you go upstairs.'

'Mu-u-um.' Sabrina did the eye-roll thing again. 'I've got homework.'

'Yes, we heard you the first time, but it'll only take a few seconds to carry your plate from the table to the sink, rinse it, and put it in the dishwasher.'

'Do I have to do *everything* around here?' was their daughter's muttered response.

Robin finished his meal shortly afterwards too, and took his plate to the sink without being asked. 'If Morgan is allowed to watch cartoons, can I?'

Henry heard the unspoken subtext of how it wouldn't be fair if Morgan was allowed to watch TV after tea, and Robin wasn't. The kids were very quick to spot the slightest unintentional preferential treatment of one over the other.

'Only if you let Morgan watch something he wants to watch,' Lottie said. 'Have you got any homework?'

Robin shook his head vigorously and Henry guessed he was fibbing.

He sat down in Robin's newly vacated chair and put his elbows on the table, resting his head in his hands.

'I've finished, Mummy,' Morgan declared, his bowl of food only half eaten.

'Good boy.' Lottie lifted him down off the chair and sent him into the living room with a pat on his bottom.

'I told him he had to eat it all,' Henry objected, lifting his head and looking at his wife.

'I know you did, but he's eaten enough. He's never had much of an appetite, and I always give him too much in the hope he'll eat more. Are you hungry?'

Henry most definitely wasn't, but he knew it would look odd if he said no so he nodded and Lottie reheated the pasta and the sauce, and retrieved some rather dry-looking garlic bread from the oven.

With the plates on the table, she slid into her seat opposite and picked up her fork. 'Did you want some wine to go with this?' she asked.

'Are you having some?' It was unusual for her to have a drink on a week night.

'It's been one of those days,' Lottie said.

'Why's that?'

Before she could tell him, there was a loud bang from upstairs and Lottie froze, a forkful of spaghetti halfway to her mouth. An ominous silence followed.

Lottie took a deep breath and let it out slowly. 'I'd better go and see what's happened.'

She leapt up and was out of the room before he could move, so Henry used the opportunity to empty half of the spaghetti into the bin, thinking he could probably manage to eat the resulting portion.

His wife came back into the kitchen, shaking her head, with Sabrina and Robin hot on her heels.

'He did it on purpose, Dad,' Sabrina said. She looked smug.

'I didn't!' Robin's face was red and he seemed close to tears.

'What's happened?' Henry asked, not sure if he really wanted to know.

Lottie told him, 'Robin has managed to break his bed. He was jumping up and down on it, apparently.'

'I wasn't.' Robin now looked sullen, his little cheeks puffed out in a pout, his eyes narrowed. He folded his arms across his chest.

'Beds don't just collapse by themselves,' Lottie pointed out. 'Somebody must have been doing something.' She sat down and picked up her fork again, eating a mouthful of the rapidly cooling spaghetti and grimacing. She chewed, swallowed, then pushed her plate away. Henry felt like doing the same – he'd only taken a couple of bites of his and it had felt like eating straw.

'It's because he wants a new one,' said Sabrina.

Instead of denying it, as Henry would have expected, Robin was strangely silent, and he guessed his daughter had hit the nail on the head. 'Can you fix it?' he asked Lottie, praying she'd say yes. He didn't want to shell out for a new one.

'There are a couple of slats broken, but I've got some wood in the shed that should do the trick,' she said.

Henry smiled to himself when he saw Robin's face darken further. 'Did you break it on purpose?' he asked his son.

Robin shook his head, but refused to meet his father's eyes.

'Beds don't grow on trees,' Henry said, aware the child was fibbing, but unable to prove he'd broken it deliberately. 'They cost money, and if Mummy can't fix it you won't have a bed at all.'

'I can mend it,' Lottie said, with a sigh. 'Let's just hope Father Christmas doesn't get to hear about it.'

Robin glared at Lottie, turned smartly on his heel and stomped out of the kitchen, Sabrina following closely behind.

Henry heard the sounds of his daughter taunting his middle child as they galloped up the stairs, and he waited for the noise to subside before he asked, 'What was all that about?'

'This is why I need that glass of wine,' she said, going to the fridge and taking out a bottle. She grabbed some glasses from the cupboard and poured them both a measure. 'Callum, one of his friends in school, told him he's got a new bed in the shape of a fire engine.'

'And now Robin wants one?' Henry tried not to guzzle his wine too quickly.

'It seems so, and he probably could do with a new one, but I can't justify the expense if I can repair the one he's got,' his wife said.

Henry agreed with her; not because he was a particular advocate of Lottie's mantra of not buying anything new unless it was strictly needed, but because he didn't want to spend the money. How much did new beds cost? Especially ones in the shape of fire engines?

Even if they could afford it, Henry knew that if he suggested treating Robin to a bedroom makeover, Lottie would probably refuse on the grounds there was nothing wrong with their son's room the way it was. She'd always been thrifty and preferred to mend or repurpose what they already had, rather than buy new, but Henry was filled with such guilt that he couldn't do something as simple as make his little boy's bedroom into a magical place for him to retreat to, that for the second time that day he wanted to cry.

Something must have shown in his face, because Lottie said, 'There's nothing wrong with the bed Robin has got; nothing that a few planks of wood and some screws can't fix. I know we're saving every penny we've got towards the extension and there's Christmas coming up, but I'm sure I can think of something to brighten up his bedroom. I could maybe paint a mural on the wall, and I've got some plywood somewhere that I could cut into some kind of a shape. Possibly not enough to make a fire engine, but I could certainly do something. His room *is* rather babyish, isn't it?'

Henry bit his lip when she mentioned the extension. If he wasn't able to walk from one job into another straight away, their timeline would be pushed back and he knew how much Lottie had set her heart on having a bit more space. It was almost laughable that a four-bedroomed house could seem so small, but it did. The rooms themselves were snug, and with five people, it felt as though they were living on top of one another, and the acoustics were dreadful. He used to joke that if a spider broke wind in the living room, it would be heard all over the house.

It had got to the point that romantic encounters with his wife had been few and far between since Morgan's birth. His room was right next to theirs and Henry suspected the master bedroom and Morgan's room had once been one larger room. Whoever had split them in two should have used some decent soundproofing. Not only that, Morgan was a light sleeper at the best of times, so the slightest noise would wake him up and have him calling for his mummy.

Henry couldn't remember the last time he and Lottie had made love, and he knew they desperately needed some space and some time to themselves. The new bedroom in the extension promised to give them that – *if* it ever got built.

Chapter 2

Lottie

Pins to Elephants was one of Lottie's favourite places. The shop sold an eclectic mix of household stuff, such as vacuum cleaner bags and pepper pots, items for the garden, electrical goods, and – Lottie's weakness – DIY things. Where other women became gooey-eyed over shoes and handbags, Lottie had her head turned by glue guns and ceramic tiles.

She recognised this wasn't usual behaviour for a woman in her thirties but she didn't care. With a whopping mortgage, three kids and a husband whose salary fluctuated like the weather, she felt she had little choice. Making do and mending was a part of her life, and if it meant she'd become a dab hand at fixing things, then so be it.

Today she was on the hunt for L-shaped brackets to repair Robin's bed. She had no doubt that her middle child had jumped up and down on it in the hope it would break and she'd be forced to buy him a new one. One part of his wish had come true; the other part, not so much.

After selling their souls to buy the house in Applewell over a decade ago, money had been very tight indeed for her and Henry and she'd quickly taught herself how to do a variety of things. Repairing furniture had been one of them.

For the first couple of years, Henry had accompanied her to boot sales and they'd had fun picking up bargains, especially when they became pregnant with Sabrina, and the cost of bringing up first one child, and then a second, had sent all thoughts of furnishing their home with expensive and stylish items out of the window. But for Henry, the novelty of buying other people's unwanted items had worn off.

Sometimes she felt Henry resented her ability to make do and mend. It might save them a small fortune, but she got the impression that he hated they had to do it in the first place.

Lottie handed over a ten-pound note to Tony behind the counter and popped the brackets in her bag, exchanging a few words with him as she did so. She had the feeling she might be the man's favourite customer: she spent more time in Pins to Elephants than she did in any other shop, except for the charity shop down the road. Which reminded her, Sabrina needed new school shoes soon.

Lamenting that she had to buy those new – she religiously had the children's feet measured and fitted whenever they needed their footwear replacing – she called in to the charity shop anyway. She often did, on the off-chance she'd find something that would come in useful. At this time of year she was especially on the lookout for toys and other gifts, although it was becoming harder to buy second-hand things for Sabrina. Robin and Morgan were easier – last Christmas she'd bought Robin a bicycle which looked almost as good as new, and a couple of years before that she'd bought a doll's house for Sabrina, and had spent ages doing it up in the shed after the kids had gone to bed. It still had pride of place on top of Sabrina's chest of drawers, although Lottie didn't think her daughter had played with it for a long time.

'Morning,' Catrin trilled, chirpily. She was the manager of this particular branch of UnderCover, which was a charity for the homeless and had shops in various locations throughout Wales. Catrin ran her shop with the help of a couple of volunteers and copious amounts of good cheer. Lottie didn't think she'd ever seen the woman with a frown on her face. 'We've just had an old gramophone player in – would you be interested?'

'I don't think so, as lovely as it is,' Lottie replied, gazing at the machine and seeing a stack of records next to it. She picked one up. Vinyl was supposed to be coming back into fashion, but despite liking anything vintage, Lottie knew her kids would look at it with horror. She couldn't justify the expense, either.

'How's things?' Catrin asked, folding a Welsh blanket and adding it to a pile of similar ones.

Lottie eyed it with longing – she loved those traditional woollen blankets and had a couple which she wrapped herself up in on those evenings when it wasn't quite chilly enough to warrant lighting their wood-burning stove.

'Robin broke his bed yesterday, so I've been buying some brackets,' she said. 'I swear to God he did it on purpose. He was only just telling me that one of his friends has a new bed in the shape of a fire engine.'

Lottie was the first to admit that her son's bed wasn't exciting, but at least he had one. *Think of all those poor children in the world who don't have a bed*, she'd felt like telling him, but had held back, knowing he would neither appreciate nor understand. At six, he was more interested in what his friends had than what some abstract kids who he'd never met didn't have.

'I used to want a four-poster when I was young,' Catrin said. 'I never got one and it didn't do me any harm, so stop beating yourself up over it.'

'Is it that obvious?'

'Yes. Just because kids want something, it doesn't mean to say they should automatically have it.'

'That's true. Although, to be fair, my children often ask for things and don't get them.'

'Are they healthy and happy?' Catrin asked.

'I suppose so.'

'Well, then, you're doing your job. Fancy a cuppa? I've got biscuits...' She waggled her eyebrows and Lottie giggled.

'Go on, but I can't be long. I've got some planks of wood to saw.'

'And I've got three black bags of donated goods to sort out. We lead such exciting lives.'

–

After a welcome cup of tea and a custard cream, Lottie was on her way back home. Her mind kept drifting to the contents of her shed.

She called the large outbuilding *hers* because Henry rarely ventured inside and hadn't done for years, and he didn't have a clue what was in there. Lottie, however, did, and right then she was thinking about two four-inch by four-inch posts she knew were in there. The finish on them was crude because they were meant for outside use, but maybe she could sand them down and paint them, or cover them in fabric... Catrin mentioning a four-poster had started her thinking that Sabrina might like to have her bed updated – after Lottie had managed to do something with Robin's, of course. Lottie had an image of a fairy-tale princess concoction for one brief nostalgic moment, before she realised Sabrina would consider it too babyish.

She'd have to have a think and, while she was at it, she needed to root through some of the stuff in the shed and see if she could find something with which to magically transform Robin's bed.

Lottie and Henry had always been careful with money but since their little scare last year when Henry had been made redundant, she'd been even more conscious of their precarious financial situation. Thankfully he'd found another job more or less straight away, so they'd put his modest redundancy payment into a savings account until they had enough funds to start the extension. She wasn't looking forward to all the upheaval, but she was sure it would be worth it in the end, although Henry seemed to want it more than she did.

She could tell he was cross about Robin breaking his bed yesterday evening and guessed it wasn't solely because it would have to be repaired or replaced. He was irked because they didn't have any spare cash to throw around and, like any parent, he wanted to be able to give his children nice things. Just as she did. But Catrin was right, kids didn't need everything they wanted, and Robin didn't *need* a fire engine bed.

She could see the end in sight, though. They were being sensible and not taking out a loan to fund the extension. They wouldn't begin building it until they had enough savings to pay for it, and they were almost there. Henry's brother-in-law would be doing the build (on the side), so it wasn't going to be nearly as expensive as it might have otherwise been.

Lottie wasn't looking forward to her house being a building site, with all the disruption that went with it, including having to move Morgan in with Robin for the duration. He'd have Robin awake at stupid o'clock, which meant she'd have a tired and grumpy six-year-old on her hands for what could be months.

It was OK for Henry – he didn't have to deal with the chaos of mornings in the Hargreaves' house. Getting three children dressed and out of the door in time for school – nursery in Morgan's case – wasn't easy. And neither was it any easier after they came home. Making sure the two eldest did their homework was a feat in itself; then there were the after-school clubs and activities, which had to be walked to because there weren't enough funds for her to have a car of her own, which sometimes meant bundling up two children and trekking back to the school gates – where she'd already stood outside once that day – to collect the third.

She supposed Sabrina was old enough to make her own way home from the cute little primary school in the heart of the village, but Lottie simply couldn't bring herself to allow her daughter the freedom. Not yet – she wasn't ready. Lottie wasn't, that was: Sabrina was more than ready, as she often let her mother know in no uncertain terms.

As soon as Lottie got home, she began clearing away the debris from that morning's mad dash to get the kids out of the door. They'd almost been late again, which was a daily occurrence ever since Morgan had informed her that he wanted to walk and was too big a boy to use the pushchair. *Dawdle* was the term she used, not *walk*, but she had to forgive him because he was so young and he only had little legs. More than once she'd had to send the older two on ahead because they were going to be late for class, her heart in her mouth as they galloped along the pavement, she and Morgan hurrying behind as best they could.

Morgan had recently started attending nursery in the mornings for two and a half hours a day, three days a week, and today was one of those mornings. Lottie relished being able to wander around the village without a toddler in tow, and she also revelled in having the house to herself, however briefly.

With the toys and assorted clothing gathered up, the breakfast things put away, and the vacuum cleaner given a swift outing in the living room, Lottie was ready to take a proper look at Robin's bed. She'd had to wrestle the mattress onto the floor last night, and he'd got under the duvet with a blend of excitement and dismay on his face. She could just imagine him boasting to his friends that he'd broken his bed and had to sleep on the floor. Conversely, she could also imagine him complaining to Mrs Campbell, his long-suffering teacher, that he'd been forced to sleep on the floor, leaving Lottie half expecting to hear a knock at the door and find a couple of social workers on the step.

It didn't take long for her to measure up the planks of wood and cut them to size. Once they were in place on the frame, she used the brackets to secure them, then pressed down hard on the planks to check they wouldn't give way, before heaving Robin's mattress back on the frame and remaking his bed.

Dusting her hands off, she put her tools away, then went to fetch her youngest son from nursery.

'Goes quickly, doesn't it?' her friend, Delia, said to her as she approached the school gates and joined the crowd of other parents, who were stamping their feet and complaining about the cold. Thankfully yesterday's smattering of snow had disappeared overnight, much to the children's dismay. 'It's the fastest couple of hours in the week.'

'I know what you mean.' Lottie laughed. 'But at least Morgan will be knackered, so I might get some peace after he's had his lunch.'

Morgan was at that stage where he sometimes had an afternoon nap and sometimes didn't. When he did, Lottie had an awful job to get him to go to sleep at his usual bedtime, but when he didn't he was as cranky as could be, and she would spent most of the early evening prodding him to keep him awake until his proper bedtime.

'Fancy going to the park tomorrow?' Delia asked. 'The weather forecast looks decent enough and as long as we dress up warm, we should be all right. I find it helps if I wear out Tyrone in the morning. If I don't, he can be a right little so and so by mid-afternoon.'

They made arrangements to meet at ten o'clock, which would give Lottie enough time to drop Sabrina and Robin off at school, get back home to quickly tidy up, put a load of washing on and pop it on the radiators to dry, make some snacks – Morgan would be sure to be hungry – and dash out of the door again.

Slightly resentfully, she thought of Henry's calm exit from the house that morning. He'd rolled out of bed while the children were eating their breakfast, had taken an uninterrupted shower, then had eaten his own peaceful breakfast while she wrestled with three reluctant children, trying to get them dressed. By the time she was downstairs with them, he was ready to leave.

She pushed the irritation away firmly. She sometimes begrudged the amount of time Henry had to himself without the constant worry of looking after the children, and she knew he occasionally resented that she didn't go out to work and was able to stay at home all day, but they'd played the who-has-the-worse-end-of-the-stick game for far too long.

They each had their roles and they each realised the necessity of them – but both of them could still have a tendency to think the other one's grass was greener. To be fair to Henry, he was a very hands-on dad and it wasn't his fault that the majority of the childcare fell to her. But sometimes she couldn't help being annoyed that he was able to walk away for several hours a day, and she wasn't. To her shame, she was actively looking forward to when Morgan was in school full time, but unfortunately that was still well over a year away.

She felt even more ashamed when she thought she should be enjoying this time when her children were young. It was a time you could never get back – once it was gone, it was gone, and she did relish it, she honestly did, but sometimes it became a little overwhelming.

It hadn't helped that last night Henry had been distant and surly. She'd put it down to Robin having deliberately broken his bed, but it wasn't as though Henry had been forced to get his screwdriver out and mend the damned thing himself; she'd taken care of it, the way she always took care of everything.

There it was again, that little bubbling pool of resentment deep inside her.

If she wasn't careful, the pool would turn into an ocean
and it just might drown her.

Chapter 3

Henry

John Porter's farm was the other end of the village to Henry's house, at the top of Oak Lane, which turned into a sort of a dirt track and ended up at Porter's Farm. Henry's predecessor had been going there for years, which was quite funny in a way, considering Henry lived less than half a mile away. John had always bought his feed from the company Henry was working at now, and farmers were often conservative in some respects, and loyal too. If they found a company, a salesman, or a brand they liked, they tended to stick with it, come hell or high water; although there was a trend, and a growing one at that, for more innovation in the farming industry, and unfortunately this innovation was impacting on sales – so Henry wasn't surprised when John shook his head after shaking Henry's hand.

'I don't think I'm ready to order from you yet,' John said, taking his cap off and scratching his head, before putting it back on again. 'I'm scaling down the dairy herd, see.'

'You are? Why is that?' Henry asked, although he was pretty sure he knew the answer: simple economics. No matter how much a farmer loved their animals, if they didn't pay the bills they couldn't continue to farm them.

'Come and see.' John walked away across the yard and into the barn, where cows could be heard grumbling noisily amongst themselves.

Henry followed. He'd automatically put his wellies on as soon as he'd pulled up into the yard, so he was happy enough to traipse into the barn and see what John was talking about.

A long row of black, bovine faces peered at him through the bars of some sturdy fencing, contentedly munching a pile of hay. They were Welsh Black cattle and Henry's heart sank. He mightn't be a farmer himself, but he'd been in the agricultural industry long enough to know what Welsh Blacks signified. A hardy breed, they usually over-wintered outside, where they birthed their calves with the minimum of fuss. Unlike most other breeds, they could withstand brutal temperatures as long as they had enough fodder, and they didn't need rich, green grass either as they were quite happy with rough grazing, eating more or less anything growing on a hillside or in a field. As a result, they didn't need to be brought into the barns during winter, with all the additional expense that brought to the farmer, and it meant they only needed the occasional bale of hay, and maybe a sack or two of cattle nuts now and again. Their need for supplementary feed was nothing when compared to the Friesians John Porter had favoured in the past.

'I got 'em mainly for beef,' John said. 'But they'll give some milk, too, and with both the meat and the dairy, we can keep the farm shop going.'

'I didn't know you had a shop,' Henry said. 'I knew you supplied some of the local outlets with butter and milk…'

'We're converting one of the sheds. Come and have a look.'

Once more Henry was led across the yard, towards the farmhouse this time, although they didn't go in; instead they swung past it and around the side, stopping beside a building with a relatively new roof, new windows and a new door.

'We've got the necessary paperwork to sell our cheese, butter and milk on-site, as well as our own beef products. I'll still be running a dairy herd, but it won't be half the size it was. I'm thinking of branching into pigs, too.'

'You are?'

'Not as fussy as sheep; they don't need so much messing with. You've always gotta be dipping sheep, or clipping their hooves, or shearing, or doing something or other with them. You don't have that with pigs. And we can sell the pork alongside the prime beef I'm gonna get from my Welsh Blacks.' John's smile faltered. 'We've got to make changes,' he said, 'else we're gonna go under.'

'Oh, dear.' Henry was well aware of the difficulties farmers faced. It was either intensive farming on an industrial scale, or they ran the risk of going to the wall. Small farmers like John found it hard to compete, so Henry understood perfectly why the man was branching out and trying to cut his overheads.

'You've got to diversify to make a living in this game,' John said. 'Have a unique selling point.'

'I understand.' It wasn't the first time Henry had heard this story. He'd lost count of the number of times he'd been to farms, over the course of his career, only to discover that the farmer had gone out of business. He'd forgotten the statistics, but it was quite alarming how many farm businesses folded in one year alone.

'We've still got a bit of work to do in the shop,' John was saying. 'We haven't finished kitting it out yet, and there's still some stuff to shift.' He pointed to a huge pile of rubbish on one side.

Henry was impressed by the man's drive and dedication. Farming was hard work, and he was certain he didn't want to do it, but he supposed if you were born into it and it was in your blood, you carried on regardless, if you could. It was just a shame that it would affect his own livelihood. With fewer and fewer farmers owning and breeding fewer and fewer animals, the need for agricultural feed was shrinking. Henry knew the big conglomerate farms had deals with companies like his, but the middling farmers were gradually being squeezed out economically. And their loss was also his loss.

Feeling rather sad and quite depressed Henry turned to leave, but just then his eye caught something in the pile of discarded items. It was a wooden rowing boat. *Dear God, the things you find in old barns*, he thought to himself.

'Thinking of taking up fishing as well, are you, John?' he joked, jerking his head towards the old boat.

John laughed. 'She'll never be seaworthy again. The only thing it's good for is firewood. You wouldn't believe all the stuff that's already been taken out from here. That's the problem with farms – you never throw anything out in case you can find a use for it. A bit like George down the lane, but on a bigger scale.'

Oh, yes, Henry had forgotten about George Nightingale's penchant for hanging onto things. According to Lottie, the man's mantra had been 'waste not, want not', and consequently his bungalow, his garage, his shed and God knows what else had filled up with all kinds of stuff – most of it rubbish, as far as Henry was concerned. He remembered the man had organised a sort of lawn sale a while ago, but he hadn't been selling anything – he was giving stuff away for free. Lottie had come home smiling like a Cheshire cat because she'd acquired several tins of paint and some other bits and pieces from him. She'd put them in the shed and he guessed they were probably still there. The thought flitted through his mind that maybe his wife was turning into a female version of George Nightingale.

'Lottie is a bit of a make do and mend person, and doesn't throw much out,' he said to John. 'It comes in handy sometimes, though,' he added, and proceeded to tell him about Robin and his bed-breaking escapade of the day before.

Henry had no doubt Lottie would have fixed the offending item by now, but it was a damn shame the boy couldn't have a brand new one. The one he was sleeping in had been second-hand when they'd bought it, although the mattress was new – he distinctly remembered Lottie bringing the bed home in bits in their car one Saturday afternoon. She'd discovered it on a website called Free-cycle, where people gave away unwanted stuff for nothing. Although Henry appreciated what she did, it didn't make him feel very good about himself that he earned so little his family had to make do with other people's cast-offs.

John chuckled. 'I remember my granddad telling me that Granny made a crib for my Uncle Arthur out of a drawer once. She didn't do anything fancy to it, just shoved some blankets in, and bingo. She only had the one cot, see, and my dad was still sleeping in it, so she had to find somewhere to put the new baby.' He shook his head, a faraway look in his eyes. 'Kids these days don't know they're born,' he said. 'I mean, they get everything brand new, and nothing is built to last.' He jabbed a finger at the boat. 'Take that old boat – it's at least eighty years old.

Mind you, it probably hasn't seen water for about seventy of them. In my granddad's day, they probably would have shoved a mattress in it, and called it a bed.'

In the abrupt, ensuing silence, Henry looked at John, and John stared back at him. A thought popped into his head, but he didn't say anything. From the look on John's face, Henry guessed John might be thinking the same thing.

John took his cap off again, scratched his head, and replaced it. 'It would make a fine bed for a little boy, if someone was clever with their hands,' he said, slowly.

Henry knew John wasn't referring to him. He could put up a shelf and screw flatpack furniture together, but it was his wife who had the singular skill of turning what he would have sent to the skip into something fresh and useable.

'You can have it, if you can make use of it,' the farmer offered.

Henry was sorely tempted. He could see how it would look in Robin's bedroom, imagining an old anchor on the wall above for decoration, or a ship's wheel. As John said, in the right hands, it would make a fine bed indeed.

'Surely it could be made watertight again?' he said.

John barked out a laugh. 'I haven't got the time nor the inclination to mess about with boats. Got enough to do here. Take it – I'll drop it down to you next time I'm in the village. It probably won't fit in your car.'

Henry squinted at it and was certain it wouldn't. He was also certain that he wasn't too keen on taking the boat and not paying for it. It felt too much like charity for his liking. 'Let me give you something for it.'

'Don't be daft. I don't want nothing. If your Lottie can make use of it, that's better than it sitting behind the cowshed for another seventy years, because that's where it'll end up. You ought to go and see what's behind there already.'

Henry didn't, just in case John offered to give him anything else. 'In that case, thank you,' he said.

Lottie would be in raptures – he hoped. It was a big project and he prayed she was up to it, otherwise it would sit in his own garden and quietly rot there, instead of behind John Porter's cowshed.

Henry thanked him once again and they said their goodbyes, but as soon as he was back in the warmth of the car and trundling down the lane towards the village, despondency struck and he pulled over outside Mairi Edwards' bungalow.

Dear God, how had things come to this?

He leant forwards and folded his arms on top of the steering wheel, rested his head on them, and took a shuddering breath.

They should never have gone in for such a big mortgage, but he'd wanted to stay in the village where he'd been born and bred, and there hadn't been much else on the market at the time. If they'd waited another six months or so, one of the little terraced cottages off Applewell's main street might have come up for sale, but oh no, they'd been young and impatient, and full of glorious optimism. He wondered where it had gone, all that youthful enthusiasm and the certainty they could achieve anything they set their minds to.

Now, over a decade later, he was saddled with an obscenely large mortgage, a job he didn't particularly like and would shortly be out of, and a family to support. Not only that, he'd been reduced to accepting the kindness of relative strangers so his boy could have a new bed. And he didn't even know whether Robin wanted a nautical theme for his bedroom. For all Henry knew, his son might have his heart set on a damned fire engine, like his friend.

Henry sat up and slapped the steering wheel, suddenly furious, torn between the knowledge he should be thankful for what he had – a gorgeous wife, three wonderful children, and a nice house (albeit one they shortly wouldn't be able to afford) – and feeling hopeless and overwhelmed. 'Sort yourself out,' he muttered, gruffly.

Instead of wallowing in self-pity, he needed to be more proactive. Jobs didn't drop out of the sky and fall in one's lap: they had to be actively sought out and applied for, and that's what he must do. Starting now. He didn't need to be at his next appointment for an hour, so he had time to do a quick trawl of the job sites. He could hardly do it at home – with his children vying for time on the family's clunky computer, and the risk of him not wiping his search history properly (he'd tell Lottie, of course he would – but not just yet), he'd be better off using his mobile.

Unfortunately, when he checked the usual job sites, he saw that there wasn't a great deal out there when it came to his type of job and the location he needed.

Telling himself that something would come up soon, he started the engine and moved off. But in his heart all he felt was dread and a crushing sense of defeat.

Chapter 4

Lottie

The last thing Lottie had expected Henry to announce when he'd arrived home from work that evening was that she would shortly be taking delivery of a boat.

For a moment she'd thought he'd lost his marbles. Despite living only two miles from the sea, the family hadn't had much to do with it. Other than numerous and very lovely trips to the beach or walks along the coastal path, none of them had done much more than paddle in it. If the weather was particularly good and if he was feeling adventurous enough, Henry sometimes swam in it, but he never went more than a few metres from the breaking waves and, to her knowledge, he'd never been on a boat in his life.

But when he'd told her what it was for, she didn't know whether to kiss him, laugh incredulously or weep. That he had such belief in her abilities was humbling. And because he'd hadn't taken much interest in her penchant for rescuing bits and pieces for the last few years, it was also rather unexpected. But nevertheless welcome. She'd seen his expression when she'd told him she'd fixed Robin's bed, and she guessed what had been going through his mind – he'd wanted to be able to take his son to a shop and tell him to pick whichever bed took his fancy, but he

35

was so intent on saving for the extension that he couldn't, so he was doing the next best thing, and hoping she was up to the job.

As did Lottie herself.

–

'Where do you want it?' John asked, manoeuvring the boat out of the rear of his livestock trailer and hefting it over his shoulder. He grunted a bit and Lottie quickly offered to help. 'I can manage. Where's it going?'

'In the shed, please.' She showed him the way to the large outbuilding at the back of the house, swiftly opening the door and moving stuff out of the way. Her shed was neat and tidy, and quite large, but there was no way a ruddy great boat was going to fit in there without her shifting things. Looking at it, she didn't know how it was going to fit in Robin's room, either. She was tempted to paint it and stick it in the garden for the kids to use as a sandpit, but the beach was only two miles away and she'd be forever sweeping up sand…

She helped John lower it to the floor, and stood back to take a good look at it. It didn't appear to be in too bad a condition and, thankfully, she couldn't see any evidence of woodworm.

'Thank you so much for this. I know you told Henry you didn't want anything for it, but please let me give you something,' she offered.

'Pleasure, that's what you've given me – I hate seeing things go to waste. And an invite to see it once it's done.'

No pressure, then, she thought wildly. 'Of course. We'll crack a bottle on her,' she joked.

After waving him off, Lottie turned her attention back to the boat. It was about eight foot long and four wide at the middle, tapering into a squared-off end at the back and a pointy bit at the front. It had two planks of wood across the middle which she assumed would have been used for the occupants to sit on, and it still had the metal bits on either side where the oars would have gone in. She made a mental note to see if she could find some – they'd look brilliant above the bed.

Oh, listen to her – it looked like she was definitely going to do this, and a shock of excitement shot through her. She couldn't wait to get started, but first she had to make up her mind exactly what she was going to do with it.

Thinking furiously and scribbling some notes on a pad, she strolled around it, looking at it from every angle. Thank God the boat wasn't a big one; she could just about cope with the size, but to double-check she grabbed her measuring tape, noted down its dimensions, then raced inside to check if it really would fit in Robin's room.

Seeing that it would (just about) she blew out her cheeks and sagged against the wall. Her son's room was a little short on storage and, as she gazed around it wondering how it could be reconfigured to make the best use of the space, an idea came to her that sent her dashing outside and into the shed once again.

She knew precisely what she was going to do and where she needed to start, although the mattress would be a problem. Or would it...? Lottie pulled the tape measure out of her jeans pocket and measured the inside of the boat. After darting back into the house to measure Robin's single mattress, she made a mark on the inside of the boat where it would fit. To her dismay, although it would sit nicely at the squared-off end, there would be some space at the sides where they curved out and quite a lot at the front where the pointy bit — the prow, she suddenly remembered — was.

She debated taking the front off — but then it wouldn't look like a boat any more, and considering that was the purpose of it, she knew she'd have to have another think.

The first thing she should do was to put a base in the bottom of the boat for the mattress to sit on, then she'd cut a hole in the side to allow access underneath and use the space for storage. Similarly, she could keep the prow shape, but open it up from the front to make shelves.

The more she thought about it, the more she knew it would work. Excited, Lottie took some photos and uploaded them to Instagram. She'd started the account a couple of years before after following several people who upcycled things, and now she had a respectable 2,000 or so followers. Some of them were friends and acquaintances, but the majority were strangers. It was rather thrilling to receive likes and comments about her projects from people she'd never met.

She was happily beavering away, a sanding block in her hand, when she realised she needed to hurry if she wasn't going to be late picking Morgan up from nursery. The two and a half hours had flown by. Hopefully he'd settle down after his lunch for a nap, and she could carry on working on the boat. Now that she'd started, she didn't want to stop.

Drat — when she went to wash her hands in the downstairs loo, she noticed she was wearing a fine film of wood dust over the parts of her face her mask hadn't covered, and her clothes and her hair were coated in the stuff. She looked a mess, so she swiftly splashed some water on her face and scrubbed her skin with a flannel. The resulting red tinge to her cheeks, forehead and chin was possibly worse than the dust.

She grabbed her keys and once she was outside, she jumped up and down, frantically slapping at her clothes to try to shake off as much wood dust as she could. God knows what the neighbours would think of her if any of them happened to look out of their window.

Keeping her head high and pretending she didn't care that she looked a fright, she collected Morgan and took him home, hoping he'd have one of his increasingly rare naps.

No such luck — he was crankier than usual and refused to settle, and she ended up sitting on the floor and playing with his farm set instead of working on the boat-bed, until it was time to fetch the other two.

The school runs punctuated her weekdays, bracketed by nagging her children to put their school uniform on before they went, and nagging them to take it off when they got home. By the time Sabrina and Robin needed to be collected, Lottie had tidied herself up somewhat from that morning's debacle and she wasn't looking half as dusty, although her scalp still felt gritty. Ruefully, she acknowledged that she'd never be a yummy mummy, unlike some of the women congregating at the school gates. It wasn't in her nature to dress up and put on make-up merely to walk her kids to and from school; some days it was a miracle she managed to change out of her pyjamas for the occasion.

And talking of yummy mummies — Lottie was a bit taken aback when, at the school gates, Natalie Sharp deigned to turn to her and demand, 'Are you really going to make Robin sleep in a *boat*?'

Lottie heard a titter from the woman's cronies. 'Only as much as you make Callum sleep in a fire engine,' she retorted, mildly. Instagram had its downsides, and Natalie Sharp viewing Lottie's photos was one of them. She'd considered blocking her, but Natalie would know she'd been blocked and that would cause more trouble than it was worth.

'It looks…' The woman shuddered, words to describe the horror of the boat-bed having failed her. She grimaced and shrugged.

'Wonderful?' Lottie supplied.

'Hardly. And I'll have you know that Callum's bed was from Nighty Night.'

Lottie hated the one-upmanship that seemed to be in abundance when it came to mums and their kids. 'I want Robin to have something unique, not something off the shelf,' she retorted, as coolly as she could manage.

'Oh, it'll be unique, all right.' More tittering from Natalie's gang.

Delia swept in and dragged Lottie away. 'Ignore her, she's only jealous. You've got a skill and talent, and what has she got?'

'A cushy job in the doctor's surgery? This skill and talent of mine doesn't bring in any income.'

Lottie caught sight of Sabrina as she waltzed out of the Year 5 classroom along with her friends, trying to pretend Lottie wasn't there. She supposed she could allow her eldest to walk home on her own, but it would be rather silly considering Lottie still had to be there to collect Robin. The group of girls flitted around each other like burgundy butterflies in their school sweatshirts, their giggles and chatter contrasting with the squeal and yell of the boys as they leapt on each other's backs, or spun their friends around by their backpack straps.

Robin launched himself at her, his enthusiasm on seeing his mother in direct contrast to the lack of it from his sister.

'Oof!' Lottie grunted as he headbutted her in the stomach, thrust his bag and coat at her, then dashed off to race around the playground.

'Yes, but if you make something it stops you having to buy it, so it's almost like having an income.' Delia carried on seamlessly after her son, Mick, thrust his schoolbag into her hands. 'It's almost as good as having a job, and why shouldn't it bring in some money? You could sell some of the things you make.'

'No one wants other people's cast-offs.' Lottie caught Sabrina's bag as her daughter handed it to her as she swept past. She always ended up carrying backpacks, coats, PE bags, artwork, a half-eaten sandwich left over from lunch... she often felt like a packhorse.

'You have heard of eBay, haven't you?' Delia persisted. 'And what about Etsy, Facebook Marketplace, and boot sales? You've told me yourself that you've picked up loads of stuff over the years for the house and the kids from boot sales. If other people can sell things they don't want, why shouldn't you?'

They rounded their children up and began the familiar walk home, the mums holding on to the hands of the littlest children, the older ones scampering on ahead. Sabrina and Mick were as thick as thieves, having known each other since they were babes in arms, and Robin was tagging behind, hoping to be noticed by his older sibling and her friend.

Lottie thought about what Delia said and opened her mouth once or twice to make a comment, then closed it again before saying anything.

'You don't think you're good enough, do you?' Delia observed.

Delia had a point – it was one thing Lottie doing this for herself and her family, it was quite another thing entirely doing it in order to sell it. Nothing she produced was ever perfect, and while she was realistic enough to know that nothing ever *was* perfect – there were tiny flaws in everything that maybe only the creator could see – she'd know they were there and they'd haunt her.

'What have you got to lose?' Delia was saying, as Lottie watched her son and Mick haring up and down the pavement. Sabrina now stalked in front, studiously ignoring their antics, believing she was too old for such childish things as a game of tag. Mick was good like that, happily playing with the younger child, much to Sabrina's disgust.

Delia shouted to her ten-year-old to slow down; he pretended he hadn't heard. 'Pick something up off Free-cycle,' she advised Lottie. 'Do your thing, then sell it.'

'But what if it's no good or nobody wants to buy it?'

'If you make something that you and your family would use, then whatever it is won't go to waste.'

Lottie saw the boys poking their tongues out at her daughter's back, but she couldn't be bothered to tell them off. If she intervened every time the children made fun of each other she'd be doing nothing but scolding them. She gripped Morgan's hand tighter as he tried to tug himself free to join the older boys.

'Let go, Mummy. Want Robin,' he demanded.

'No chance, buster. You're too little not to hold Mummy's hand.'

'Am not.' Morgan abruptly went limp and collapsed onto the pavement, almost yanking Lottie's arm out of the socket. He hung there like a baby chimpanzee on a branch, the beginnings of a wail issuing from his mouth.

Lottie scooped him up and balanced him on her hip, trying to avoid his flailing feet. 'He didn't have a nap,' she explained, when Delia caught her eye with a sympathetic smile. 'When they get to this stage, I'm always torn between trying to get them off to sleep in the afternoon so I don't have to put up with this, or being relieved he'll drop off at seven instead of still being awake at nine.'

'The next couple of hours will be interesting,' Delia agreed. 'Trying to keep them awake until bedtime when they're like this is always fun.' She pulled a face and Lottie laughed. 'I'm serious, Lottie,' she said, returning to their earlier conversation. 'You've seen all those programmes on TV where old things are brought back to life. People are interested in that kind of thing.'

'Yeah, to do it themselves.'

'Some people will want to, of course; but others will want the items but won't have the time, the patience or the skill. They'll just want the finished results.'

'Surely they'd just go and buy new?'

'Like Natalie Sharp, you mean? As I said, she's jealous.'

Lottie wasn't convinced about any of it – from Natalie's supposed jealousy, right through to selling the bits and pieces she transformed. She also knew how much work went into producing the pieces she made; it would never be cost-effective. If she seriously wanted to contribute to the family's finances, she'd be better off going out and getting a proper job. Unfortunately, she didn't feel able to do that until Morgan started school: she'd fork out more in childcare than she'd earn. Besides, it wasn't easy finding a job that fitted in with school hours, and the school holidays would be a nightmare to manage. Her parents lived too far away to be of any help and they both still worked, and although Henry's parents lived in Applewell, they had full-time jobs, too.

The only option open to her was to work in the evenings when Henry was at home and could look after the kids. But she was knackered enough already by teatime — goodness knows how she'd cope if she had to go out to work just when the children were off to bed.

Thinking of Henry must have set something in motion, because just then her phone trilled with an incoming text. Smiling at Delia, she waved goodbye as her friend turned into the road she lived on, and Lottie checked to see what Henry wanted.

Going to be late, she read.

That figured — this past week or so he'd been late more often than not. It looked like she'd have to deal with the kids by herself again this evening.

As she let them into the house, the children darted in front of her, discarding shoes, coats, sweatshirts and a stick (Robin had brought it home for some inexplicable reason) as they went. She followed them inside, calling for them to come and pick their stuff up and put it away, continuing with the usual nag that they change out of their school uniform or they wouldn't have the snacks she'd prepared for them.

Lottie sighed dramatically as her words fell on deaf ears. *Groundhog Day* had nothing on her.

Chapter 5

Henry

Henry looked at his watch with a frown; it might be late, but he couldn't prevent himself from checking yet another job site. The library was quiet at this time in the evening, hardly a soul in it apart from the librarians themselves, but he glanced around quickly, almost furtively, to check there was no one who knew him. Improbable, he realised, but he didn't want to take any chances. When he thought about it logically, he was hardly likely to meet anyone he knew in Lampeter Library, and if he did, they wouldn't be peering over his shoulder to see what he was doing. But still...

Over the course of the last few days he'd popped into a library on the way home from work to make use of their computers. That evening the nearest one had been in Lampeter, and so far he'd applied for two jobs – but he wasn't particularly hopeful about either of them.

There were jobs around, but very few in this area: it was bad enough being on the road most of the day as it was, without having to spend nights away from home, living out of a suitcase. Besides, if he took a job where he had to do that, he would have to pay those overnight expenses himself, and he wasn't quite that desperate. Not yet.

He'd been mostly concentrating on vacancies with agencies who specialised in agricultural sales – surprisingly, there were several of them in what one might assume would be a very niche market. This latest trawl had shown him very little of interest, although he seriously considered a marketing executive job, before he realised that his CV would probably be thrown straight in the bin.

He checked the time once more, dismay running through him when he realised how late it was. Lottie would be cheesed off again. Since Redundancy-gate, as he referred to it, he'd been late home more often than he'd been on time, and he could tell Lottie was becoming a little fed up with him.

Reluctantly, because he felt compelled to keep looking no matter how tired he was or how futile the search, Henry removed the memory stick from the computer and slipped it in his pocket. The stick held his CV, which he'd recently updated, and a covering letter, which he was careful to tailor to each application. The other day he'd forgotten to take it out of the library's computer, almost reaching his car before he'd realised and had to dash back inside to fetch it. Henry's mind was still very firmly on job hunting when he walked into his house some time later, shrugging his jacket off at the door and dropping his briefcase at the bottom of the stairs. He hung his jacket over the newel post and walked into the kitchen, flinging his car keys onto the worktop near the microwave.

'Lottie?' he called, keeping his voice low. Morgan would undoubtedly be in bed at this hour, Robin too. Only Sabrina would be up, although Lottie would be doing her level best to encourage their daughter to have a bath and get ready for bed, because Robin wouldn't settle if his sister was still bumbling around. Robin claimed it was unfair that she was allowed to stay up later than him, and he didn't give a hoot about their age difference being a sound and logical reason for the discrepancy.

Henry didn't receive a reply, but there were noises filtering down from upstairs so he guessed his wife was still seeing to the children. The aroma of onions and garlic lingered in the air, and he wondered what she'd made for dinner.

Opening the oven, he saw a plate and he peeped underneath the foil covering. With a grimace, he hastily shut the door – homemade burgers and vegetable fries, with a side of yet more vegetables in the form of corn on the cob. A filling, healthy meal and one Henry had no doubt would have benefited from being eaten freshly cooked. He noted the solitary plate and guessed Lottie had eaten hers already.

He didn't blame her. He couldn't expect her to wait around for him to get home, especially when he was so late.

Not feeling in the slightest bit hungry, he poured himself a glass of wine, walked into the living room and slumped onto the sofa. The kids had been watching a cartoon channel, so he flipped over to something more grown up, then wished he hadn't as a close-up of a crying woman filled his vision.

'You're home, then,' Lottie said from behind him, and Henry nearly jumped out of his skin.

'Blimey! Don't creep up on me like that!' he cried, a hand over his thudding heart.

'I didn't creep. You were too engrossed in whatever you're watching to hear me.'

'I wasn't, and yes, clearly I'm back.' She was being sarcastic, so he answered in kind. He knew it was unwarranted, but honestly, he could do without his wife's passive aggression. He had enough on his plate at the moment.

'Your tea is in the oven,' she said, dropping into the chair opposite with a loud sigh.

'I'm not hungry.' He ignored the momentary flash of annoyance that had appeared on her face, and he stamped down on the urge to ask her whether she'd fancy eating a dried-up meal. It wasn't her fault he was late and at least she'd made him something, even if it did look inedible. And he wasn't lying when he said he wasn't hungry.

Since Paula from HR had informed him his services were no longer required, his appetite appeared to have deserted him. The only things to pass his lips recently were endless cups of coffee and antacid tablets. And wine.

He drained his glass, debated whether to have another on an empty stomach and decided one more wouldn't hurt. It might even help him sleep.

Henry got up, went back into the kitchen and poured himself a second. Feeling guilty, he poured his wife one, too, all the while trying not to glance at the oven, feeling its blank, accusing stare as the uneaten contents berated him.

Lottie took the glass from him with a muttered thanks and downed half of it in one go. It looked like her day had been as bad as his, but he couldn't for the life of him work out why. It wasn't as though she had to get up and go to work, and today Morgan had been at nursery in the morning so she'd had a good couple of hours without any of the children bothering her. He wished *he* could have a couple of hours to himself just to do nothing.

Occasionally, when they were really going at it, Lottie would shriek at him that perhaps they should swap places and he could stay at home and be a house-husband, and she could go to work and see how he liked it. He thought it sounded wonderful, but he never actually said so. Deep down he knew how hard she worked, and some mornings he was glad to get out of the door unscathed and leave the chaos of the school run behind.

Aware he was being unfair and not wanting her to delve into the reason why he was late home yet again, he decided to head her off at the pass. 'How is the boat-bed coming along?'

'It's good,' his wife said, with a shrug. 'I've done the sanding down and put a base in the bottom ready for the mattress to sit on. There's still quite a lot of work to do, though, but I think it's going to look good. I can't believe you found it, and I can't believe John Porter didn't want any money for it. Result!'

Henry pulled a face. It still didn't sit well with him that John had just given it to them, even though he knew the farmer would never use it and it would just sit there behind one of the sheds and rot. He felt good that they were saving it from oblivion, but he couldn't shake off the impression he was being treated as a charity case, even though John couldn't possibly be aware of their impending financial circumstances. Hell, his own wife didn't even know...

'You'll have to come out to the shed and have a look at it,' Lottie said. She smiled warmly at him.

Henry blinked in surprise. They'd been so uptight with each other lately that it was a shock to see such an open smile directed at him. It was unexpected and rather disconcerting. He couldn't remember the last time she'd smiled at him like that. Which didn't say much about the state of their marriage, did it? Although, come to think of it, she probably wasn't smiling at *him*, but at the thought of how the boat-bed was coming along.

Henry was the first to admit that the state of their marriage was probably his fault. He was the one being distant and uncommunicative, but he had so much on his mind that he didn't feel able to share with her. Although he continued to stick to his original plan of not telling her about this latest redundancy until he had a new job lined up, he knew he was being a miserable git, but he couldn't seem to help it.

There was very little further conversation as the evening trundled on, and eventually Henry let out a huge yawn. That was another thing – he was exhausted all the time, yet he didn't seem able to sleep. There was a time, not so very long ago, when he wouldn't wake up even if a bomb went off outside, but not these days. He seemed to lie awake for hours now, cursing Lottie who dropped off to sleep the second her head hit the pillow, and when he did eventually enter the land of Nod, it was to be kicked out of it repeatedly as he woke several times during the night.

'I'm bushed,' he announced. Seeing Lottie's answering yawn, he switched the TV off and they both made their way upstairs.

Henry crept along the landing and into their bedroom, careful not to make any noise which might disturb their sleeping children, and flopped down onto the bed as he waited for Lottie to get ready. Their nightly routine followed the same pattern – she had a shower first because she spent ages afterwards plastering her face and body with all kinds of creams and potions while he had his, often shaving at night because it saved time in the morning, meaning he had a few precious extra minutes in bed. Light from the half-open door showed his wife's shadow on the wall of the landing as she went into the bathroom, and he heaved a deep sigh, his mind whirling.

He barely noticed Lottie coming back into the bedroom and letting her towel fall to the floor as she reached for a bottle of something gooey and nice-smelling. Instead, he heaved himself off the bed and took his turn in the bathroom, crossly wiping the mirror free of condensation and wondering how one woman could generate so much steam. He'd be lucky not to scrape half his face off if he couldn't see his reflection properly when he shaved, and he opened the window wide to try to air the bathroom out.

By the time he'd finished and returned to the bedroom, Lottie was under the covers with the duvet up to her chin. He knew she'd be wearing fluffy PJs and he hopped into a pair of pyjama shorts, earning himself a 'Shh!' from his wife as his feet thudded on the floor.

Henry held his breath and waited for a wail from Morgan, which thankfully didn't come.

Closing the bedroom door with a soft click, he plunged the room into darkness and felt his way around to his side of the bed, climbing in with a low groan. Exhausted didn't begin to describe how tired he was, and he prayed he'd get more than a couple of hours' kip.

'Henry?' Lottie sounded odd.

He turned onto his side and propped himself up on his elbow. 'What's up?'

'That's what I was going to ask you.'

'What do you mean?' He worried he might have let something slip.

'You seemed a bit distracted lately,' she said. 'Is there anything wrong?'

Henry swallowed and forced himself to remain calm. 'Of course not! Whatever gave you that idea? Everything is tickety-boo.' Even as it left his mouth, he cringed: never in his life before had he used the term *tickety-boo*.

He waited for her to say something else, but she didn't. Instead, she squirmed around so she was facing him, and her arm slipped around his waist. He could feel her warm breath on his cheek and in the darkness he saw the pale oval of her face, inches away from his own.

She nuzzled into his neck and he felt her lips on his skin, as her hand moved from his waist to caress one of his buttocks.

If she'd made such a move even as little as a week ago he would have been seriously up for it, but right now the last thing he could think of was making love to his wife. He was far too tired for one thing, and, for another, he wasn't in the mood. Panicked, a part of him briefly wondered if he'd ever be in the mood again, before he dismissed the ridiculous notion. All he needed was to sort out a new job and everything would be fine.

He pulled away slightly and removed her hand, giving it a squeeze. 'Sorry, Lottie, not tonight. I'm absolutely bushed. It's been a long day.'

Lottie stiffened for a second, before scooting away to the other side of the bed. 'That's OK,' she muttered. 'I understand.'

But from the tone of her voice Henry knew she was hurt. Trying to make amends, he shuffled over to her side of the bed, the knobs of her spine pressing against his chest as he cuddled into her and put his arm around her waist. She gave a long drawn-out sigh and he kissed her shoulder. 'Night, night,' he murmured, but even as he lay there spooning his wife, he could feel the tension simmering between them, and it was a long time before either of them fell asleep.

Chapter 6

Lottie

The following morning Lottie stomped up the stairs and flung open Sabrina's bedroom door. 'Wakey, wakey,' she trilled, then she did the same to Robin, listening on the landing to ensure both children had stirred before she returned to the kitchen to make their breakfasts.

'Mummy cross?' Morgan asked her from the lofty heights of his three-cushioned seat. He'd progressed from a highchair to a proper chair, albeit with some help, several months ago, and Lottie had difficulty getting used to his newfound freedom. At least when he had been in his highchair she'd known he'd still be there when she came downstairs after waking his siblings. Only yesterday morning she'd walked into the kitchen to find him pouring milk all over the table. Apparently, he'd wanted some on his toast, the way he did on his cereal.

'Mummy's not cross,' she lied, and tried on a cheerful smile. It was a poor fit for her mood.

'Mummy *is* cross,' her youngest insisted, and she realised there was no pulling the wool over his eyes.

'Only a little bit,' she admitted.

'With me?' Morgan poked himself in the chest with his spoon, leaving a blob of porridge on his pyjamas. Thank goodness she always insisted the children ate their breakfast before getting dressed. There were only so many loads of washing she wanted to do in a day.

'Never with you, my cherub,' she declared, swooping down to kiss his curly head. The look he gave her was far too knowing, so she amended her statement to, 'OK, sometimes, but not today.'

'Robin?' He sounded gleeful.

'Not Robin, and not Sabrina, either,' she added hastily. The relish Morgan displayed when one of his siblings was in trouble was quite bothersome. She'd have thought the kids would stick together in the face of parental ire, but that was not the case. All three seemed happy to snitch on each other given half the chance.

'Daddy!' her astute son announced, having correctly determined the reason for her annoyance.

'Not Daddy,' she replied automatically, not wanting their children to think there was anything wrong between them. The look Morgan gave her told her she'd not been successful in her denial that she was cross with Henry.

Cross was too short a word to express the way she was feeling – hurt, unwanted, undesirable – and that was only the result of his rejection of her last night. Add neglected, unappreciated, ignored and abandoned to the list, and it was starting to be more accurate.

Lottie walked to the bottom of the stairs and yelled at the top of her voice: 'Sabrina! Robin! Get your backsides down here this second!'

'Mummy's cross,' she heard Morgan mutter as she marched back into the kitchen and poured herself a much-needed cup of coffee.

She heard the children thunder down the stairs – why they couldn't walk down them like normal people was beyond her – then they pushed and shoved their way through the door and launched themselves into their usual seats.

Wordlessly, she poured milk into two bowls of cereal and added some sliced banana and a handful of blueberries.

'Mummy cross,' Morgan informed his siblings. 'With Daddy,' he added, for good measure.

Robin looked a little alarmed, but Sabrina only looked curious. 'What did he do?' she asked.

'I'm not cross with Daddy,' Lottie said through gritted teeth, hearing the shower kick into life in the bathroom overhead. She glanced up at the ceiling and rolled her eyes. As usual, it was left to her to get the kids fed, dressed, and out of the door without one of them killing another. That she'd been up with Morgan since five thirty didn't help her mood. Trust Henry to have slept through it, despite her nudging him in the hopes he'd let her have another hour in bed.

No such luck.

No wonder she was cross – she was tired and fed up. The way things were at the moment, she might as well be a single parent for all the use Henry was around the house.

'Daddy, you've been naughty,' Morgan told his father as soon as Henry waltzed into the kitchen, his hair still damp from the shower, the faintest hint of stubble on his face, smelling of the aftershave she'd bought him for Christmas.

It was only because Lottie was staring at him, thinking how handsome he looked (and how deeply unfair it was that she needed at least two cups of coffee and more slap on her face than a clown would wear before she looked half-decent at this time in the morning) that she saw a flash of panic on his face.

It was gone so quickly, she wondered if she'd imagined it. And, as he crouched down beside his youngest son – a safe distance away, she noticed – his expression was one of mild interest so she knew she must have done.

'Why is Mummy cross with me? Did she say?' he asked, with a smile. He didn't look at her, and she narrowed her eyes in irritation.

'No. Have you been naughty?' Morgan was waving his spoon around and Henry hastily drew back. This time she was positive she hadn't imagined the odd look on her husband's face. So if she hadn't imagined this one, she surmised that she hadn't imagined the first one, either.

Knowing she needed to think about it but not having the time right then, she shelved the thought and got on with chivvying the children into washing their faces, brushing their teeth and getting dressed. Morgan, despite her doing all his dressing for him, was always the last one to be ready. He preferred squirming out of her grasp and haring into the other kids' rooms to annoy them, his turn of speed impressive. Vaguely, she hoped they might have an Olympic runner on their hands, and if she hadn't been quite so exasperated she would have smiled.

Eventually, though, she'd wrangled him into his clothes and the older two were dressed and as ready as they could be without her double checking their bags. She'd packed them with everything they needed the evening before, as she always did, but more often than not something would be missing even though she knew she'd put it in there. Plimsolls were the most frequent of the missing items when it came to Sabrina (she didn't like PE), and Robin usually managed to 'forget' his spellings book.

Just a typical day, then.

With her two eldest safely dropped off at school, Lottie gave a sigh of relief. Despite loving those few short hours when Morgan was in nursery, she also enjoyed the time she spent alone with him. He was bright and funny, and a handful, and it was important he had some one-to-one time with her.

It's a pity his father doesn't feel the same way, she thought sourly, as she grasped Morgan's hand tightly and prepared to cross the road. And she wasn't just referring to Henry spending time with Morgan. It would be nice if he and Lottie spent some time alone as a couple. She was still smarting from his rejection of her last night. They hadn't made love for ages – which she had to admit was more down to her than him, but she was usually so tired that as soon as she put her head on the pillow, she was asleep.

He hadn't been up for it last night, though. Far from it. He'd made it crystal clear he wasn't interested, and the cuddle hadn't made up for his brush-off.

'Can I have sweeties?' Morgan asked hopefully, as she opened the door to the general store and grabbed a basket.

'Not today,' she replied, as she nearly always did. It was rare she bought the children sweets, and she also tried to regulate what they bought with their meagre pocket money, not wanting them to waste it on sugary rubbish that would only rot their teeth and make them hyper. 'You can have some strawberries,' she said, her voice as hopeful as her son's.

He shook his head firmly. 'Want sweets.'

'Nope. Sorry. No sweets.'

Predictably, he went all limp and floppy, throwing himself down on the ground and beginning to wail.

'I remember the "terrible twos",' a voice said, and Lottie looked up to see Mairi Edwards, accompanied by her neighbour Nessa Millbrook, gazing sympathetically at her. 'My Alison used to make a right show of me when she was that age.'

'Hello, Mrs Edwards. How are you?' Lottie ignored her screaming child, as the parenting books advised she should.

'Not so bad. I've got my helper with me today.' The old lady pointed to Nessa. 'I don't know what I'd do without her.'

Mairi, who lived in the bungalow next to Nessa, had suffered a stroke a while back. Nessa and her fiancé, George, were Mairi's unofficial carers, even though the old lady lived alone in her own home.

'She's doing ever so well,' Nessa said, and Mairi beamed at her.

'Now then, young man, what's all this fuss about?' Mairi asked, holding onto Nessa's arm as she bent down to speak to Morgan.

Morgan stopped wailing and stared up at her.

'You must have a magic touch,' Lottie said, shaking her head. 'He can carry on screaming for ages.' As if to prove her right, Morgan started screaming again, his little feet kicking the floor. 'Sorry, he wants some sweets, but I've said no.'

Mairi laughed. 'Watch this.' She put a hand in her pocket, pulled out a cola cube, showed it to Morgan, then popped it in her mouth. 'Mmm, I love sweeties,' she said to the incredulous child, who yelled even harder at the unfairness of this strange adult eating sweeties in front of him.

60

Then Mairi cried, 'Oh, no!' She put her hand to her mouth and suddenly she was toothless. She grinned at Morgan, who abruptly stopped crying and stared at her with wide eyes. 'Too many sweets make your teeth fall out,' she gummed at him. 'And if your teeth fall out, you will never be able to eat sweets again. Or much of anything else, for that matter,' she added.

Morgan's bottom lip trembled, and Lottie saw he was close to real tears this time. Mairi certainly had an unconventional way with children, and Lottie hoped the old lady hadn't scarred him for life.

'Grape?' Mairi asked, plucking one out of a punnet in Nessa's basket.

Morgan took it and scrutinised it doubtfully. After a second or two, he put it in his mouth and ate it.

'Thanks,' Lottie said, grateful her son's tantrum had ceased, but not entirely convinced about the method Mairi had used to achieve it.

'Are *you* all right, my dear?' Mairi asked her.

'I am now he's stopped screaming,' Lottie said. So much for spending quality time with her youngest.

'I meant generally.'

There was something in the way Mairi said it that made Lottie frown. 'Yes, why do you ask?'

'It's probably nothing, but about a week ago I saw your Henry sitting in his car outside my bungalow and he seemed upset, so I wondered if everything was all right.'

'We're good,' Lottie said, thinking furiously. That must have been when Henry called up to John Porter's farm, the day he spotted the boat. She wondered what could have upset him, because whatever it was seemed to have continued to upset him over the past week or so.

He had been moody even before then, and she thought back to last night. She'd known there was something up with him, but he'd denied it. And immediately afterwards, he'd brushed her off when she'd tried to initiate some passion.

Henry, she suddenly thought, *is acting like a man who has something significant on his mind; something he doesn't want to share with me.*

The question was, what was he hiding?

But Lottie, to her chagrin, discovered she wasn't sure she wanted to know.

Chapter 7

Henry

'I'm going to have to borrow the car,' Lottie announced the following Saturday morning. 'Sabrina needs new shoes and I can't put it off any longer.'

Henry groaned inwardly – school shoes weren't cheap. He knew he could kiss goodbye to the best part of forty quid. Nor was there what Lottie termed a 'proper' children's shoe shop in Applewell, so she would be taking Sabrina to Aberystwyth, where the possibility for spending increased exponentially.

The family wasn't quite on the bread line, but he was acutely aware he only had two weeks left to find another job. Two weeks until his final pay. Then they'd have to live on fresh air if they weren't to touch their extension funds. Sabrina's need for new shoes couldn't have come at a worse time.

'How long will you be?' he asked, hoping Lottie was only making a flying visit. If she parked the car, bought the shoes, then drove straight back home there wouldn't be any opportunity for Sabrina to talk Lottie into popping into Sparkle and Glitter for a look at all the girly stuff they sold. Because it wouldn't be just a simple 'look', would it?

'Why? Do you have something planned?' Lottie's question was sharp.

'Nothing. I assume you want me to have the boys?' He'd be glad to have them, if only to mitigate any chances of further spending, because no doubt one of the children would be hungry or thirsty, and eating out wasn't cheap.

'Is that a problem?' Lottie had her hands on her hips, and for a second or so Henry tried to think what had put her back up.

'I was just checking – you might have been planning on taking them with you.'

His wife shot him an incredulous look. 'Do you honestly think I'd want to take the boys shoe shopping, when the shoes wouldn't even be for them?' She shook her head and rolled her eyes. That's where Sabrina got it from, he saw now – the eye-rolling thing. Females were so much better at it than males; it was as though they were born with an eye-rolling gene.

'Are you looking after us today, Daddy?' Robin asked, appearing at his elbow. 'Can we go to the cinema?'

Good Lord, no – it was far too expensive, and Henry didn't fancy trying to keep Morgan in his seat when the little boy would doubtless lose concentration after ten minutes and would want to go exploring.

'I'll take them to the beach,' he called to Lottie's retreating back, as she made her way upstairs. It looked to be a decent day outside, fine if cold, and at least the beach was free, so hopefully the kids would wear themselves out.

'Good idea,' she threw over her shoulder. 'But try not to tramp sand or mud through the house. The path down the valley will be as muddy as anything, so they'll need their wellies.'

Henry tried an eye-roll on for size and decided it fitted rather well. 'Come on, guys, let's find your wellies – we're off to the beach to look for crabs.'

No matter what the season, his children loved dibbling around in rock pools, and winter storms often flung up interesting things, depositing them at the high tide mark.

'Yay! Can I have a new net?' Robin asked, leaping up and down.

Morgan jumped around, too. 'New net! New net!' Why did his youngest son only ever seem to speak in exclamation marks?

'No one needs a new net. If you two get dressed in some warm clothes, I'll fetch the nets and buckets from the shed.'

Robin tore up the stairs, narrowly avoiding Lottie who was coming down them, Sabrina trotting after her, her expression one of hopeful excitement.

Henry knew it wasn't because of the prospect of new shoes.

He waited for Morgan to thump up the stairs after his brother, ruffled Sabrina's hair (much to her annoyance) and debated whether to kiss his wife.

The moment passed as Lottie bent down to straighten the leg of her jeans, so he simply wished them a good trip and took himself off to the shed.

Henry guessed the large outbuilding had been put up around the time the house was built. It was made of grey bricks covered in smooth render – the reason he was aware of the colour of the bricks was that some of the render had come off and had yet to be replaced. It was another little job that needed doing at some point in the dim and distant future, when the rest of the more essential jobs in the house had been completed.

He unlocked the double doors and stepped inside, coughing as dust motes swirled around his head, illumin-ated by the weak winter sun streaming in through the windows. The first thing to catch his eye was the boat. Or the bed – because although it still retained the rowing boat shape, Lottie had already done a significant amount of work on it.

All the old varnish had gone, revealing the bare wood underneath. A solid base had replaced the planks people would have previously sat on, and both sides of the boat had sections cut out and little doors put in revealing storage spaces underneath. The prow had been transformed into two shelves. It appeared that all she needed to do was to paint it, and he noticed a couple of pots on the workbench. Blue and white – perfect.

Henry looked at the bed for a while, pride filling him. His wife had talent, and it put his pathetic attempts at DIY to shame. Nevertheless, he was delighted he'd seen the potential, even if he had initially been reluctant to accept the boat. Robin would be thrilled – Henry would bet that the little boy with the fire engine bed wouldn't be able to boast that his bed was made out of a *real* fire engine.

Lottie was doing a grand job and Henry couldn't wait to see the finished result. She'd mentioned something about displaying a pair of oars on the wall above the bed, and he reminded himself to speak to John Porter in the hope that there may be some oars knocking around the farm.

Quickly he found the nets and brightly coloured buckets, and went back inside – to discover Robin wearing his swimming shorts and nothing else, and Morgan stuck half-in and half-out of his Spiderman outfit and bawling his eyes out.

'Sorry, mate, we won't be going in the sea today, it's too cold,' he told Robin, as he pointed him in the direction of some fleecy jogging bottoms and a jumper, before turning to his youngest son.

It took him a while to extricate Morgan, calm him down, and dress him in what he was supposed to be wearing. By that time, Robin announced he was hungry, and Henry was faced with the prospect of never getting out of the door.

'If you can wait, I'll make us a picnic and we can eat it on the beach. How does that sound?' he suggested.

From the excitement that ensued, Henry deduced the boys liked the idea, so he made some sandwiches, grabbed a few pieces of fruit out of the bowl, added three cheeky packets of crisps to their impromptu lunch, and nearly forgot some drinks, having to race back into the house to fill a couple of water bottles.

Finally, they were on their way, Morgan stopping every few paces to examine something or other. Henry didn't mind, although Robin was getting slightly angsty, wanting Morgan to hurry up so they could get to the beach more quickly. But Henry was content to allow Morgan to stop and stare as much as he pleased. After all, there was no rush, and if it took them two hours to make what should have been a forty-five minute walk, then so be it.

After a while, though, Morgan began to flag so Henry picked him up and put him on his shoulders. He wished he could carry both his sons, and maybe he'd have to on the way back – which would be an interesting exercise in logistics – because Robin was getting cranky, too. *How does Lottie cope when she walks with the children to the beach?* he wondered, then an image of the folded-up stroller in the porch popped into his head and he groaned. Of course!

Feeling as useless as a chocolate teapot, he chivvied Robin along until they eventually dropped down into a steep-sided, wooded valley with a stream trickling at its base. Lottie had been right about the path being muddy, and Robin had great fun squelching through it. Morgan was more interested in the golden beach with sparkling blue water that could be seen through the trees, and he kept kicking Henry, urging him on.

As soon as they reached the sand, Henry put Morgan down and rotated his shoulders, wincing at the unaccustomed ache and wondering whether he'd have any bruises from his youngest son's hard little heels. He watched the two boys scamper off to pick a spot to have their picnic, and he paused to take in the view.

The cove was a small one, bordered by cliffs on either side – both with navigable paths to their tops – and the valley to his back. In front of him lay an expanse of sand and the sea. The tide was out, unveiling rocks with their intriguing pools, and the water glittered as the sun shone on its surface.

Robin had the stick end of his net firmly planted in soft sand in a suitable spot, so Henry spread out a couple of old towels to sit on and took the picnic out of his rucksack. He discovered he was just as hungry as the boys, and they fell on the food, demolishing it within minutes. Henry wished he'd had the foresight to bring a flask of coffee with him; he remembered Lottie always packed a flask when they went out for the day, but it hadn't occurred to him. At least he'd remembered hats and gloves.

Once fed and watered, the children were eager to dabble in the rock pools, urging him to turn over large boulders to see what was underneath. He had great fun pointing out crabs, periwinkles, cockles, limpets, tiny fish and the varieties of seaweed. They even saw a starfish in one of them, which made Morgan's day. Once Henry had counted to five on his own fingers to indicate the arms on the starfish, Morgan took great delight in holding up his own little starfish hand and shouting 'Five!' at the top of his voice.

After rock pooling, the boys decided to make sand-castles using the buckets (Robin), and then stamping on them (Morgan), which seemed to be their favourite things to do when they visited the beach, while Henry dug a moat and a trench leading to the incoming tide.

Finally, as the sea inched closer and closer, Henry took them to the water's edge, and they had fun splashing through the wavelets and jumping over them, squealing when the cold water sloshed into their wellies.

Eventually, though, the children were exhausted. Henry hefted his youngest son onto his shoulders once more, and the three of them made their slow way home again, the promise of a gingerbread man from the bakers stifling Robin's grumbling about being too tired to walk and wanting to take turns on his father's back.

It was only when he set Morgan down to walk the last few hundred yards to their house that Henry realised he hadn't once thought of his impending redundancy. His previously buoyant mood quickly evaporated.

Oh, well, it had been nice while it lasted; it had certainly been lovely spending time alone with his sons, and Henry resolved to do it more often. He hoped his wife and daughter had had a successful afternoon, and hadn't bickered too much over the type of shoes to buy – Sabrina always wanted something fancy with a low heel, and Lottie always insisted on practical and plain flats. He also hoped they hadn't cost too much… the minute the thought popped into his head, he hated himself for thinking it.

Thankfully, his previously good mood hadn't disappeared entirely by the time they arrived home, and he busied himself with sorting the boys out – very early baths, with the two of them in the tub at the same time – and he'd even made a start on preparing the evening meal when Lottie and Sabrina returned.

His wife and daughter bustled into the hall, Sabrina chattering nineteen to the dozen, and Henry heard Lottie's tinkling laugh and he smiled to himself. Everything was going to be all right – he had a wonderful wife, three happy, healthy children, a roof over his head, and—

'Blimmin' heck, what have you bought?' he demanded, seeing Lottie enter the kitchen.

Her laughter died and her expression hardened. She held up one of the bags she was carrying. 'Shoes for your daughter. A new school jumper for your daughter. Knickers for me – is that OK?' She carried on, before he had a chance to say anything: 'Two new pillows for our bed, because I'm sick of tossing and turning all night on those pancakes we've currently got. Oh, and a sledge.'

'How much did that cost?' He eyed the wooden sledge with mistrust. It was old and didn't look particularly safe, although he knew Lottie would make sure it was before she allowed the children to have a go on it.

'All of it, or just the sledge?'

'Er...'

'I bought the sledge from a charity shop near the pier. Hang on, I've got the receipts for everything in my purse.' Lottie dropped the bags on the floor. 'Sabrina, can you take your things upstairs, please? Where are the boys?'

'In the living room, watching—'

'Good. Here you go.' She slammed a fistful of receipts down on the worktop.

Henry looked at them but made no move to pick any of them up.

'Go on,' she urged, her face tight and her voice low. 'Make sure I didn't spend too much of your hard-earned wages.'

'That's not what I meant,' he protested, even though that was exactly what he'd meant. Not the hard-earned wages bit, but the spending too much bit. 'I thought we were trying to save for the extension?'

'We are, but we don't have to live on bread and gruel while we're doing it. And apart from the blasted sledge, everything else was essential. I wish I hadn't bought it now,' she muttered. She was about to leave the room, when she halted and said, 'It's not as though I throw money away, and I do save in other ways. If it's going to cause this much of an issue, the extension can wait – it's hardly essential.'

Neither is buying a sledge, he thought. Especially considering there wasn't any snow and hadn't been since that flurry a couple of weeks ago, on the day he'd been informed of his redundancy.

He turned back to the stove, his hunger gone, and he continued cooking with his stomach churning and a sour taste in his mouth, as he heard Lottie leave the room.

'Tea's ready,' he called up the stairs ten minutes later, and although the children zoomed in on the table like the creatures from *Alien* when they discovered prey, Lottie took her time to appear. Just when he was beginning to think she wasn't going to bother, she drifted into the kitchen and poured herself a glass of water before greeting the boys.

'Why are you in your pyjamas already?' she asked Robin and Morgan. Her voice was a bit croaky and her face was blotchy. He wondered if she'd had a quick nap while he'd been slaving over a hot stove. Her eyes were slightly bloodshot and her hair was mussed, so he thought she probably had.

'We had a bath before tea, me and Morgan,' Robin said. 'We were covered in sand and Daddy said we had to wash it off or you'd be cross. Are you cross, Mummy?'

Henry nearly answered for her, but he shoved another forkful of mashed potato in his mouth instead.

'Why is everyone so fascinated about whether I'm cross or not?' Lottie asked, irritably.

'Mummy's cross,' Morgan stated.

'Oh, for—' Lottie stopped abruptly and took a deep breath. Henry wondered what was going through her head. 'Did you have a good time at the beach?' she asked the boys.

'I caught a starfish and Morgan had to be carried,' Robin said.

Morgan waved his chubby hand in the air, fingers outstretched. 'Five!' he yelled.

'I taught him that starfishes have five arms, like his fingers,' Henry said, anxious to dispel the atmosphere.

'Daddy forgot the buggy, and we had a gingerbread man. Mine was a reindeer face and Morgan's was Father Christmas. When is Father Christmas coming, Mummy?'

'Not for ages, yet,' she replied, staring at Morgan's almost untouched plate of food, then she looked at Robin's. He'd made very few inroads into his meal and was busily digging holes in his potato with his fork and making engine noises. Henry winced – he was in the dog-house again, it seemed.

'When did they have the gingerbread?' his wife asked him, and he heard the exasperation in her voice.

'On the way back.'

'Just before you got home, you mean? And what time was that?'

'About an hour ago, maybe less.' Henry groaned inwardly.

'That will explain why they're not eating their tea.' Lottie glared at him.

Henry bit his lip. It seemed he couldn't do anything right. He'd thought he was giving them a treat, and now Lottie was berating him for it.

The sour taste in his mouth increased.

He put his fork down and pushed his plate away. Getting to his feet, he said, 'I'm going out.'

Robin stopped digging at his mashed potato and stared at him with big eyes. Sabrina paused, a forkful of food halfway to her mouth. Only Morgan seemed oblivious to the escalating tension between their parents.

'Where?' Lottie asked.

'Anywhere. The pub.'

'Oh, so you don't want *me* to spend money on *our* children, but *you* can spend money in the *pub*?'

'One pint, that's all. Do you begrudge me one sodding pint?'

Lottie turned away, her mouth set in a straight line, her jaw clenched, but not before he saw the gleam of tears in her eyes. Morgan began to wail, Henry's raised voice having startled him.

For pity's sake, now he'd upset the kids. *What the hell kind of a father does that?* At that moment, he didn't like himself at all, and he suspected Lottie liked him even less.

He really did need to get out of the house, if only to stop himself from causing them any more distress than he already had.

Tears prickled the back of his eyes as he dashed into the hall, hooking his waxed cotton coat off the banister as he went past.

He heard the front door slam loudly behind him and he flinched. It sounded as though he'd stormed out and slammed it shut in temper, when he'd actually only pulled it a little too hard as he'd shot through it.

Debating whether to go back and explain to Lottie that he hadn't meant to slam it, he hesitated on the step, then he shrugged. It would look even worse if he went back in now, then left again. It was better to just leave and return when he could face his family once more.

At least she didn't have to bath the boys, he thought – at least he'd done *something* right. And Robin and Morgan had had a whale of a time at the beach. They'd had a good day – until he'd spoilt it.

His feet took him along the coastal path, in the opposite direction to the pub. He hadn't been serious when he'd said he was going for a pint – primarily because he suspected he wouldn't stop at just the one, and how much of a hypocrite would that make him if he drank their money away?

Wanting to avoid people, he headed across the fields towards the coastal path. It was almost dark and there probably wouldn't be anyone else daft enough to be on it.

The moon was rising behind him, giving him sufficient light to allow him to pick his way along the path, and the air was still and calm, nature holding its breath. It was quiet enough to hear the boom of the waves as they crashed into the cliff face long before he unlatched the kissing-gate separating the field from the rugged path.

Now that he'd reached the cliff top, the wind picked up, carried across the Irish Sea to cool his cheeks and ruffle his hair. It smelt of wilderness and freedom, and escape.

As he turned left, his footsteps carrying him away from Applewell and home, he wondered what it would be like to keep walking. The coastal path stretched for nearly one and a half thousand kilometres around the Welsh coastline. He was standing roughly at the mid-point and he was currently heading south, the land on his left, the sea to his right, the water black against a midnight sky, the ground beneath his feet barely visible.

Heaving a despondent sigh, Henry came to a halt.

Running away wasn't an option, no matter how appealing it seemed. Instead of walking aimlessly and risking falling in the darkness, he stepped nearer to the cliff edge, careful not to get too close, found a flattish patch of grass and sat on it. Drawing his knees up to his chest, he wrapped his arms around his legs and dropped his chin to rest on them, staring out to sea.

Henry felt incredibly small and insignificant. Right there, right now, his troubles were nothing more than specks of dust on the wind.

Feeling calmer and cleansed, he didn't know how long he stayed there, but when he clambered stiffly to his feet, his backside numb with cold, his fingers and toes freezing, it was with a renewed sense of purpose.

He'd get another job and quickly, and then he'd explain to Lottie why he had been acting the way he had. Vowing to be a better husband and father, and not allow his work worries to impact on his private life, he made his slow way home to the family that he loved more than anything else in the world.

Chapter 8

Lottie

The trick to appearing to be asleep was in the breathing, Lottie decided. She'd watched her children sleep enough times to know the rhythm of it. Long ago, another life ago, she used to watch Henry sleep too, marvelling that this slumbering hunk of a man was all hers.

Deeper breath in, shallower breath out; repeat steadily for as often as necessary.

It was eleven fifteen when she heard the unmistakable squeak of the front door and she listened intently for the soft tread of her husband's footsteps through the house. The fridge door opened as she strained to listen, followed by the glug of something being poured into a glass; Lottie was amazed at how far sound travelled in the darkness.

She imagined him standing in the kitchen, one hand resting on the worktop, the other tipping a glass up to his mouth, and she wondered how many pints he'd sunk, who he'd been with, and what he'd spoken about.

She'd never been so shocked as when he'd stormed out earlier, abandoning his barely touched meal, leaving her with her mouth open in surprise and their children with large eyes and fearful expressions. Sabrina had flinched when he'd slammed the front door, and Morgan had cried in earnest.

The familiar creak of the third stair and then the seventh told her he was coming upstairs, and she shuffled down into the bed, pulling the duvet up to cover as much of her head as she could tolerate. She closed her eyes and began the sleep-breathing – deeper breath in, shallower breath out.

If he thought she was awake, he might want to talk and she couldn't face it. She was too tired, physically and emotionally, to deal with him, even though she guessed sleep might be a long time coming.

She heard him go into the bathroom and the sound of running water told her he must be in the shower, and she knew she'd find his clothes puddled on the floor in the morning.

A spill of light as he opened their bedroom door almost made her wince, and she willed herself not to react. Deeper breath in, shallower breath out...

There was silence and no discernible movement for a moment, and she wondered what he was doing. Then she heard a sigh, and knew he was going around to his side of the bed. The mattress depressed as he sat on it and he slipped his legs under the duvet before sliding down. Lottie could tell he was trying not to wake her – maybe he was as reluctant as she to start a conversation – and she allowed herself to go floppy, concentrating on her breathing.

He shuffled gently for a while, plumping his pillow, shifting until he found a comfortable position, and she speculated whether he could tell she was awake but was happy to go along with the charade. Eventually, though, she felt him twitch as sleep took hold, and she let out a long, slow breath and turned onto her back to stare at the ceiling. His breathing deepened and she wondered if he was faking it too, then decided he wasn't as he let out a little snort.

Lottie turned again, this time towards him and tried to study her husband in the darkness, wishing she knew what was going through his head. There was a time when she could read him as well as she read Morgan, and she tried to work out when he had become such a closed book.

As she lay there, listening to Henry sleep, something niggled at her. Lottie frowned, and she raised herself onto her elbow. What was it...?

It took her a while to figure it out, but when she did, her frown deepened further. Underneath the tang of toothpaste, she should be able to smell the sourness of second-hand alcohol.

It was disturbingly absent. If he'd been to the pub, he must have had soft drinks.

If he'd been to the pub.

Carefully, so as not to wake him, she eased herself out of bed and crept towards the door, opening it only wide enough for her to slip through. The landing light always remained on as Morgan refused to go to bed unless it was, but Henry didn't stir at the momentary brightness flooding the room. He was so used to her having to get up in the night to see to one or other of the kids that it didn't register with him. It never did. She was the one who always dealt with the nightmares, the requests for the toilet, the fevers, the thirst... And sometimes it got her down that Henry didn't have to.

That said, she couldn't blame him, because when Sabrina was born they'd agreed that Lottie would stay at home and do the lion's share of the childcare. She understood how hard it was for him to be out on the road all day after having night after night of broken sleep. It was dangerous and unsustainable, so it was only right she saw to the children at night. But now and again it would be nice to have him get up, and let her sleep.

Going into the bathroom, Lottie found Henry's clothes piled on the floor as she'd expected. Wondering if she was being silly and admitting that she was, she picked up the sweatshirt he'd been wearing and sniffed it.

The Busy Bumble, like most pubs she'd been in, had a certain aroma – stale beer, cooked food, the faint hint of smoke from those people clustered outside the front door having a cigarette…

Henry's sweatshirt smelt of the sea, of cold winter air and the outdoors.

She sniffed again, working the fabric across her face, not quite sure what she was trying to find. Some hint of where he'd been? Because as sure as God made little green apples, she didn't for one moment think he'd been to the pub.

Picking up his jeans, her hand delved into the pockets, but she found nothing more than a handful of loose change. She was about to let the jeans fall to the floor – he could pick up his own clothes – when she noticed something odd: there were grass and mud stains on the backside.

She knew they had been clean on today. She'd only ironed them yesterday and he'd been wearing old joggers this morning to go to the beach, so he must have changed into them when he'd come home. Which begged the question, where had he gone this evening to get muck all over his backside?

Lottie crept downstairs, her curiosity well and truly piqued.

Not quite knowing what she was searching for, she examined his jacket, the one he always wore, but there was nothing in the pockets except for a memory stick in the inside one. She took it out and looked at it thoughtfully, turning it over in her fingers. It probably held work stuff, which didn't interest her in the slightest.

Next, she checked his wallet, all the while thinking that she couldn't believe she was doing something like this. But now she'd started rifling through his things, she couldn't stop. She wasn't even sure what she was looking for, although a little niggle in the back of her mind argued she knew exactly what she was searching for and praying with all her heart she wouldn't find it. Apart from a couple of ten-pound notes, a receipt from a petrol station dated a few days ago, his bank card and a library card (when did he get one of those?), there was nothing of interest.

Never in a million years did she think she'd be the kind of woman who didn't trust her husband; she never thought she'd have to be.

Lottie, aghast at what she'd just done, went back to bed, telling herself she hadn't found anything because there wasn't anything *to* find. She knew she was being paranoid; but despite arguing that she was being silly, her gut feeling continued to tell her something was wrong. And she intended to find out what.

Just because she hadn't discovered any evidence he was having an affair, didn't mean he wasn't. It just meant she hadn't looked hard enough.

There was something else that niggled at her, too – if he was seeing another woman, who the hell could it be?

It wouldn't be anyone who lived in Applewell: keeping a secret in a small village such as the one they lived in was nigh on impossible. Therefore it must be someone at work. Or someone he'd met through work, considering head office was a fair drive away. A farmer, maybe? Or how about someone who owned a stables?

Once the thought had lodged in her head, she was unable to shift it. Did it explain why he was so late home recently? Was he playing around?

Did she want to know? Or could she turn a blind eye and allow life to go on as normal?

Lottie's heart filled with dread and her stomach with knots, and it was a long time before she finally drifted off to sleep.

Chapter 9

Lottie

Lottie stabbed her brush into the pot of paint with barely controlled venom. She wasn't quite imagining her husband's cold, black heart as being the recipient of her paintbrush attack, but she wasn't far off it. He'd said hardly a word to her all day yesterday, although he had played a game of tag with the kids in the garden, so his relationship with his children seemed to have been repaired.

She said *seemed*, because every so often she'd catch Sabrina watching her and Henry with a wary expression in her eyes. Their daughter hadn't forgotten the little contretemps on Saturday evening, although the boys seemed to have. The four years between their eldest and their middle child made all the difference. Sabrina had always been far more observant than Robin, and that didn't help either.

Although Lottie had tried her best to appear normal, Henry wasn't making it easy. Yesterday morning when she'd asked him, 'How was the Busy Bumble?' his brusque reply of, 'All right, I suppose,' hadn't done anything to allay her suspicion that he hadn't gone to the pub at all.

'Damn it!' Now look what he'd made her do! Instead of concentrating on the job in hand, she'd been so busy being annoyed at Henry that she'd overloaded the brush and had dripped white paint over the blue paint.

Cursing soundly – under her breath, because she never said words like that aloud in case the children were in earshot – Lottie dabbed off what she could, throwing the used rag into a bag. She'd rinse it under the outside tap later, when she washed the brush.

The boat-bed was looking pretty good, even if she said so herself. Henry still hadn't been out to the shed to look at it, which upset her a little. She would have thought he'd display some interest, considering he was the one who'd found the boat in the first place. If the shoe had been on the other foot, she'd have been demanding daily updates. The whole thing only served to highlight the growing distance between them.

Lottie checked the time. 'For fu—four fat snakes,' she amended. Grabbing her phone with paint-smeared fingers, she found Delia's number. 'Hi, it's me, Lottie. You wouldn't do me a huge favour, would you, and pick Morgan up from nursery? I'm running late. I can meet you at the corner.'

'No need, I'll drop him round to yours.'

'Would you? That's so kind. How about if you and Tyrone stay for a spot of lunch?'

Delia was more than happy to, and Lottie made a quick phone call to the school to let them know Delia would collect Morgan. Once that was done, she hastily cleaned up after herself and changed out of her overalls. She'd picked them up in UnderCover one day last week, and they were a godsend, allowing her to peel them off in a matter of seconds and reveal clean, non-paint-spattered clothes underneath.

Lottie was in the kitchen when she heard Delia's 'Coo-ee!' as she knocked and came straight in, Morgan and Tyrone racing ahead and hurtling into the kitchen, bringing with them a blast of chilly air. The temperature was steadily dropping and Lottie was thankful she had a heater in the shed, otherwise she'd never be able to work in there over the winter. Although, it was a wonder Henry hadn't whinged about the amount of electricity she was using.

Lottie braced for impact as her son barrelled into her, and she dropped into a crouch to accept his enthusiastic kisses, in between his almost incoherent reports of what he'd done in nursery that morning.

When he ran out of steam, she straightened up, stroked his hair, gave Tyrone a hug, and kissed Delia on the cheek. 'Thank you so much for fetching him for me – I owe you, big time.'

'You can pay me in coffee and sandwiches,' Delia replied, her attention on the plate of food Lottie had just finished preparing. Lottie had even ripped up some parsley leaves from a plant on the kitchen window sill and sprinkled them on for added colour. 'They look yummy. Did you do this for me, or do you garnish every meal like this? Stephen wouldn't know what had hit him if I garnished his curry and rice. He'd think I'd been abducted by aliens and one of them had taken over my body.'

Lottie pulled out some chairs and everyone sat down at the table. The kitchen table was another one of what Henry called her 'make do and mend' projects, and she was rather pleased with it. It was amazing what a lick of paint, some old tiles for the tabletop and recycled and re-covered cushions – courtesy of Gracie Stewart, who was a brilliant seamstress – for the seats, could do.

'I don't think I could be bothered. Henry is one lucky fella,' Delia said, as she accepted a plate and popped a couple of sandwiches and some grapes on it before handing it to her son.

'I wish he thought so,' Lottie muttered, shoving a plate at Morgan. The two children tucked in hungrily. Lottie served herself but didn't have much of an appetite and her sandwiches remained untouched. She slumped back in her seat and let out a sigh.

'What's up?' Delia asked, around a mouthful of food.

'Henry is behaving oddly.'

Her friend shot her a sharp look. 'In what way?'

'I'm not sure. There's something going on, but...'

'Another woman?'

Lottie could feel the colour draining from her face. Hearing someone vocalise her fears made them seem horrifyingly real. She nodded, unable to speak for fear of bursting into tears.

'What makes you think that?' Delia asked, putting her sandwich down and giving Lottie her full attention.

'He's moody, distracted, distant...'

'That describes my Stephen to a tee, but I can assure you he's not playing away.'

'Who's playing, Mummy?' Tyrone asked.

Delia pulled a face. 'The men on the telly. Cricket.' She waited for her son to turn back to Morgan, and shook her head. 'He's as nosy as I am, but one ball game he doesn't like is cricket, so if he thinks we're talking about batting averages and legs before wickets, he'll not pay us any attention.'

'Batting averages?'

Delia shrugged. 'It rubs off on you – like cat hairs. Stephen watches so much of it I'm sure it's in the air and I breathe it in.'

'At least you know what Stephen is up to when he's glued to the TV. Henry and I had a row on Saturday night and he stormed out. He says he went to the pub.'

'You don't believe him?'

'He had grass stains on the bum of his jeans. And he didn't smell like he'd had a pint.'

'That's hardly grounds for thinking he's having an affair,' Delia pointed out, reasonably.

'There's more. He's getting home later and later, and Mairi Edwards said she saw him parked up outside her house and she thought he was upset. And...' She paused, knowing what she was about to say sounded daft, but the thought had sneaked into her mind and was hanging around, stubbornly refusing to leave. She lifted her chin. 'You know the boat he found, the one I'm making into a bed for Robin—?'

'Ooh, how's that going? I meant to ask. Can I see it?' Delia interrupted, clapping her hands together.

'It'll be finished in a couple of days, and of course you can see it. As I was saying—'

'Sorry.' Delia placed her hands on the table, wrapping the fingers of one hand around the other, her expression sombre.

'I think he gave it to me to keep me busy,' Lottie finished.

To her surprise Delia burst out laughing. 'Do you honestly think that?' She reached across the table and patted her on the arm. 'I actually think he was being rather sweet and thoughtful. Robin wanted a new bed, a *different* bed, and Henry saw an opportunity and took it. I think it's lovely he has such faith in you. Stephen does all the DIY in our house, but I'd never dream of shoving an old rowing boat under his nose and asking him to turn it into a bed. Now' – she rubbed her hands together – 'can I see it?'

Lottie led her outside and dragged open one of the shed doors. That was another thing that needed fixing – the sagging shed doors.

'Wow!' Delia's eyes were round. 'I mean, *wow*! Are you sure this is the same boat you put on Instagram?' Her mouth had dropped open.

Lottie smiled. 'I'm sure.' The two women moved into the shed. 'Careful, I only just finished painting the white bits this morning. It's usually dry in half an hour, but what with it being so cold out here it might take a little longer, and I don't want to take any chances of you getting it on your clothes.' She stuck her head out of the door and checked on the children. They'd followed the adults outside and were happily playing with a digger and a truck in her wintry flowerbeds, so she left them to it.

'It's fabulous. You're so talented and I'm so jealous. It'll look wonderful in Robin's room. Has he seen it yet?'

'No one has except you.' Lottie sounded wistful and sad, and she winced.

'Maybe Henry is waiting for you to tell him it's finished,' Delia suggested. 'Have you asked him to take a look?'

Lottie dropped her gaze to the floor and nodded. She hadn't asked him as such – what she'd said was that he should come out and look at it some time. That was the same night he'd refused to make love.

'He doesn't want to have sex,' Lottie blurted.

'What! Not *ever*? Since when?'

'Last week. I tried to initiate proceedings, but he turned me down.'

'How often has this happened?'

'Just the once.' Once was enough. He'd never turned her down before.

'Once?' Delia snorted. 'Are you telling me that your husband hasn't said no to sex with you before now?'

'He hasn't,' Lottie protested.

'Do you ever say no to *him*?'

'Not often.'

'But you still refuse sometimes?'

Lottie nodded. It was rare: Henry seldom initiated anything when she wasn't in the mood, and vice versa. Until she'd misjudged the situation the other night.

'So why isn't he allowed to say no to you? I'm sure he has days when he's too tired, doesn't feel well, can't be arsed. We all feel like that sometimes – why not Henry?'

Delia had a point, Lottie realised. 'It's just that it's never happened before.'

'Blimey! How long have you two been married? Stephen and I tend to give each other the brush-off more often than we get to do it. I thought that was the norm. Are you telling me it's not?'

Heat crept into Lottie's cheeks, and she knew her face was turning beetroot.

Delia slung an arm around her shoulders. 'Look, my lovely, from what you've said, I don't think you have anything to worry about. So what if Henry is moody and preoccupied? Do you think it might be a work thing? Have you asked him?'

She had asked the same night he'd knocked back her advances. 'He said everything was tickety-boo.'

'Well, then. Don't go jumping to conclusions, eh? Henry loves you and the kids. He's not the type to go sneaking around behind your back.'

'I'm sure you're right.' Lottie sighed. 'It's probably just me being silly.' And with that, she vowed not to go trawling through his pockets again.

No more thinking that her husband was up to no good. Delia was talking sense – they had been married a long time, and she shouldn't expect everything to stay the same. It was only natural their relationship would evolve as the years went on, and they weren't the same people they'd been, pre-kids.

Lottie could see that they'd been taking each other for granted perhaps, and they each had their separate issues to deal with. But that shouldn't drive them apart, so she vowed to try to make some time for each other outside the family. They could do with some date nights in their life – not a quick fumble in bed after a long day when both of them were exhausted.

She'd start with getting a babysitter for Friday evening, and perhaps they could have a meal out. They hadn't done that in ages, and she found she was looking forward to it.

Chapter 10

Henry

Henry almost whooped with joy. One of his many applications had led to some interest he read, with growing excitement as he rapidly scanned the email. This one hadn't been through an employment agency, but direct to the company concerned. He hadn't held out much hope that he'd get anywhere with them because Allinson's speciality was fertilisers not feed, but they seemed to like the cut of his jib enough to drop him a line to say the sales director would be in touch in the next few days.

Deciding it called for celebration, Henry knocked off early for the day. He'd been to all the appointments he needed to, so now he could scuttle off home and hopefully be back in plenty of time for tea.

He wasn't known for whistling, but he caught himself whistling along to a couple of tunes on the radio and he even tapped his fingers on the steering wheel once or twice when something livelier came on. Feeling the most upbeat and optimistic than since he'd been told he was being given the push, Henry found himself looking forward to spending some time with his family. He saw his wife and kids daily, but for the past couple of weeks he'd felt as though he was there in person but not there in spirit. He guessed Lottie might have come to the same conclusion, and he vowed to make it up to her.

He was almost tempted to tell her what had been going on, but this job was far from in the bag and he didn't want to tempt fate by announcing it and then to have it fall through. There'd be time enough to tell her when he had a firm offer under his belt.

On seeing the sign for Aberaeron ahead, he considered popping into the library for half an hour since he had plenty of time, but he changed his mind. Checking job sites daily was a thankless task, as they needed time to refresh. Every other day, or every third day was enough, but he'd felt so desperate he'd trawled through them obsessively every single day, even if he had to use his phone to do so, which wasn't ideal. There was a lingering taste of that desperation in his mind now, but it wasn't as sharp as it had been before he'd read the email.

Sally Chisholm, that was the sales director's name, and he couldn't wait to talk to her. Selling was one thing he was good at, no matter if it was pony nuts or himself, even though he hated being interviewed. Even so, every job he'd managed to get an interview for, he'd been offered. Throughout the course of his career it was only three, but the precedent had been set. His main problem this time around would be that he wasn't applying for a sales job in animal feed – but, honestly, it shouldn't be hard to make the transition between selling one kind of agricultural product to another. Henry beat his fingers once more to a tune on the radio.

Five minutes later, however, he was suddenly assailed by the idea that the change might prove impossible. For one horrible moment, as he negotiated some sleeping policemen, he wondered if he'd lost his touch.

Almost immediately, he shoved the notion out of his mind. It simply didn't bear thinking about, so he turned up the volume on the radio and for the remainder of the journey he sang along to the songs on Radio 2, doing the la-la-la thing when he didn't know the words.

—

'Sh—sugar!' Lottie exclaimed, as Henry barged through the front door and nearly knocked her over. He put a hand out intending to steady her and caught her around the waist instead, pulling her into him.

She came up against his chest with an audible 'Oof!' and he laughed out loud.

'What time is it? I haven't started cooking tea yet. Oh, damn. Sorry...' Lottie looked delectably flustered, and he laughed again, earning himself a rather incredulous look.

Henry kissed the top of her head and released her. 'I'm early,' he explained. 'It's only ten to four.'

'Thank goodness for that! I thought I'd lost a couple of hours, for a minute. Let me take this upstairs' – she nodded at the now-crumpled pile of ironing she was holding – 'and I'll get tea started. It's chicken wraps, so it shouldn't take more than half an hour.'

'Where are the kids?' he asked.

'Robin's got football and is having tea at Joffrey's house. Sabrina is in her room and Morgan is doing a jigsaw in the kitchen.'

As though he'd heard his name mentioned, Morgan came hurtling down the hall and threw himself at his father. Henry grabbed him by the arms and lifted him up. 'What have you been doing today, my little monkey?'

'I helped Mummy clean Robin's room. Shh, we're not supposed to tell him. It's a secret.'

'It is?' Henry glanced at Lottie for confirmation.

She nodded. 'Actually, I'm glad you're back early, as it would be an ideal time considering Robin is out of the house, to bring his boat-bed in from the shed. That's why Morgan was helping me clean his room. Can we do it now, before I start cooking?'

'I'll just get changed. Give me a sec.' Still dangling Morgan by the arms, Henry made his way upstairs. It looked as though being home early was fortuitous.

He wondered why Lottie hadn't said anything about finishing Robin's bed, but when he thought about it, neither of them had said a great deal to each other over the past few days, since he'd stalked out of the house on Saturday.

It was time to apologise.

Lottie was already in the shed when he entered the kitchen, Morgan hot on his heels. His son had stuck to him like a limpet, following him into the bathroom and back out again, into their bedroom and back out again, chattering all the time. Henry listened to him with a mixture of incredulity (did Morgan ever pause for breath?) and delight. He realised how much he missed this. He'd hardly been at home lately, and had been so preoccupied…

'I love you, mate,' he said to his son, scooping him up and throwing him over his shoulder.

Morgan squealed in delight, his heels and his fists drumming a beat on Henry's torso.

'I've got a sack of spuds,' he declared to Lottie as he walked into the shed, holding Morgan firmly in place. 'Where do you want them?'

'I'm not a spud!' Morgan shrieked indignantly. 'Put me down!'

Henry popped the child down on the floor, only for the little boy to immediately demand to be picked up again.

'Can you go and ask Sabrina to open Robin's bedroom door, please?' Henry asked. The tactic worked, as Morgan scampered out of the shed and into the kitchen, yelling for his sister at the top of his voice.

'I've already opened the door,' Lottie said.

'I wanted a quick word without Mr Big Ears listening,' Henry said, and drew in a deep breath. 'Sorry, Lottie. I've been an arse.'

'You've only just realised?' His wife's expression was arch.

'I've got no excuse for behaving so badly.' He pulled a face. 'It was a work thing preying on my mind, but whatever it was I shouldn't have taken it out on you and the children.'

'No, you shouldn't have,' she agreed, and he wondered if she was going to forgive him. 'Is everything OK now?' she asked.

Henry risked telling a porkie. 'It is.' It wasn't quite yet, but he hoped it soon would be. And even if it wasn't, he didn't intend to act like such a prat again. So much for him not wanting to worry her – dashing out of the house in a fit of pique hadn't exactly helped.

He held his arms wide and she stepped into them, snuggling against him. God, but he loved this woman. Even if they did squabble now and again, it was never over anything major and it never lasted long.

Her perfume wafted into his nose and he inhaled the flowery scent of her, thinking how good she felt. He was just about to discover if she tasted as good as she smelt when Morgan came hurtling into the shed.

'I want kisses, too, Mummy, Daddy,' he demanded, and the mood was broken.

Henry brushed his fingers down her arm as he released her, and whispered, 'Later, Mrs H.' Her wicked answering smile almost made him melt, and he hurriedly cleared his throat. 'Shall we get on with it?'

'It's heavy,' Lottie warned. 'I'm not sure the two of us can manage it on our own.'

'How did John Porter get it in the shed? Did he have some help?'

'No, it was just him.'

'Then I'm sure we can manage it between us,' Henry declared. But he'd not taken John Porter's farming muscles into consideration, and by the time he and Lottie had navigated the repurposed boat out of the shed and into the kitchen, sweat was beading on his brow and his T-shirt clung to his back, despite the temperature outside.

'Good Lord, I didn't realise I was so unfit,' he said. 'I think I'd better start going to the gym.' Or maybe not the gym: running was free and there were plenty of places he could go for a jog right on his doorstep.

Eventually, though, they managed to tilt it this way and that, and get it through the kitchen and up the stairs, with Morgan dancing excitedly around them. Sabrina stuck her head out of her bedroom once to see what all the fuss was about, then retreated hastily in case she was asked to help.

By the time Robin's bed was in his room, the only thing Henry wanted to do was to go and lie down on his own bed. He was worn out, but he gamely helped Lottie dismantle their son's old bed, and put the original mattress on the new one.

'When did you do that?' he asked, noticing that the walls had been painted a fresh light blue.

'Last week.'

'Oh.' Henry felt idiotic for not noticing. He'd been so wrapped up in himself... 'You've done a fantastic job on that old boat,' he said, standing back to admire it.

'Do you think?' She sounded doubtful.

'I most certainly do. How much would something like that cost if you bought it in a shop?'

'I don't know. A lot.'

'It's really professional.' He walked over to her. She was stuffing a pillow into its case and plumping it up. 'I'm so proud of you.'

Lottie stopped what she was doing and turned to face him. 'Are you?'

'I don't tell you enough, do I? I also don't tell you often enough how much I love you.'

'Aww, what's got into you, you big softie?' She stroked his cheek and Henry pressed his face against her hand. 'Do you want to show me how much you love me?'

Henry smirked. Oh, yeah, this was what he had been talking about in the shed earlier. 'You bet!'

'Can you make tea, while I finish sorting Robin's room out? It's still a bit of a mess.'

'Right. Er, yeah, of course. Do what you've got to do. Wraps, you said?'

'Thanks, hon.' She'd already returned to her task of making the bed.

Deflated, he picked up Morgan and balanced him on his hip. 'I'll give you a shout when it's ready,' he said.

'Henry?'

'Yes?'

'I can think of another way you can show me,' she said, and she blew him a kiss, leaving him in no doubt as to her meaning.

Shaking his head at her, he went downstairs with a smile on his face. Things were definitely looking up.

Chapter 11

Lottie

Walking on air didn't begin to describe how Lottie felt the next morning as she and Morgan trotted down Applewell's main street. It was amazing how reconnecting with her husband had boosted her mood, despite having had less sleep than usual. She didn't mind late nights if they were all like that. They'd even shared a proper kiss before Henry left for work earlier, much to Sabrina's disgust. Robin hadn't been too impressed either, taking his cue from his sister, who'd pulled faces and had made gagging noises.

All Lottie had done was smile at her serenely, and pray that if and when her daughter fell in love, it would be with someone who loved Sabrina as much and who made her as happy as Henry made Lottie. Even after all this time together and three kids, they were as in love today as they'd been when they first married.

Of course they'd had bumps along the way – and they'd just hit one and come out the other side – but so did every couple. Sometimes it took one of those bumps to bring two people back together.

Listen to her! She was exaggerating the bump business. They'd had a bit of a squabble, that was all, and she'd jumped to conclusions. It had taken Delia's sensible viewpoint to put things into perspective. Lottie just thanked God they were back to normal. Actually, more normal than normal, according to last night's antics, and she giggled to herself.

'Mummy happy?' Morgan asked, and she giggled again. It was a change from being asked if she was cross.

'You look pleased with yourself,' Eleri Jones from the cafe said, as Lottie and Morgan walked past. 'Good news?'

'Hi, Eleri. Oh, you know...' She stopped for a moment to chat.

'Do you fancy coming in for a minute? A hot chocolate and a slice of Christmas cake on the house? I'd like to pick your brains.'

Lottie wasn't one to turn down an offer like that. It would be such a treat – rarely did she pop into a cafe, and with the extension to pay for, and Christmas fast approaching (she still had some presents to buy, although she'd been picking things up throughout the year so there weren't too many left to get) she didn't have the spare cash to splash around on coffee and cake out.

'Hi, Gracie,' she said, seeing the woman who'd made her cushions for her sitting at a corner table. 'How are you?'

'Good, thanks, and you?'

They exchanged pleasantries for a minute or so, until Eleri placed a tray down on a spare table and beckoned her over. 'Here you go, a hot chocolate and slice of Christmas cake for you, and a milkshake and a reindeer biscuit for Morgan.'

Morgan had been tugging restlessly at her arm, not interested in the conversation of adults, but on seeing the goodies he clambered onto a chair and sat nicely.

'Thanks, this looks delicious,' Lottie said, tucking into her cake. 'Mmm.' She closed her eyes in bliss as she chewed, then opened them again slowly. 'It tastes even better than it looks,' she declared. 'Now, what do you want to pick my brains about?'

'Look around you,' Eleri said. 'What do you see?'

Lottie frowned, wondering what the cafe owner was getting at. As far as Lottie could tell it looked the same as it always had apart from the recent addition of a Christmas tree and assorted decorations. There was a counter off to the side, the chiller beneath displaying sandwiches, baguettes, pasties and other snacky lunch-time food, which she knew would all have been freshly prepared that morning on the premises. There was also a cabinet holding assorted cakes and pastries. Behind the counter was a coffee machine, being worked by Olive, one of Eleri's employees, and shelves filled with mugs, plates and other items like teapots and cake stands. On the wall behind the counter was the daily specials board, with a selection of home-cooked meals. Today's was carrot and coriander soup with sourdough bread, jacket potatoes with various fillings, or lamb hotpot. Despite it being nowhere near lunchtime, Lottie's mouth watered.

The cafe itself held eleven tables, although it could probably hold more if they were moved up a bit, and was prettily decorated in what Lottie thought of as a sort of Victorian tea room style, with chintz curtains and old furniture. In one corner there was a squashy sofa and a low coffee table, and in another was a book stand filled with children's stories. A wonderful aroma of coffee, vanilla and cinnamon hung in the air.

'I'm not sure what I should be looking at,' Lottie confessed, watching a couple of small children break free from their mums and head for the bookcase. She smiled, remembering occasions when her own children used to have to be bribed with a book to keep them quiet while she chatted with a friend for more than five minutes. Gone were the days when she could spend a lazy hour in a cafe catching up on news – gnats had better attention spans than her kids: no sooner had they eaten, they wanted to be off. Looking at the speed at which Morgan was devouring his biscuit, she anticipated having less than three minutes before he started clamouring to get down.

'There!' Eleri hissed and jerked her eyes towards the group of three mums and their children.

'I don't follow.' Lottie wiped Morgan's hands and face free of crumbs, and helped him guide the straw to his mouth. He sucked on it greedily, the level of milkshake in the glass dropping at an impressive rate.

'Those kids have been driving their mothers mad. None of them will keep still.'

'Are you thinking of banning children?' Lottie asked, horrified. That wouldn't be good for Eleri's business at all.

'No, silly! The opposite. We get so many families visiting the area, especially in the summer months, what with all the camping sites and the guesthouses, that I want to encourage them to come in here. At the moment, if they've got young kids they only have a quick cuppa and they're off. I was thinking of creating a kiddies' corner to encourage people with children to stay for a bit longer – maybe have a spot of lunch, rather than just a coffee and a cookie.'

'It sounds like a great idea,' Lottie said, letting Morgan wander off to check out the books. 'Is that what you wanted to ask me?'

'Not exactly.' Eleri took a sip of her drink. 'I saw the photos you put on Instagram. Your boy's bed looks fab. I can't believe it used to be an old boat.'

Lottie blinked at the abrupt change of topic. 'Thanks. I'm pleased with it. I'd like to buy some curtains and a duvet set in a nautical theme, but that's going to have to wait a while.'

Eleri bit her lip. 'Your photos got me thinking about the kiddies' area – I was hoping you could help me set it up. I'll pay you, of course,' she added, hurriedly.

Lottie's eyes widened. That was a shot out of the blue. 'Gosh. I'm, er, flattered, but—'

'I've seen what you can do with old furniture,' Eleri interrupted. 'I've got some bits and pieces I thought I could use. You see, I don't have a great deal of money to spend on this, and I was hoping…?'

Lottie's heart sank; she knew how much time it took to upcycle a piece of furniture. She wanted to help, but it would take hours and hours, and she was anxious to get on with repairing the sledge she'd bought, and using its template to make two more, before any decent amount of snow fell. The money would come in handy though, and she wondered how much Eleri would pay. Not enough to compensate for the amount of time it would take if she was to be paid by the hour, but anything she received could be put towards buying those last few Christmas presents she had yet to purchase. Or she'd save it towards new bedding for Robin. Or maybe not – she couldn't justify purchasing new when there was nothing wrong with the duvet cover he already had.

'What did you have in mind?' she asked, daunted and intrigued at the same time. If Eleri was willing to pay, then Lottie would be able to feel she was helping to contribute to the family finances.

'Look.' Eleri turned her phone towards her, and Lottie examined the photos she was being shown. 'When I saw your before and after pictures of the boat, it got me thinking.'

'That's an old TV stand, isn't it?' The photo showed a piece of alarmingly orange-coloured pine furniture which had a space for a TV, a small cupboard on the one side which was probably for DVDs or CDs, a larger cupboard on the other side with deeper shelves, and two doors underneath with yet more storage space.

What made her wince – and set her imagination on fire at the same time – were some photos of how the cabinet had been transformed into a child's play kitchen. The way it had been converted was ingenious and Lottie was eager to get started on it, but she also knew how much time it would take to make the 'before' into the 'after'.

Eleri said, 'There's an almost identical piece of furniture to the old TV stand in the photo, in my gran's house that she wants to get rid of. I thought I could do something with it.'

'You can,' Lottie agreed.

'But…?'

'It'll be cheaper to buy a new play kitchen.' Lottie felt obliged to point out. She wouldn't feel right taking Eleri's money, when the woman could purchase a new one for probably less than it would take to upcycle the cabinet.

'Really?'

Lottie nodded.

Eleri looked crestfallen. 'How much would something like this cost new?' She focused on her phone for a moment, then looked up. 'I should have checked first,' she admitted. 'This one is about a hundred pounds. I bet it won't last, though. Are you sure it would cost this much to do up the TV stand?'

'Not if you were to do it yourself, but if you paid someone to do it…'

'Ah, I see. That's a shame. And there are other bits and pieces in my gran's house I was hoping I could use, too. Never mind.'

Lottie had a thought. 'How about if I show you how to do it yourself? I'll cut out the hole for the sink and do any woodworking because I've got the right tools, but you can do all the sanding and painting yourself. That's the time-consuming part.'

'I'll pay you,' Eleri insisted again, but before Lottie could say anything a voice from another table piped up.

Gracie Stewart said, 'I'll make you a duvet cover and a pair of curtains. I've got some lovely fabric with boats and beach huts and lighthouses on. It should be enough to make a single duvet set and a pair of curtains.'

Lottie stared at her. Gracie was well known in Applewell for her sewing skills. She was also a collector of fabric and could frequently be seen in UnderCover rooting around for unusual patterns. Catrin also often gave her any items that were too worn or damaged to be sold in the shop, and it was astounding what uses Gracie could put them to.

'That's very generous of you,' Lottie said cautiously, thinking it was a lovely gesture but wondering why Gracie had offered. Lottie knew how eager the residents of Applewell were to help each other out, but Gracie had a business to run and couldn't afford to work for nothing.

Eleri was far quicker than Lottie to catch on. 'Lunch every day for two weeks?' she said to Gracie, and Gracie grinned.

'Deal!' the woman cried.

Lottie squinted at the pair of them. 'Is this, like, bartering?'

'Yep. Good, innit?' Eleri rubbed her hands together. 'Gracie re-covered my favourite armchair for the same price.'

Gracie grinned. 'It saves me cooking. I'm hopeless at it. So, this way I get a decent meal, Eleri gets her TV stand made into a kitchen, and you can finish your little boy's room off.'

'Deal,' Lottie agreed firmly, thinking what a marvellous system it was.

After rounding Morgan up — he was trying to get behind the counter to help himself to another biscuit — Lottie arranged to call around to Eleri's grandmother and take a look at the TV stand. She was quietly excited about the prospect of helping Eleri turn the old piece of furniture into something useful, and receiving a hand-made duvet set and curtains in return seemed like a good deal.

'Guess what?' she squealed to Delia down the phone on the way home.

'You've won the lottery? You've been swept off your feet by a hunky pirate...?'

Lottie took her mobile away from her ear and stared at it for a second. Did she just hear Delia correctly? 'A *pirate?*'

'Yeah, sorry, we watched a re-run of *Pirates of the Caribbean* last night.'

'I see. Erm, no, no pirate. It's better than that.'

'Better than Captain Jack Sparrow?'

'Yes, now be quiet so I can tell you. I've been asked to make a play corner for Eleri's cafe, using old bits of furniture from her grandma's house. I'm getting a duvet set and a pair of curtains in return.'

'Eh? You'll have to run that by me again.'

Lottie laughed, and went on to explain what had happened.

'Wow, Lottie, that's fantastic! I said you were good, didn't I? Are you thinking of making a business out of this?'

'No chance! It's OK for me to upcycle stuff for my own use, but selling it is a completely different ballgame. There's the time element for a start. Not only that, but if I have to buy things to work on, it would eat into any profits I make. I was just lucky John Porter gave Henry the boat for nothing.'

'Talking about Henry, how are things between you?'

Lottie was glad she wasn't on a video call to her friend, as a heated blush swept into her cheeks. 'Good, they're good,' she muttered.

'I see,' Delia said, with a chortle. 'I'm glad about that. But have a think about the business thing, yeah? You can always try using Etsy a bit more. It'll keep you busy until Morgan is old enough to start school and you decide whether or not you want to go back to work.'

'We'll see,' Lottie said, meaning, *I'm not going to think about it at all*. Still, it was nice for Eleri to have asked her. And it was even nicer that Lottie was able to help. Her philosophy regarding reusing and repurposing things might have originated out of necessity, but it had swiftly become more about not wanting to be so wasteful and throw things away; and if she could help someone else do that, then she'd have done her good deed for the day.

Chapter 12

Henry

Henry could feel himself sliding down the slippery slope towards grumpiness again. It might have only been three days since he'd received the email from Allinson's but it felt like at least a week. Tenterhooks didn't begin to come close to describing his emotional state.

He'd still continued to trawl the internet for anything suitable, and he'd continued to fire off CVs and application forms left, right and centre in the hope one or more of them might produce a result. But so far the only one to have done so was his application to Allinson's and they were taking their sweet time in moving on to the next stage of the process.

What if they'd changed their minds? It had been known to happen – if they'd received a couple of applications that matched their remit better, then they might be interviewing those people first. If so, instead of a phone call from this Sally Chisholm, the best he could hope for would be a thanks-but-no-thanks email.

Some companies wouldn't even bother with that.

Or maybe they'd decided to withdraw the position. He'd known that to have happened, too. Or—

His jumbled thoughts ground to a halt and he grimaced. There was no point in going over and over it in his head; he'd hear from them in due course, or not at all, and trying to anticipate what was likely to happen wasn't doing his mood any good.

The last thing he wanted was a return to the way he'd been feeling. Now that he was back on an even keel with both his wife and the children, he had no intention of rocking the boat.

All those nautical references made him remember that he had been meaning to pop up to Porter's Farm to have a word with John about some oars. Robin's bedroom was nearly finished, but not quite, and the oars, along with new curtains and bedding, would set it off a treat.

When Lottie had told him at dinner the other night – yet another evening when he'd made it home in time to eat with his family – that she'd swapped her upcycling expertise for a length of fabric and Gracie Stewart's sewing skills, he'd been dumbfounded. He'd not known that bartering was still a thing – he'd assumed it had gone out with the Middle Ages.

He'd also been amazed when she'd told him she was helping refurbish a corner of Eleri's cafe. It was just a pity she wasn't getting paid for it. Good hard cash was what the family needed now. Unfortunately, he couldn't explain that to Lottie without having to share the reason why.

He'd had his P45 through yesterday, along with his final payslip, and both documents now resided safely in his briefcase, along with the formal letter from Baldwin Ltd advising him of his redundancy. He'd had a bit of a moment when he'd seen the envelope sitting on the kitchen table, but he'd opened it when Lottie was out of the room and then had shoved it in his briefcase. She never looked in there.

Breathing hard, he wondered if it was time to come clean. He didn't know how much longer he could keep this up, and once he'd received his final wages at the end of December he'd have to tell her. He wouldn't be able to keep it a secret when there was no longer any money going into their account. If he hadn't managed to secure another position by the New Year, he'd put in a claim for benefits and tell Lottie. Until then, he'd pray and hope.

'How's that old boat coming along?' John asked, after Henry had pulled into the yard and tracked John down – the noise of a hundred or so sheep in the pens adjacent to the biggest barn had given him a clue as to the farmer's whereabouts.

'It's finished,' he declared proudly, 'and it looks great. Here.' He took his phone out of his pocket and showed John the finished result. 'Robin was absolutely ecstatic – he couldn't wait to go to school and tell his friend Callum all about it. A real boat trumps a pretend fire engine any day. Although it was only six in the evening, he insisted on going to bed and staying there.'

'It does look grand,' the farmer agreed.

'You'll have to come and see it next time you're in the village. Lottie would love to show it to you.'

'Aye, I'll do that,' John said. 'Now, what can I do for you?'

'I hate to ask, but I was wondering if you had any oars to go with that boat you so kindly gave me?'

'What do you want them for? You can hardly row the damned thing.' John took his flat cap off and scratched his head. He seemed to do that a lot when he was speaking, Henry noticed, with a smile.

'To put on the wall above the bed. For decoration,' he said.

John gave him an odd look. 'Right. Hmm, well, I've not seen any around for years. They might have gone for firewood, or the like. I'll keep an eye out for them, though, and if I see them I'll give you a bell.'

'That would be great, thanks.' It had been worth a try. Maybe he could have a scout around some reclamation yards, he thought, until he remembered his precarious financial situation. If he had to pay for them, the oars would have to wait until he'd landed himself a new job.

John spoke. ''Ere, can you make use of this? The missus wanted a new door in the porch, so she had one.' John didn't wait for a response, but turned smartly on his heel and led Henry back across the yard and into one of the sheds. 'I've got no use for it. Maybe your Lottie can do something with it.'

Henry found himself gazing at a glass-panelled interior door. Most of the glass was still intact but a few panes were cracked, and one had disappeared completely.

'Um…' What on earth would Lottie be able to do with an old door? 'That's wonderful – thanks.'

'I'll help you load it in your car. You'll have to put the back seats down as far as they'll go.'

'Right, yes, I'll do that.'

'You grab that end and I'll take this.' John lifted one end of the door and waited for Henry to get a grip on the other.

Henry did as he was told and together they walked to Henry's car. After some fiddling around, they slid the door in through the hatch at the back.

'Well, thanks for that,' Henry said, nodding at the door he had no idea what to do with. 'I'd best leave you to your sheep.'

'Aye, I'd better get back. Their feet won't trim themselves.'

Henry watched him go, then got in his car. Lottie would think he'd gone mad. He knew she was good at recycling, but he was pretty certain the only thing you could do with a door was to use it as a door. Or... he had a thought. Without the glass in it, he supposed it could be used as a trellis. But the Hargreaves' household didn't need either a door or any trellis.

He'd leave it up to Lottie – if she took one look and demanded he take it to the nearest household waste depot, that's what he'd do.

That would teach him to try to get something for nothing.

Chapter 13

Lottie

'Why?' Lottie asked, after Henry informed her he had a door in his car.

'John Porter,' he replied, as if that explained everything, when it explained diddly-squat.

'Nope. I'm not getting the connection,' she said.

'I dropped by his farm to see if he had any oars to go with that boat.'

'And you came away with a door instead? Are you expecting me to make oars out of it?'

'Can you?' His hopeful expression was endearing.

'I doubt it.'

'So what *are* you going to do with it?'

'I don't know – you tell me.'

Henry shot her a despairing look. 'Surely you can do *some*thing with it?'

Lottie hesitated. She possibly could find a use for it that didn't involve it being hung as a door, but honestly – why was he bringing her other people's rubbish? At least they'd been on the same page when it came to the boat. This time they weren't even in the same library.

'You'd better stick it in the shed,' she sighed.

Something she'd thought of a few days ago came back to her, but she dismissed it. Still, the idea lingered, despite knowing it was ridiculous to even contemplate that Henry might be bringing her things to upcycle just to keep her occupied. She was a mother to three children, she had a house to run and a husband – she didn't need anything else to keep her busy.

As she watched Henry wiggle the door out of the car, huffing and puffing as he did so, she noticed an expression of chagrin on his face. It seemed to her that he was a little bit put out at bringing her a present and her dismissing it. She supposed her reaction *had* been somewhat akin to that of the owner of a cat being presented with a mouse, and she wondered if cats could tell that their owners were being ungrateful.

Chastened, she tried to make amends. 'It's very kind of you,' she said to him. 'I'm sure I can do something with it.' She was sure the internet would offer up all kinds of weird and wonderful suggestions.

It wasn't as if she didn't have anything to do, though: with Eleri asking her to revamp furniture to create a children's play area in the cafe and the sledges she wanted to make, Lottie had more than enough on her plate. Another thought occurred to her – had Henry been listening at all when she'd told him about what Eleri had asked her to do? She suspected not, otherwise he wouldn't have brought her a door.

I ask you, she thought to herself. *Other husbands would give their wives flowers, or chocolates.* Not hers – he brought her a *door*. She realised he was being thoughtful, because the chocolates would only go to her thighs and the flowers would soon wilt and die. And he was trying to support her in her quest to upcycle rather than discard and buy new. The problem was, she didn't particularly want a door, they didn't need a door, and she hadn't got a clue what to do with it.

Oh, well, it could sit in the shed until she found a use for it, but the thought gave her pause as she recalled the village hoarder, George Nightingale. Although she applauded his waste not, want not ethic, what she didn't want to do was to turn into a female version of him.

Her principle of mending or fixing what she had rather than discarding it straight off the bat was different, as the boat being turned into a bed testified. Robin's old bed wouldn't go to waste, either. She'd find a use for it sooner or later. Preferably sooner.

With the door safely stashed, Lottie and Henry went back into the house. Now might be a good time to tell her husband that she'd arranged a date night for them. He might not be a flowers and chocolates man, but he had clearly been thinking about her, and it warmed her heart.

'Guess what?' she said, biting her lip in what she hoped was a provocative manner.

'Hmm?' Henry appeared to be a little distracted.

'I said, guess what?'

Henry's gaze when he looked at her was blank for a moment, then he focused with an effort. 'I've no idea.'

Disappointed that he wasn't going to play along, Lottie stopped trying to be provocative because it obviously wasn't working, and told it to him straight instead. 'We're going out tomorrow evening.'

'We are? Where?'

'Nowhere exciting. Just the Busy Bumble for supper, but I thought we could do with an evening away from the kids.'

A vertical line creased his brow and his gaze sharpened.

'Before you say anything,' she hurriedly continued, 'your mum is coming to babysit, in case you were worried about the children.'

'Dinner? Out?'

'Yes, that's OK, isn't it?'

For some reason, Henry didn't look as if it was OK. He looked alarmed.

'What's wrong?' she asked.

'I thought we were trying to save money,' he replied.

'We are, but not to the extent that we can't have a bite to eat in the pub now and again. It's not as though we make a habit of it.' She couldn't remember the last time they'd gone out for a meal.

'I don't think so,' he said, walking away. It seemed that Henry considered the matter closed.

Lottie, however, didn't. There was something more to this than simply not wanting to spend the money. Meals at the Busy Bumble were hardly expensive, and it wasn't as though they would sink a bottle of the pub's finest wine. She'd have half a lager like she always did, and Henry would invariably have a pint of ale. They weren't exactly big spenders.

In that case, what was his problem?

She dashed into the hall and was about to ask him – confront him might be a more accurate description – when his phone rang.

Henry was halfway up the stairs as he fished it out of his jeans pocket, and he slowed to a halt as he looked at the screen. 'Hello?'

There was a short pause, then he said, 'Er, hang on a sec, I'll, um...' Henry walked back down the stairs and along the hall to the front door. He didn't look at her once.

His expression was blank, but she knew her husband too well. The best way she could describe him was 'unnerved'.

'Shifty' was another word that sprang to mind.

She watched him hurry outside, pulling the front door shut behind him, and trot down the drive, where he eventually stopped and began talking. Lottie strained to hear what he was saying, even going as far as pressing her ear to the glass, but all she heard was the sound of her own whooshing pulse.

Giving up on trying to listen, Lottie darted into the living room and peered out of the window. Henry had his back to the house, shoulders hunched, one hand in his pocket, the other holding his phone. He kept scuffing his feet, reminding her so much of Robin that if she hadn't been so concerned she would have smiled.

She waited for him to end the call and, as soon as he turned towards the house, she leapt back and scuttled into the kitchen, where she pretended she'd been preparing the evening meal all along.

'Important?' she asked casually.

'Nah, just work.'

The words themselves might have been offhand, as was the manner in which they were delivered, but Lottie sensed suppressed excitement coming off him like heat from a radiator. His mood had lightened too, and he didn't look as miserable as he had when he'd arrived home.

Lottie persevered. 'Anything to worry about?'

He shook his head. 'Not at all. Everything's tickety-boo.'

She flinched. He'd used that phrase again, the one that didn't sound as though it should be coming out of his mouth. *Tickety-boo, indeed.* She couldn't help wondering where he'd got it from, because it wasn't like him to be twee.

'In fact,' he continued, 'maybe we *should* go to the pub on Friday after all.'

'Great. I'll confirm with your mum.' *But it isn't great, is it?* Lottie thought. There was something going on with Henry. She didn't know what it was, but she was determined to get to the bottom of it.

Chapter 14

Henry

Finally, he was getting somewhere with finding another job, Henry thought, as he got ready to go on their date night. It was the only reason he'd agreed to go out at all, because he didn't feel quite as guilty now about spending the money. He had an appointment to meet Sally Chisolm in person next Tuesday. She'd sounded nice on the phone – although it was difficult to tell what someone was like until you met them, and sometimes you didn't truly find out what they were like until after you started working for them. But he was hopeful. And he'd been sadly lacking in hope lately.

It had been rather awkward that she'd called while he was at home, and even more awkward that Lottie had been only a few feet away. He was pretty sure his wife didn't suspect anything, though. After all, he'd been home slightly earlier than normal and officially he should still be working, so it wasn't unexpected that he might receive the odd phone call. It was quite common for him to get a call from one of his clients asking him to pop in, or wanting to speak to him to place an order. Lottie should be used to it.

When he came to think of it, Henry concluded that employing travelling salesmen was quite an old-fashioned way of doing things. No wonder Baldwins was shedding staff. These days it was so much easier to pick up a phone direct, or to order online. Some of the more traditional and older farmers preferred to have a bloke they knew and trusted popping around every few months and telling them what was new on the market, or leaving them with a complimentary bag of feed for them to try. Whichever way he looked at it, though, the writing was on the wall for him regarding sales jobs. He just hoped he could find another one which would last him a few more years, until he could figure out what he really wanted to do.

Being an agricultural feed salesman hadn't been one of his top five choices of profession when he was in school. It probably hadn't featured in his top one hundred. He'd wanted to be a deep-sea diver, based solely on a few holidays abroad where he'd enjoyed snorkelling in the warm waters of the Med. He'd looked into it once, and had even considered taking PADI courses in his local swimming baths, but that had been as far as it went.

Looking back, he still wasn't completely sure how he'd got into sales in the first place, and into agricultural feed sales at all. It had just kind of happened – a friend of a friend's dad knew someone, who knew someone, who was looking for... Yep, that's how things often had a way of working. And here he was, seventeen years later, still selling cow nuts. Hardly exciting, was it?

Oh, well, it put a roof over their head and paid the bills. They were hardly going to get rich from it, but at the moment he'd just be grateful to get any kind of job at all. He'd give himself a few months to settle in, and then he'd have a serious think about what he wanted to do with the rest of his life. Because he couldn't, in all honesty, see himself doing a sales job until he retired.

It wasn't all bad, though: he loved being out and about. He loved the travelling as long as it wasn't too far and didn't involve any overnight stays, and he loved visiting different places and meeting new people. What he didn't love was trying to flog them something. Which was a bit of a drawback, he had to admit, if you were a salesman.

He'd been doing it for so long it was second nature. Even though it was hard work and a thankless task sometimes, it wasn't too much of a chore. It was just that he didn't want to do it any more.

He put all these thoughts behind him as he stared into the wardrobe. Lottie didn't deserve to have a distracted husband, not when she was going to such an effort. He couldn't remember the last time they'd been out as a couple, and certainly not when they'd been out for a meal. Lottie was a pretty good cook, and she often said she resented spending money on pub grub when she could cook just as well at home. But he guessed that sometimes she needed a break from it, and they both needed a break from the house and from the children.

What he'd really like, and would be a *total* break, would be a night away. How fantastic, just him and Lottie and wild rampant sex, without the worry of trying to keep quiet in order not to wake the kids.

Henry pulled a shirt out of the wardrobe and slipped it off its hanger. He usually lived in T-shirts and sweatshirts, and thick jumpers in the winter – farmyards were cold and often draughty places – but this evening he thought he'd make a bit of an effort, and his blue Oxford button-down was perfect with a pair of dark navy chinos. He even had a decent pair of shoes somewhere – tan leather brogues that he'd had for at least ten years but had hardly worn, so they still looked practically brand new.

Lottie, he was delighted to see, was also making an effort. Not that she needed to, he thought hastily, just in case she could read his mind. She was beautiful anyway; she always had been and she always would be. To his eyes, she still looked about eighteen, the tiny lines around her eyes were barely noticeable, and neither were the odd grey hairs in her honey-coloured locks. He guessed she'd be one of those women who grew old gracefully, and would still look just as wonderful at sixty as she did at thirty-five.

He watched her brush out her hair, which was long and straight, falling to just below her shoulders. She normally wore it in a ponytail or a messy bun, but in honour of the rare occasion of them going out, she was wearing it loose. He also noticed that she had make-up on. She didn't need it, but she always looked that little bit more coquettish with mascara-covered eyelashes and pink lips.

'Is that new?' he asked, looking at her dress.

'*What?* No! This old thing? I've had it ages.'

He cocked his head at her and gave her a knowing look.

'Really,' she protested. 'I *have* had it ages. I'm surprised it still fits. I bought this when Sabrina was about two but I've hardly worn it, so in some ways it does feel like it's new. Do you like it?' She did a twirl and he wolf-whistled at her.

'Come on, hurry up. Mum will be here in a minute. I'm bloody desperate for a pint.' Gallantly he opened the bedroom door for her and ushered her through it.

He didn't know about his wife, but he felt like a kid getting out of school early. It was like he was truanting, sneaking out without the children. He probably shouldn't feel that way, but he couldn't help it. He loved his children more than life itself, but he wasn't averse to having his wife to himself, while supping a child-free pint.

His mum, predictably, had brought little gifts for the children: colouring books and crayons for the two younger ones, and a notepad and gel pens for Sabrina. Henry guessed it might keep them quiet for all of ten minutes.

'Go on, get off with you,' his mum said, shooing them out of the door. Henry sped through it, towing a slightly reluctant Lottie behind, who was still trying to explain about teeth-brushing routines and favourite stories.

'Mum knows all that,' Henry said. 'They'll be fine.'

He was beginning to wonder why Lottie had been so anxious to go out, when she was now clearly so anxious to stay in. Didn't she think his mother could cope with three children? It wasn't as if she'd not done it before.

Finally, though, Henry managed to hustle Lottie down the road and into the heart of the village. With each step further away from their house he could see her visibly relax. He was relaxed too, although part of his mind was still on the interview next week, and he assumed that Lottie's was half on the children. Nobody told you that being a parent meant you'd never have a worry-free moment ever again. But he was determined to enjoy the evening, and the first thing he did when they stepped inside the Busy Bumble was to head straight to the bar and order them both a drink.

'This is more like it,' he said, after taking a long swig and smacking his lips.

Lottie giggled, wiping his upper lip with her thumb. 'Foam moustache,' she told him.

'I know how to attract the ladies,' Henry joked. 'If you want to find a seat, I'll grab us a couple of menus.'

'Awright, Henry? Long time, no see.' Henry turned to see Donald Mousel at his elbow.

'It certainly is,' Henry agreed.

'Them kids keeping you busy?'

'As always. And how are you?'

'Can't grumble,' Donald said, and then went on to do precisely that, with Henry nodding and smiling in the appropriate places, or shaking his head and commiserating in others. He was eventually able to escape and join Lottie.

She was busy chatting to the couple on the next table, Nessa Millbrook and George Nightingale, him of the hoarding fame, although nobody ever mentioned it. Personally Henry didn't have an issue with owning a garage full of stuff. If it wasn't for the fact that the shed was Lottie's domain, Henry would probably have escaped to his on a more regular basis. He could also see the attraction of an allotment for the very same reason – as somewhere to disappear off to for hours on end, doing a bit of digging, then hiding in the potting shed with a copy of *Motor Weekly* and a sneaky hip flask full of sherry.

Nessa smiled at him as he sat down. 'Eleri was telling me about how Lottie is going to help her renovate some old pieces of furniture for the cafe. Your wife is so clever.' Nessa beamed at George. 'And so is George – he repainted all the cupboards in my kitchen. I'm useless at things like that. I can't even hang a mirror straight.'

Henry *was* immensely proud of Lottie. 'Has she told you about the boat we got from John Porter?' he asked. 'She's only gone and turned it into a bed for Robin. You ought to see it! She's done a fantastic job. Lottie' – he nudged her – 'show Nessa and George the photos.'

Lottie was blushing, but she did as she was asked and scrolled through her phone to show them. She was pleased at the praise, but he could see she was embarrassed to be the centre of attention.

'You *are* very clever,' George said, and Lottie beamed.

'You haven't got any ideas what I could do with an old door, have you?' she asked.

'Hang it?' Nessa suggested with a smirk.

Lottie pulled a face at the woman's teasing. 'We don't need it – we've got enough doors of our own, and it's not in good enough condition to sell. Henry brought it home for me.'

Henry could feel Nessa's eyes on him.

'You men are a strange lot,' she said. 'My George tried to woo me by painting my kitchen cupboard doors. I know I haven't lived in Applewell for very long and I might be missing something, but is it a thing for the men around here to present their women with doors, rather than jewellery or tickets to the theatre?'

Lottie giggled. 'It certainly appears to be that way although, to be honest, I don't get to wear jewellery very often, and I'm not too keen on the theatre.'

'Hey, I thought I was being nice,' Henry protested.

'You were, darling.' She patted him on the knee.

George cleared his throat. 'I'm sure I could find a use for it,' he said, and visibly shrank in his seat when Nessa sent him a ferocious glare.

'Oh, no, you don't, George Nightingale. We don't need a door, and when we do need one, we'll just go and buy one. You're not starting that again.'

George looked sheepish, but he gave Lottie a little smile. Lottie smiled back.

Their meals arrived and as Henry and Lottie tucked in, the conversation between the two tables ceased. But as he ate, Henry's thoughts turned once more to the issue of redundancy and the possibility of a job with a new company. He knew he wasn't living in the moment, but he couldn't help it. No matter how much he tried to tell himself that this job was his for the taking, he was still worried he wouldn't get it.

Another worry was the amount this meal was costing. The Busy Bumble was inexpensive, but it was still money they could do without spending, if only Lottie knew it. But that was where the problem lay – he didn't *want* Lottie to know it.

Not for the first time he wondered why he was so adamant about not telling his wife he'd been made redundant again. And not for the first time he came to the conclusion he didn't want her to think he was a failure. Losing one job was unfortunate; losing two in the space of six months was careless. Deep down, he knew how unfair he was being on himself, but he couldn't help it. The thought kept circling in his mind that he wanted to be able to tell her he'd stepped from one job to another almost seamlessly, and that he could provide for the family. He hated that she'd had to make do with so little for so long, even with him being in steady employment; what depths would she have to plumb to keep the family afloat if he failed to find another?

She'd done an absolutely fantastic job on the old boat, and it looked spectacular in Robin's room, but there was a part of him that wished she hadn't had to do it, that she should have been able to just go into a shop and buy one. He didn't want her to have to scrimp and save. He wanted her to be able to afford whatever she liked.

He knew it was ridiculous, and unless you were mega-wealthy no one could simply afford anything and everything they wanted; compromises always had to be made. But he thought Lottie took compromise to the extreme. Take this latest bartering thing, for instance. She was doing work for someone else in order for a third person to provide them with soft furnishings for their home. Was this what his family had been reduced to?

'Penny for them,' Lottie asked, breaking him out of his reverie.

'Huh?'

'You looked as though you were away with the fairies,' she said. 'Are you OK?'

'Yes, fine.' He put his knife and fork down, realising he'd cleared his plate without having tasted a thing. *Bloody hell, what a waste.* He'd polished off his meal without really being aware of what he was eating. It was a bit like when you drove home from work along a familiar road, and when you got there you couldn't remember a thing about the journey. It felt like that, only worse because he had to pay for this. He hadn't even enjoyed it, and for a moment he struggled to remember what it was he'd ordered. Ah yes, he'd fancied steak, but he'd gone for the cheapest thing on the menu, which was scampi and chips.

He was still somewhat distracted by the time they got home, and he prayed Lottie hadn't noticed, but knowing his wife she most certainly had. If she asked him again if anything was wrong, he'd blame it on work problems. He wouldn't exactly be lying, would he?

After Lottie gave Meryl a peck on the cheek and thanked her, she went upstairs to check on the children, while Henry saw his mum out.

'Did you have a good time?' Meryl asked.

'Yes, thanks, it was lovely.'

'What did you have to eat?'

'Scampi and chips.'

'I'd have thought you would have gone for steak, like you usually do.'

'I fancied a change.'

'Are you all right, Henry, love? You don't seem yourself.'

'I'm fine.' His answer was rather tetchy so he tried to soften it with a smile.

His mother didn't seem convinced by his performance, and neither was he. He wasn't fine; but he would be. He just needed to get this interview out of the way and be offered the job, and then he'd be totally fine.

But nothing was totally fine, as he discovered after he and Lottie went to bed. Recalling the events of the other night, Henry was feeling a bit frisky. He wasn't sure if it was *despite* his worry about his job or whether it was *because* of it, but he wanted to feel a deeper connection to Lottie, so he snuggled up closer and put his arm around her.

Lottie uttered a little noise, almost as though she was asleep, but he knew she couldn't possibly be because he'd watched her get into bed mere seconds before him. He kissed her shoulder and his hand travelled lower over her stomach, heading south.

'Mmmph,' she muttered, shrugging him off.

Surprised, he moved away, inching across the bed until he reached the other side. After their love-making the other night and the way she'd insisted on a date night this evening, he'd hoped they would carry things to the logical conclusion. But Lottie clearly wasn't interested.

She was probably tired, he reasoned. And full from the meal. And she'd had two halves of lager. Early mornings didn't help, either.

But even as he thought those things, he was conscious that something was awry in their marriage and it was all because of him. He'd hardly been *datey* this evening, had he? So he couldn't blame her for rejecting his advances. All he hoped was that everything would be resolved once he'd secured another job.

Chapter 15

Lottie

'A door?' Natalie Sharp scoffed as Lottie approached the school gates the following Monday morning. 'You're seriously going to waste your time on that?'

Lottie had uploaded a photo of the door onto Instagram as part of her before and after collection, as she usually did but, after seeing the scorn on Natalie's face, she wondered why she'd bothered. The woman was right: Lottie was also beginning to think it was a waste of time. Still, the boat-bed had received loads of likes and several comments – not one of them from Natalie, though.

'She's seriously going to waste her time renovating the kiddies' corner in Eleri's cafe,' Delia piped up, sarcastically. 'It's nice to be paid for doing something you love, isn't it?'

Lottie widened her eyes at her friend and as soon as Natalie, with a sneer on her face, moved out of earshot, Lottie asked, 'What was all that about?'

'Natalie stuck-up Sharp hates her job. It's something to do with having to deal with patients and their germs. I've heard she wants to pack it in and become a lady of leisure, but she likes having an income of her own so she can buy what she wants without her hubby complaining. Don't let her get to you – she's just jealous.'

'I'm not bothered about her,' Lottie said.

'So why the frown?'

'Men, kids, chores… the usual.'

'This is *me* you're talking to. Men, kids and chores have been part of our lives since we met, but you don't usually look so down about it.'

Delia was right. They'd met at the local mother and baby group not long after Sabrina and Mick were born, both of them new mums and both of them struggling with breastfeeding and sleep deprivation. Men, kids and chores were nothing new.

Lottie stared into the distance, wondering where she should begin, or even if she should begin at all. She'd already chewed Delia's ear off once about her suspicion that Henry was having an affair, and Delia had talked her down. And for a few days afterwards Lottie had been convinced she'd been jumping to silly conclusions, but since Thursday evening when Henry had gone outside to take a phone call and his mood had changed on a sixpence, plus him being distant and reserved when they were out for a meal, his mind on something – *someone?* – else, her suspicions had reared their ugly little heads again.

It wasn't unusual for him to have work phone calls when he was at home – but unless the kids were making a noise, he usually just answered regardless of whether she was in earshot or not. It wasn't like him to go outside to take it. It was as if he hadn't wanted her to hear who he was talking to. And then there was that odd change of mood…

She may not have found any evidence he was having an affair, but that didn't mean to say he wasn't. All it meant was that he was being very cautious, and she wasn't looking hard enough.

She hadn't forgotten the daft door he'd brought home for her, either. Actually, it wasn't that daft, after all; she'd spent some time on the internet and she knew what she was going to do with it. She didn't want to keep it herself, but she was going to convert it into a coat rack combined with an oversized photo frame – using each of the sections where the panes of glass had gone to hold one photo. Turned on its side, and with hooks on the bottom and a shelf on the top, it would make a fantastic piece for a decent-sized hall. She already had paint she could use, and there were a few knobs and hooks somewhere in the shed, together with a piece of wood that would make a perfect shelf. Upcycling it would cost her nothing but her time.

But that was where the issue lay. Look at her now, thinking about renovating doors instead of thinking about her marriage. If this was what Henry had wanted to achieve by bringing someone else's discarded items into her life, then it looked like he was succeeding. Which was something else that made the hairs on the back of her neck stand up and her heart feel heavy: the more distracted she was – as if she wasn't distracted enough by having three children under the age of ten – she supposed he reasoned the less attention she'd pay to his comings and goings, his moodiness, and his unusual behaviour.

If Delia had described those exact same things to her with regards to Stephen, Lottie would have thought Stephen was having an affair. That it was Henry who was behaving in this manner shouldn't affect her powers of deduction, or her common sense.

'You still believe Henry is playing away, don't you?' Delia asked astutely.

Lottie worried at her bottom lip. 'Maybe.'

'I thought you'd decided you were overreacting?'

She gave herself a mental shake. There was no point in discussing things any further with her friend, and certainly not with Henry, until she had concrete proof. She was probably just being oversensitive and silly. It didn't prevent her from being unable to shake her suspicions, but that was something she'd have to deal with on her own.

'I am, I know I am. It's just me being silly,' Lottie said, chewing at her lip.

'Do you fancy a day out?' Delia asked suddenly, her eyes lighting up. 'That'll cheer you up.'

'Where?'

'Remember I told you we were going to the Winter Fayre at Penygraig Castle tomorrow? Stephen can't make it, so it's just me and Tyrone. Unless you want to come too? Kids under five go free, so it won't cost you anything. Please say yes – I don't fancy going on my own and if we don't go it'll be such a waste. There's a Santa's grotto...?' Delia waggled her eyebrows.

'And that's supposed to entice me?' Lottie smiled.

'Just imagine the kids' faces! It's the other side of Builth Wells and will take about an hour and a half to get there, so if we leave at about eight thirty we can be there for ten and come away about four o'clock. I think six hours is probably enough.'

Lottie thought hard. She could arrange for the two older ones to go to the school's breakfast club at eight, and she could always ask Henry if he could finish early and pick them up from school. If that wasn't possible, there were other favours she could call in, or she could ask Henry's mother. It was definitely doable, and the more she thought about it the more she found she was looking forward to a day out – and she knew Morgan would simply adore looking around the castle and seeing Santa. Not to mention all the stalls where she might be able to pick up some of those last-minute presents she still needed to get. It would be a wonderful start to the festive season and hopefully would get her in the mood. Delia was right, though, six hours would be enough, especially with over an hour spent travelling each way. The little ones would be exhausted, but as long as she took the pushchair for Morgan, he could get in it when he was tired. A change of scene would do her good.

'If you're sure, we'd love to come. Thank you so much for asking us.'

Feeling better than she had done all weekend, Lottie gave Morgan a resounding kiss before he dashed off into the nursery, and she hurried home to start work on the door. The sooner she got it done, the sooner she could advertise it and maybe get a few pounds for it.

But at the back of her mind, doubt and suspicion continued to linger. Was this going to be the last Christmas they'd have together as a family? The thought terrified her, but now it had lodged in her head she couldn't seem to drive it out, and the more she tried to dismiss it, the more she figured Henry just might be holding off until after Christmas before he admitted he was having an affair and was going to leave her. After all, he wouldn't be so horrible as to spoil Christmas for the kids, would he?

Naturally her thoughts moved on to imagining a life without Henry in it. He'd be an ex-husband, nothing more to her than the children's father. Would he still want to be involved in their lives? The moment she thought it, she realised how daft she was being: he loved his children unconditionally. But what about this other woman of his? Would *she* want to be involved, too?

'Over my dead body,' Lottie muttered savagely.

And even if this was only a fling – *Only? Huh!* – it sounded the death knell on their marriage, because how could she ever trust him again?

Whichever way she looked at it, if Henry was having an affair, their marriage was doomed.

Chapter 16

Lottie

She should have told Henry where she was going today, Lottie thought, as she checked and double checked the rucksack. Hat? Tick! Gloves? Tick! Change of clothes? Yes, and she'd also made sure to put in an umbrella because, although the forecast was for it to be dry and cold, one could never be 100 per cent certain that it wouldn't rain in Wales. And when she'd checked out the Winter Fayre online last night, she'd noticed that the castle had the most amazing grounds with a reindeer and elf trail to keep the little ones occupied; it would be a shame to miss it because they didn't have anything waterproof with them.

The number of snacks and drinks she'd packed could have fed a small army, and she'd also felt around in the bottom of the backpack for the first aid kit she usually kept in there, and counted the plasters and packets of Calpol. One of the boys was certain to fall over or develop a poorly tummy. It was almost a given.

With a quick check of her stock of wet wipes and tissues, she was finally ready. *Blooming heck*, she thought, not for the first time, *going on a day out with a young child takes as much time, effort and forethought as I used to give to packing for a week in Majorca when I was single*. Minus the Calpol, obviously.

She walked the children to school early for the two oldest to take part in the breakfast club, and left Sabrina and Robin with a kiss and a command to behave themselves. The sour looks she received in return made her smile; she felt a little guilty about not taking them, but the autumn term hadn't ended yet, and she didn't want them to miss anything. Besides, she'd have to pay for Sabrina and Robin's entry into the castle and its grounds, and taking two more children meant considerably greater expense because no doubt they'd want to go on something, buy something, or demand something to eat that wasn't wrapped in tin foil and came out of her rucksack.

Once back in the house, she encouraged Morgan to have a wee, then she waited impatiently for Delia and Tyrone to pull up outside.

The journey was uneventful, if somewhat long, and after the first half-hour ringing with choruses of, 'Are we there yet?' and, 'Mummy, I'm hungry', both boys dropped off to sleep, leaving Lottie and Delia to chat amongst themselves and enjoy the scenery.

–

When they reached the outskirts of Builth Wells, the town nearest the castle, Lottie reached into the back of the car and gave the children a nudge, wanting to allow them plenty of time to wake up before they arrived. They parked the car and made their way up a slope towards the impressive and immense main entrance to the castle. Already Lottie could smell mulled wine and roasting chestnuts, and her mouth watered. Built in red stone, the castle perched on a hill, and had gardens sloping off on three sides. As she waited for Delia to present their tickets at the gate, Lottie could hear the excited squeals of children and the sounds of carols being played, and despite her worries she felt the familiar excitement that the anticipation of Christmas brought. She almost felt like a child herself as the four of them strolled under the enormous stone archway and into a courtyard packed with stalls selling all kinds of wonderful crafts and food. A man dressed in a Victorian costume and balancing on stilts was handing out maps of the castle. A choir, the women wearing red cloaks and black bonnets, the men in capes and top hats, was standing off to one side, and the jaunty refrain of 'Deck the Halls' filled the air.

'Shall we have a hot chocolate and a mince pie first, then have a look around the castle?' Delia suggested. 'Many of the rooms have been reconstructed exactly as they would have been several hundred years ago.'

Penygraig Castle wasn't a medieval ruin. It was more along the lines of Windsor Castle, and the family who owned it still lived there, although most of it was open to the public and Lottie was looking forward to seeing inside.

The boys were more than happy to have a drink and biscuit each before beginning their exploration, and were soon clambering up staircases and trotting through huge rooms crammed with valuable furniture, artifacts and paintings. Lottie especially loved some of the bedrooms, which had four-poster beds and sumptuous soft furnishings. The boys, typically, loved seeing the armour and the swords on display. A coat of chainmail that they were allowed to touch, much to their delight, proved to be a firm favourite.

Attics at the top of the castle held the servants' rooms, where the corridors were narrow and the rooms so much smaller than the ones below, which would have been occupied by the nobility. Lottie joked that if she had been alive then, she'd have been one of the servants and not one of the aristocracy.

'Yeah, but look at the fabulous views they'd be missing,' Delia said, hoisting first one small boy and then the other to look out of the windows and down onto the gardens below.

Trust Delia to see the brighter side of things, Lottie thought fondly. 'Come on, let's go and see the dungeons.'

There weren't any as such, but there were huge kitchens (two of them), a laundry room, and school room, which still had old desks with inkwells in them.

Finally, though, the boys were tired and ready for a spot of lunch, which they ate in the orangery prior to visiting Santa in his grotto. As soon as their batteries were recharged they darted off in the direction of the reindeers, which were in a pen not too far away.

'I want a reindeer,' Morgan stated firmly when Santa asked what he wanted for Christmas. 'And a sword, and a rugby ball. And a—' The list was comprehensive and some of the items on it were new to her, but as Morgan changed his mind every time the words 'Christmas' or 'Santa Claus' were mentioned, Lottie wasn't too bothered. She'd seen a plush reindeer on one of the stalls, so she'd buy him one if Delia could distract him, and she had a bit of wood that she could turn into a sword without too much difficulty, and she'd already bought him a rugby ball. Robin had one of his own and although she always encouraged the boys to share, Robin loved his ball to bits and guarded it jealously.

By the time they'd walked around the gardens following the reindeer and elf trail, where the boys found clues, all four of them were exhausted. They'd walked for miles, and their senses had been assaulted by so many sights, sounds and smells that they were ready to call it a day. Six hours was plenty, although it wasn't anywhere near enough time to see everything there was to see. Lottie wished she could have brought the two older children because they would have thoroughly enjoyed themselves, and maybe even Henry, although it was difficult to say these days what would please him and what wouldn't. Maybe they could all go together as a family next year?

Feeling as though she'd been away from Applewell for a few days and not just a few hours, Lottie made her way outside the castle, following Delia as they headed towards the car park.

'That was bloody brilliant,' Lottie said. 'I had a fantastic time, and Morgan did too. Thank you for bringing us.'

Morgan, bless him, was sitting in his pushchair with a glazed expression on his face and sucking his thumb, something he only did these days when he was upset or tired. She knew he'd sleep on the journey back. Once he was in his car seat, he gazed sleepily out of the window and she smiled. It was rare that she managed to wear her youngest son out this early in the day. She knew she was in for a tricky evening, because he'd have a nap on the return journey and probably quite a decent one at that, so he'd be refreshed and raring to go by the time they got home. Unfortunately Lottie wouldn't be. She couldn't fall asleep in the car (it wouldn't be fair on Delia, who was driving) and she wouldn't be able to nap when she got home either, because she'd have to prepare the evening meal. At least Meryl had offered to give Sabrina and Robin their tea after she'd picked them up from school, so that was a bonus, but no doubt Henry's mother would want to chat when Lottie went to collect them. Unless she could persuade Henry to do it…?

A small flame of discontent and resentment flared in her stomach. Yesterday, when she'd asked Henry if he could possibly collect the children from school, he'd looked flustered and rather put out, telling her he had an appointment he simply couldn't miss, and that she'd have to make other arrangements. He hadn't even asked her where she was going, and by that point Lottie seriously didn't feel like telling him.

Although she'd really fancied telling *him* where *he* could go.

As if Morgan was privy to her thoughts, he said, 'Daddy.'

'Yes, darling, we'll see Daddy when we get home.' She rested her head against the back of the seat and sighed deeply. Delia was weaving her way through the traffic in Builth Wells, and was concentrating hard, and Lottie fought to stay awake and keep her friend company.

'Mummy, look. Daddy.'

Lottie twisted around in her seat to peer over her shoulder at her son, wondering why he'd gone from semi-comatose to wide awake, and saw Morgan gazing intently out of the window. He jabbed at it, leaving a smear of sticky fingerprints on the glass.

'No, it's not Daddy.' Lottie didn't even bother to look.

'It is!' Morgan insisted. 'It *is* Daddy. Daddy!' he yelled, at the top of his voice.

Lottie shushed him, smiling apologetically at Delia who was tapping her fingers impatiently on the steering wheel and shaking her head at the volume of traffic, then she glanced out of the window, wondering what had set Morgan off.

The car was stationary at some lights, and she peered in the direction Morgan pointed.

Suddenly she sat up straighter, almost pressing her nose against the glass.

It was indeed Henry, opening the door to a rather smart coffee shop and gesturing for the woman behind to go in ahead of him. What was Henry doing in Builth Wells? He hadn't mentioned he'd be out this way today, although she knew he covered a fairly large area. What a coincidence.

Wondering whether she should rap on the glass and attract his attention, she decided she couldn't be bothered.

And then she was glad she hadn't, as the woman who he'd opened the door for turned back to Henry and gave him a wide smile. It wasn't the sort of smile a woman usually gave to a stranger who just happened to hold the door open for them; it was the sort of smile a woman gave to somebody she knew.

In the few seconds left to her before the lights changed to green and the car pulled away, Lottie scrutinised this unknown woman. She was slim, quite tall, and had bleached-blonde hair cut to her jaw and sculpted in at the back of the neck. Even from this distance Lottie could tell she was pretty. She appeared to be somewhere between thirty and forty, and was very well dressed in a trouser suit and a blouse. Lottie caught a flash of red lips and pearly white teeth, and she smarted. What she also saw just as the lights turned green and the car moved off – she had to crane her neck back to make sure of it – was the strange woman and her husband take a seat at the same table.

This wasn't a casual encounter. This was somebody Henry *knew*.

Was this *her*? Was this the other woman?

With the cafe now out of sight, Lottie slumped back in her seat and closed her eyes, trying not to cry.

'Daddy,' Morgan said.

'Yes,' Lottie agreed, flatly. 'Daddy.'

Chapter 17

Henry

Builth Wells was awkward to get to from Applewell. There wasn't a straightforward route unless you were prepared to travel for miles along single track mountain roads, over high moorland and down through sparsely populated valleys. So Henry decided to go the longer way around, sticking more or less to the main roads, and he had booked in a couple of clients along the way to keep his current employer happy.

He'd set off from his final appointment of the day in plenty of time, but by the time he arrived at Builth Wells it was already three thirty, although thankfully his appointment wasn't until four. When Sally Chisholm had suggested meeting in a cafe in Builth Wells he'd readily agreed. He could understand her reasons for choosing the location; as she'd informed him on the phone, she was popping in to see a major client who was based nearby, and it seemed an ideal opportunity for them to meet, considering the company's head office was in Suffolk, which would have been one heck of a way for him to travel.

He parked just off the main street and made his way into the centre of the town, glancing up at the signs outside the various establishments he passed to make sure he didn't miss the cafe she'd suggested meeting at.

Ah, that must be her, standing outside a coffee shop. Sally had told him she'd be wearing a navy suit and that she had short, blonde hair. She had a large handbag slung over her shoulder and was carrying a folder bulging with papers. It had to be her.

'Ms Chisholm?' he asked, stepping up to her and hoping he wasn't about to make a prat of himself.

Her smile was warm and genuine. 'You must be Henry Hargreaves,' she stated, holding out her hand. 'It's a pleasure to meet you. Did you have any difficulty finding it?'

Henry laughed. 'Not at all, I'm used to finding my way to strange places.' Not that Builth Wells was strange – far from it, it was a lovely little market town – but he hadn't been there in years as it wasn't part of his patch.

'Shall we go inside?' She gestured towards the coffee shop. 'We can have a drink and a proper chat. I want to get a feel for you, to see if we want to move it forward from here.'

Henry hurried ahead of her to open the door and she swept inside, stopping when she was just over the threshold to give him another warm smile.

'If that's OK with you?' she asked.

Henry returned her smile and nodded. At this point anything was OK with him. If she'd wanted to meet him on the top of Snowdon he'd have hiked up the mountain without a murmur. It was a bit strange she was conducting a first interview in a coffee shop, but it wasn't unheard of. He had no doubt any subsequent interview, should he be lucky enough to be invited to one, would take place under far more formal conditions at their head office.

He was glad he'd worn his suit, and he fully intended to treat this like any other interview he'd had, regardless of the location. He'd had a change of clothes in the car, as he hadn't wanted to risk getting his suit covered in cow muck or any other unsavoury substance, and after he'd left his last client he'd pulled into a service station and used their loos to change out of his scruffy work clothes and into his suit. Although he didn't have any other clients booked in after meeting with Sally Chisholm, he fully intended to change back into his usual work clothes before he went home. He didn't want Lottie asking any awkward questions.

Sally sat at a free table by the window and he joined her, sitting down. Almost immediately he stood back up again as he remembered his manners.

'Would you like a coffee? Or something else?' he offered.

'It's OK, I'll get these; they can go on expenses. And it's waitress service here, so there's no need to go to the counter.' Sally Chisholm held up two fingers and mouthed 'Coffee,' at someone behind him, then turned back to him. 'So, tell me about your present role,' the sales director said.

Coffee was fine; Henry would have preferred tea but he wasn't going to quibble and he launched into the spiel he'd prepared while in the car earlier. He'd gone over every single question he thought she could ask and had tried to come up with some answers. The question he was dreading was the one she was bound to ask, and that was why he wanted to leave his current position. All he could do was to be honest, and hope she didn't think Baldwin Ltd was letting him go because they didn't think he was up to the job. It was pure economics. People were made redundant all the time. His situation was hardly unique.

After they'd chatted for a few minutes, Henry began to relax and get into his stride. Sally seemed pleasant, she asked intelligent questions and he thought he gave her intelligent answers. He hoped he sounded knowledgeable about selling in general, although he had a fair way to go when it came to bringing himself up to speed regarding fertilisers, despite the research he'd done on it to prepare for this meeting. But he was sure he would get there eventually. With a little bit of training on product knowledge, he'd be able to hit the ground running.

Another cup of coffee and a half-hour later, when the interview was about done, Sally asked him a question which raised his hopes. 'If you were offered the job, when could you start?'

'I'd be able to start next Monday,' Henry said. He couldn't believe that three weeks had passed already since Redundancy-gate.

'Good,' she said. 'I think it's a wrap.' She stood up and offered him a hand, which he took and shook briefly, and once again he held the door open for her as they left the cafe.

'I'll be in touch,' she promised.

'Could I just ask – I'm assuming there will be a second interview?'

'I don't think so. I never see the need, although it drives HR wild.' She smiled at him with a twinkle in her eye and he nodded, trying to suppress a smile.

Hopefully, this was in the bag.

'There is one final thing,' she said, as they stood on the pavement preparing to go their separate ways. 'I didn't ask how you feel about travelling.'

'I travel quite extensively as it is,' Henry said. 'It's nothing new, although I do like to be in my own bed in the evening,' he added in a joking voice, although he wasn't joking at all. He did prefer to go home at night, and not live out of a suitcase.

'I see. Well, thank you, it's been a pleasure.'

–

That went well, Henry said to himself as he got in his car and turned towards home. With nothing else on the immediate horizon, he was pinning all his hopes on this. He didn't like being so restricted, but beggars couldn't be choosers.

As he drove, he replayed the interview in his head, hoping he'd made a good enough impression. Sally Chisholm would be his immediate boss, and he thought he could work with her. Even if he couldn't, the way things were at the moment he didn't have any choice. If she offered him the job, he'd grab it with both hands.

It took him a fair while to get home and it was nearly seven o'clock by the time he pulled onto the drive. Morgan would be in bed by now, Henry thought, but when he glanced up at the front of the house, he saw his youngest child standing on the windowsill of his bedroom, his legs and arms outstretched, and looking cute in his Thomas the Tank Engine pyjamas. He could see Morgan's mouth moving, leaving a trail across the glass, and guessed the little boy was saying, 'Daddy!'

The first thing Henry did when he stepped in through the door was to go straight upstairs and give Morgan a kiss and take him back to bed.

'Story, story, story!' Morgan chanted.

'Shh, calm down and I'll read you one. What did you do today?'

'I saw reindeers, and Santa, and a tall man, and swords, and carols.' He waved his arm about as though he was wielding a lightsaber and made whooshing noises.

Okaaay... that was random, and who was Carol? 'What story would you like?'

'I saw *you*, too, Daddy.'

'Yes, you did, didn't you? But you mustn't stand on windowsills. It's dangerous; you could fall off. Shall we have this one?' Henry held up one of Morgan's favourite bedtime stories and the little boy nodded. He snuggled down under the covers and Henry read to him, possibly going a little faster than he did normally. He was anxious to have a beer and something to eat.

When he finally went downstairs, Lottie was in the kitchen, emptying the bin.

'Had a good day?' she asked him.

'Yeah, good, thanks. You?'

Lottie stopped what she was doing, looked up and narrowed her eyes. 'Yes, it was very—' she paused. '—*interesting.*'

'Did you get any more of that door done?'

'Not today.'

'Oh, right, OK. What's for tea?'

'Chilli and rice. I've already eaten. Give me five minutes and I'll warm yours up. What did you do today?'

Henry shrugged. 'You know, the usual.'

Lottie washed her hands under the tap, wiped them dry on a towel, then switched on the ring underneath a depleted and rather sorry-looking pan of chilli. 'No, I don't know,' she said, her back to him, her hips moving slightly as she stirred the pan.

'Went to see a few clients, got some sales. That's it, really.'

'Go anywhere interesting?'

'Like where?' Henry was baffled; Lottie rarely took this much interest in his travels.

'I just wondered if you'd been anywhere where you could have picked up some more stuff for me to upcycle,' she said.

Ah... 'Not today, but I can keep an eye out, if you like. You'd be surprised what you see on farms.'

'You'd be surprised what you see in towns,' he thought he heard Lottie mutter.

He paused for a moment, trying to work out what she meant, then he shrugged it off. 'Next time I'm anywhere near the coast, I'll see what I can find,' he promised. 'Oars *would* look really good above Robin's bed. It would set the room off nicely. How are things going with Eleri?'

'I'm seeing her tomorrow evening for her first lesson. I'm not going out until seven, so do you think you can be home by then?'

'I most certainly will be,' Henry assured her, fetching a plate from the cupboard. The delicious aroma of chilli filled the air and his mouth watered. He was starving, having not eaten much at lunchtime due to nerves.

'Did you know that the Winter Fayre is on at Penygraig Castle this week?' Lottie asked.

'Is it?' He hoped to goodness she wasn't suggesting they go. It would cost a fortune.

Lottie dished his supper up and he sat at the kitchen table. 'It's not far from Builth Wells. Isn't that part of your territory?'

He said, 'It's too far east for me. Someone else does that patch.' Oh, God, she *was* hinting that she'd like to go. They *would* visit the castle – *just not this year, eh?* She nodded, but he got the feeling his wife wasn't paying attention.

'Right, I've got to fetch Sabrina and Robin from your mother's,' she said. 'Unless you want to do it?'

'No, thanks.' He pulled a face. 'I've only just got in.' He'd wondered why it was so quiet. Lottie had had an easy afternoon, then, only having Morgan to look after.

She shot him a strange look then left.

It was a pity she was still a bit frosty with him but he was confident once she knew what he'd been going through she'd be all tea and sympathy. He also hoped she'd be pleased with him for having not worried her. There was no point in both of them stressing; he was perfectly capable of carrying this burden himself.

Hopefully, by this time next week, everything would be sorted. Maybe Monday was a bit too soon to start the new job, because they'd have to get all the paperwork in place, but he was quietly confident it wouldn't be long.

Finally, things were beginning to look up.

Chapter 18

Lottie

She had laid more traps than someone who worked in pest control, and her damned husband had walked into every one of them. Lottie was so furious, she was shaking. Or was it shock at his blatant lies? Either way, she simply couldn't remain in the house a second longer.

She'd dashed out and was halfway to her mother-in-law's house before she realised she should have taken the car.

Never mind, it wouldn't do her two eldest any harm to walk. They'd probably grizzle, especially since she'd expect them to get ready for bed as soon as they got home, but the twenty-minute walk might go some way towards wearing them out. And if it didn't, Henry could shift his backside and put them to bed. He could do it all over again tomorrow, too.

'Mummy!' Sabrina appeared delighted to see her, Robin not so much, and when Lottie walked into Meryl's living room, Lottie could see why. Robin was sitting on the floor surrounded by a Lego set. Sabrina looked bored out of her mind, not enjoying the slightly childish cartoons on the TV. Meryl had a tendency to think of them as babies, which Robin still was to a certain extent, but Sabrina was growing up fast, and watching things like *Peppa Pig* wasn't to her liking.

'Fancy a cup of tea?' Meryl asked.

Lottie didn't, but neither did she fancy going home yet. It might almost be the children's bedtime, but what the hell? What did half an hour matter in the great scheme of things? Lottie had always been a stickler for routine when it came to the children, trying to make sure Sabrina was in bed by eight thirty on a school night, Robin at seven thirty, and Morgan at seven o'clock. Tonight, though, she didn't give two hoots whether they were in bed on time or not. Because the sooner they were in bed, the longer she would have to be alone with Henry without the children as a buffer.

'Go on then, just a quick one,' she said, and followed Meryl into the kitchen.

Meryl flicked the switch on the kettle and got a couple of mugs down from the cupboard above.

'Did the kids behave themselves?' Lottie asked.

'Of course they did. They always do – they're a credit to you. How was the Winter Fayre?'

'Really good.' *Apart from seeing your son with another woman*, Lottie thought.

'Did you enjoy yourself on Friday when you went out for a meal?'

Lottie shrugged. 'It was OK.'

'It's not exactly what you call gourmet food, is it? The Busy Bumble is all right just to pop in and have a quick bite to eat, but not for a proper night out. You should have gone somewhere a bit nicer.'

'We were lucky we went anywhere at all,' Lottie muttered.

'Oh? Why is that?'

'Ask Henry.'

'What's he done now?' To be fair to Meryl, she wasn't one of those mothers who thought the sun shone out of her son's backside. She was well aware he had his faults, just as she was well aware that Lottie had hers.

Lottie decided to stick with the facts as she knew them on Friday, without trying to let what she'd discovered earlier today colour the conversation. 'We had a bit of a squabble about spending money.'

Meryl gave her a sharp glance. 'Is money a problem? Because if it is—'

'It's not,' Lottie hastened to assure her. 'It's just that with Christmas and saving for the extension, Henry has turned into a right miser. It's become a bit of an obsession for him.'

'The Busy Bumble is hardly expensive,' Meryl said. 'And it's not as though you go out that often,' she added.

'I know. Try telling Henry that, though.'

'He seemed happy enough when I came over to babysit.'

'He'd come around by then,' Lottie said, omitting mentioning the reason he'd come around appeared to have had a great deal to do with a certain phone call he'd received.

As much as she hated to admit it, things were starting to stack up, and now she could add lying about his where-abouts and meeting strange women to the list. Lottie still couldn't believe he'd told her a barefaced lie about where he'd been earlier that day. It made her feel like crying.

She picked up her mug and took a cautious sip, the scalding liquid burning her mouth. 'Burnt my mouth,' she said, somewhat indistinctly. She fanned her face with her hand and hoped Meryl would think the tea was to blame when she blinked furiously to clear her imminent tears. 'Talking of Henry, he's only just got home,' she added, once the threatened waterworks had subsided.

'He's late,' Meryl observed, taking a look at the clock on the wall.

'That's nothing new. He's often late these days,' Lottie said.

Meryl leant forwards, her fingers clasped around her mug. 'You mustn't let him work too hard. Make sure you have time together as a couple. I'm always happy to babysit, you know that.'

Lottie did know, but she also knew that both of Henry's parents still worked and they had busy social lives to boot. Oh, how she wished her own mum lived nearer – Llandudno was a bit too far to pop in for a chat.

But even if her mum had been closer, Lottie wasn't sure she'd want to share her suspicions with her just yet. Because that's all they were at the moment – suspicions. When – *if* – she had something concrete, she may well need a shoulder to cry on.

Feeling teary again, Lottie gulped the rest of the tea, trying to ignore how hot the liquid was, and stood up. 'I must get the kids home; they've got school in the morning.'

'I'll get their bags and coats,' Meryl said, but as she got to her feet Lottie's mother-in-law added, 'A marriage takes work, you know. On both sides. You don't want to let it go stale.'

Lottie froze as she was putting her mug in the sink. Quickly she covered her reaction, but she had a horrible feeling Meryl knew something. Did she, too, have a sneaking suspicion that Henry was up to no good? Or – and Lottie suddenly felt drenched in ice-cold fear – had

Henry confided in his mother, and this was her way of warning Lottie and telling her to pull her socks up if she wanted to keep her husband?

Lottie bit down on any retort she was tempted to make. For one thing, she didn't think she could enter into a civil discussion right then, and, for another, if Henry *was* playing away – such an incongruous phrase for something with such dire consequences – there was no way she wanted to carry on being married to him. Lottie had always said she was a 'one strike and you're out' kind of person. If Henry could cheat on her once, he could do it again, and she wasn't prepared to put up with that – not even for the sake of the kids.

Oh, my God, *the children*; what was this going to do to them? Her three gorgeous, wonderful children would be devastated and heartbroken. They were more important to her than life itself. They should be the most important things in Henry's world too, but they obviously weren't. And it was that realisation which was very nearly her undoing as she rounded up Sabrina and Robin and shepherded them home.

–

Lottie had been right: the kids had moaned and grizzled when they realised they'd have to walk, but the novelty of being out and about when it was past their bedtime had soon made them perk up, and they had played games all the way home.

'Go upstairs,' she instructed as soon as they stepped through the door and into the hall. 'Wash your hands and face, and clean your teeth. Daddy will be up in a minute to help. Give me a shout when you want me to tuck you in.'

Getting the children ready for bed was normally Lottie's job, but this evening Henry could bloody well do it. She desperately wanted five minutes to compose herself. She also wanted five minutes to check Henry's wallet again and dig through his pockets, while he was occupied with the kids.

'Henry, please see to the children,' she said without preamble. 'I've got the uniforms to sort out and the bags to pack for the morning.' There were always things from school to sort out, so she didn't wait for Henry's reply. Instead, she gathered up the two school bags and began checking them for letters, smelly PE kit, and leftover bits of lunch that seemed to lurk in the depths of Robin's bag, despite him having a rather nice lunchbox and the availability of bins in the school dining hall in which to dispose of any half-eaten sandwiches and balled-up foil.

Lottie wasted no time: as soon as she heard Henry's tread on the stairs she reached for his wallet. But, once again, she found nothing of interest, and his jacket pockets yielded no evidence, either. She hadn't been sure what she'd been expecting to find – receipts from hotels or fancy restaurants, maybe? Surely he wouldn't be so stupid as to leave evidence like that lying around?

Next, she sniffed his jacket, but all she could smell was Henry's aftershave and a vague aroma of farmyard. When she scrutinised it for smears of make-up, the only thing she could find was what looked like moss stains (she hoped it wasn't anything more substantial) on the back of it and down the front, which wasn't unusual when farm gates and fences were leant on.

When she'd finished, all the time listening to the getting-ready-for-bed noises upstairs, she had to concede that she'd found nothing incriminating whatsoever.

Deflated, Lottie carried on sorting out clean polo shirts for the children ready for the morning, unsure whether to feel relieved that she hadn't found a condom in his pocket or upset that she still didn't know for certain whether he was having an affair.

At the thought of Henry having a condom about his person, Lottie collapsed against the washing machine. She didn't want to have an image in her mind of him being in bed with another woman, but now it was there, she couldn't shift it. The woman she'd seen him with earlier that day was playing a starring role in her imagination, and it made her feel quite sick. That Lottie was now able to put a face to the unknown woman hit her hard, and she clapped her hands to her mouth to stem the deluge of sobs wanting to break free.

'They're ready for you. Are you OK?'

Lottie let out a shriek at the sound of Henry's voice, and it took every ounce of willpower she possessed not to fall apart, knowing that if she did, everything would be out in the open – and she wasn't ready for that yet. She needed to get her head around it and find positive proof before she confronted him. She also didn't want the fireworks to go off – and there would most certainly be fireworks aplenty – when the children were in earshot.

'Thought I saw a cockroach,' she said, latching on to the first thing to pop into her head.

'A cockroach?' He sounded dubious, as well he might: the little blighters didn't like lights or humans, and would hardly be scuttling around their kitchen while either of those two things were in evidence. 'Let me see.'

Henry covered the floor in two strides and suddenly he was standing so close she could smell his skin, that familiar comforting scent that was his and his alone.

It made her want to cry.

Hastily, she pushed past him and headed for the stairs, taking them two at a time in her hurry to get away from her philandering husband. Because, God help her, she still loved him just as passionately as she'd done on their wedding day, and she had no idea how she was going to survive without him.

Chapter 19

Henry

The drive to New Quay from the A487 was along tree-lined roads, and the view of the sea once the road opened out never failed to lift Henry's mood. Until today, that was.

Even with the sweep of Cardigan Bay stretching out before him as the road dropped down into the picture-perfect harbour town, Henry's mood was sour. He was soon to be officially unemployed. The only thing keeping him going was the hope that he'd receive the phone call he'd been waiting for. It hadn't been twenty-four hours since he'd met Sally Chisholm and in reality he shouldn't expect her to contact him yet, but this waiting was driving him crazy.

Another thing bothering him was his wife. Lottie had been behaving a little oddly lately. He guessed part of it might be something to do with him – he was aware he was a little preoccupied – but he had no idea what had been up with her yesterday evening. She'd been off with him from the minute he'd got in to the minute he'd gone to bed. And beyond, because he'd felt her creep out of bed and had heard Morgan's bedroom door close.

She'd slept in their youngest son's bed all night, but Henry was fairly certain Morgan hadn't woken up. Which

163

begged the question of why she'd felt the need to abandon the marital bed. She was adamant that she slept better in their own generous bed, and she was usually tired and a tad grumpy after spending the night with one of the kids.

Unable to work her out and with other things on his mind, Henry found a place to park near the Sea Horse Inn at the top of the town, got out of the car and stretched.

Once again, his thoughts circled back to his interview with Sally Chisholm yesterday, and he checked his phone just in case, even though he knew full well he hadn't had any phone calls while he'd been driving.

He was at a bit of a loose end because over the past week, or maybe longer, work phone calls had dried up to the point where they were almost non-existent. He assumed that anyone phoning head office would be passed on to the guy who was forced to cover Henry's patch as well as his own. And with Christmas only just around the corner, leads tended to dry up at this time of year anyway. Today he only had three clients booked in, which was why he was finding himself heading towards the pretty harbour town of New Quay and the possibility of finding a couple of oars. If he couldn't do anything else, he might be able to make Lottie happy by bringing home the finishing touches for Robin's bedroom.

She'd not been at all happy lately, and it pained him to see her this way. Even acknowledging that part of it might be his fault because of his attitude and his mood, it didn't explain everything, and for what felt like the twentieth time that day he wondered what was going on with her.

The only thing that seemed to please her these days was renovating and upcycling old stuff. Namely furniture. Maybe she was getting fed up with being a housewife? With Morgan not yet in full-time school she had very little respite from parenting. It went on twenty-four hours a day, seven days a week. She was always the one who got up with the children in the middle of the night when they were ill; she was the one who attended sports days when he couldn't because he was working; she was the one who was called into school to collect them if one of the children became sick.

In some respects, he had it easier; more often than not, he managed to relax when he came home. It wasn't that he didn't play his part – he did; but his part, when it came to parenting and running the house was, out of necessity, considerably smaller than Lottie's.

Morgan's arrival had been a bit of a surprise to them both – a very welcome and very much-loved surprise, but Lottie, he could tell, had been thinking about starting to expand her horizons again. And when their most recent bundle of joy had made an appearance, she had instead been catapulted straight back into the nightly feeds and nappies stage.

He was pleased to see she was enjoying a hobby, and he wondered if it could be more than that for her. He wasn't truly aware of the amount of time which went into transforming something like a boat into a bed, but he suspected it was quite considerable, and he was fairly certain she wouldn't get a return on her investment if she factored in the hours she spent on the project. But if she could get something for nothing, do it up and sell it, then it might be worthwhile.

He wasn't entirely sure about Lottie showing Eleri what to do. As far as he was concerned, Lottie should be doing this herself, then charging Eleri, and he felt she was selling herself short. He also felt rather cross that she wasn't being paid in cash, but had been paid in soft furnishings.

Still, it was up to Lottie – it was her hobby, and it was down to her how she wanted it to go.

His boots slapping against the tarmac and his breath misting in the cold air, Henry headed down through the steep, narrow streets that would take him to the harbour. Most of them, especially those nearer the sea, had been built before motorised vehicles had become a thing. If he ignored the yellow lines on the tarmac, he could almost imagine himself being transported back a couple of hundred years.

The harbour was almost directly below him, and he stopped for a moment to admire the view. On the side of the road furthest away from the sea were shops, guest houses and an ice cream parlour, although the latter was closed. On the other side was a grassy area dotted with benches, and he strolled over to one of them and sat down, stretching out his arm along the length of the back of the seat. With the tide out, a variety of small boats lay in the sand, cocked to one side as if asleep. The harbour wall, which bustled with tourists in the summer, was mostly devoid of people apart from a few fishermen repairing lobster pots or nets, or doing whatever fishermen did.

That was where he was headed: he wanted to have a chat with some of them to ask if they had an old pair of oars they no longer used which they could donate to a worthy cause, namely his son's bedroom. It was a bit of a long shot, he realised, but he couldn't concentrate on work anyway – as his last, disastrous visit to a stable yard a few miles away had proved. He wouldn't have much commission to show for this month, but that sometimes happened, so he was sure Lottie wouldn't comment on it. At least, he *hoped* Lottie wouldn't comment on it.

He took a deep breath of briny air, smelling the fresh scent of the sea along with the tang of seaweed, and an undercurrent of fish. It wasn't a nasty smell, it was a traditional seaside smell. And surfing on the top of it was an enticing aroma of fish and chips.

His stomach gurgled.

He thought about the sandwiches he'd eaten earlier on, which Lottie had made for him, and he grimaced. He had a suspicion they hadn't been made with love: basic Marmite sandwiches didn't rock his boat, although Robin adored them. Sabrina not so much – it was safe to say that Sabrina absolutely hated Marmite. He marvelled at the differences between his three offspring. They had distinct and clear personalities of their own, regardless of gender, and he thought what a wonderful job Lottie was doing in bringing them up. Of course, he took some of the credit, but most of it was down to his wife, he acknowledged.

A tune coming from his pocket made him jump, and he scrambled for his phone, almost dropping it in the process.

'Hello?' His voice was tentative. He didn't recognise the number, but then again that didn't mean anything.

The voice on the other end was gruff and most definitely male. 'Are you the Baldwin bloke?'

Henry rolled his eyes. He'd been called worse. 'Yes, I am. What can I do for you?'

'I need some of that new stuff you dropped off with me last time.'

'Sorry, I didn't catch your name—?'

'Evans from Coed Cae Farm at Tregaron.'

'Oh, yes, hello, Mr Evans. What stuff was that?'

'Can you call in after Christmas and I can give you an order? And I read about some new-fangled supplements that's good for sheep. Helps their feet. It was in that brochure you sent me. I could do with a free sample of that, too.'

The brochure would have come from head office, but Henry knew what was in it because he'd seen a copy. His heart sank as he said, 'I'm sorry, but I won't be working for Baldwin after this Friday, but I can get head office to put you in touch with someone who can help you.'

'Will he give me a free sample?'

Henry didn't know, but he doubted it. He liked to do that for his clients as he felt it built confidence in new products, but he was aware it was a dying practice. Margins were so tight these days that giving stuff away was becoming less common.

Call ended, Henry returned his phone to his pocket, stood up and carried on walking down the hill, ignoring the enticing cooking smells coming from the pub and the aroma of the chip shop on the corner. He paused for a moment to look in the window of a gift shop that seemed to specialise in using driftwood and other salvaged materials in artistic ways. Despite there being a lack of tourists it was open, and he gazed at the prettily decorated window, festooned with sparkling lights and a small Christmas tree. It was nearly time to put their tree up. The whole family made a point of going to choose it together from a farm that grew fir trees as a seasonal sideline.

A display of jewellery caught his attention. It wasn't the usual diamond and gold, or even silver. These were pieces made from things as diverse as pebbles, driftwood and discarded fishing paraphernalia.

He knew Lottie would simply adore this place, and after checking the prices and seeing they were rather reasonable, he gave in to an impulse and went inside. He hadn't given Christmas a second thought (he rarely did, until it was almost upon him), and this year his only concern had been being able to afford it. On seeing such unique pieces though, and with the prospect of another job hoving into view, he knew exactly what he'd buy Lottie – a wonderful pin for her hair. She normally shoved anything thin and pointy into her bun to get it to stay up, from a pencil to a chopstick, but the one he'd seen in the window was perfect. A piece of card in front of it said it was made from metal salvaged from the beach, and it had a smooth, oval pebble in the most wonderful shade of orange at one end. The pebble was encased in intricate metal scrolls on which tiny beads of sea glass in similar shades had been threaded.

Lottie would love it, and it would appeal to her love of using repurposed or recycled things whenever she could. It was the ideal present for her, so Henry paid for it, trying not to flinch as he shoved his bank card into the machine, and waited for the pin to be gift-wrapped.

When he was sorted with a new job, he'd suggest a day out in New Quay. They could have chips out of a cone and play on the small but perfectly formed beach. He'd treat the kids to a kite or something and maybe they could even go on one of the dolphin-watching boat trips in the summer, when Morgan was a bit older.

As he continued on down the slope towards the harbour wall, he could see the men with fishing tackle were still there, and he gathered his courage and made his way towards them, thinking that if you don't ask, you don't get. No one was going to simply offer him a pair of oars out of the blue, were they?

'Excuse me?' he said nervously, to three men that were closest to him. 'I know this might be a bit of an imposition, but I wondered if anyone had a couple of oars they no longer had any use for. I don't mind if they're split or cracked, or have got woodworm – they'll just be for decoration for my son's bedroom. My wife has made him a bed out of an old boat and we thought a pair of oars would set it off nicely.'

The three men looked up, and glanced at each other. Two of them went back to what they were doing, which seemed to Henry's untrained eye to be repairing lobster pots.

The third sucked his teeth and said, 'Sorry, mate, I don't have any. Do any of you?'

His companions kept their attention on their work and shook their heads.

'Can't leave stuff lying about like that, see? The harbour authorities don't like it. Piles of rubbish puts tourists off.'

'OK, well, thank you anyway.' Disappointed, Henry decided to carry on walking to the end of the harbour wall. Even in the short amount of time since he'd been watching the sea, he could tell the tide was coming in. With nothing else to do, he found a seat and perched on it, ignoring the cold.

His phone rang again. This time Henry wasn't feeling quite as hopeful that it would be Sally Chisholm, but he answered it anyway. Sitting on a bench and staring out to sea while answering a phone call seemed to be the theme of the day.

'Is that Henry Hargreaves?'

Henry recognised the voice instantly and his heart missed a beat, before compensating with a rather more noticeable one immediately after.

'This is he,' he said, trying to keep the hope out of his voice and not seem too eager.

'Sally Chisholm here. How are you?' She sounded upbeat, and hope rose slowly from his stomach into his heart. She was going to offer him the job, he simply knew it.

'I'm fine, thanks, and you?'

'Good, good... Look, I'm sorry, but we don't think you're the right fit for Allinson just now.'

And that was it. In one simple sentence hope deserted him and his world came crashing down around his ears. Not wanting to listen to her platitudes, he abruptly switched his phone off and dropped it back into his pocket.

He might be being dramatic, but at that very moment all he could think about was how the hell he was going to pay his bills, without dipping into the extension fund. He would have this month's salary to carry him through to the next, but what was he supposed to do after that? With no other prospect insight, with not even a sniff of interest from any other company, he knew he had no choice but to claim unemployment benefits from Monday. And Lottie? He still had a little bit of leeway before he'd have to tell her, but not yet, not today. He needed to let this latest setback simmer for a while and settle. Once he'd got over his acute disappointment, then he'd tell her.

Unable to face going home, he sat on the bench for the rest of the afternoon and into the evening, hunched into his coat, hands in his pockets, thinking that his search for a pair of oars was a metaphor for his life – because at that moment, he really did think he was up shit creek without a paddle.

Chapter 20

Lottie

Lottie glared at the clock. Henry was late. Again. He'd promised he'd be home to see to the children so she could go to Eleri's, but there was no sign of him.

She grabbed her phone and stabbed at it. The call went straight through to voicemail again, so she guessed he'd probably turned the damn thing off. She must have rung him six times already, plus sending several texts, each one more and more annoyed in its tone. *What the hell was he playing at?* she asked herself, before answering her own question. 'Playing' was probably the operative word here. He must be with *her*. There was no other explanation as to why he was uncontactable, and why he was late.

She couldn't believe he'd chosen another woman over their own children.

Hang on a minute, he hadn't, had he? It wasn't as though she was about to leave the kids on their own to fend for themselves, was it? He knew perfectly well she'd take care of them, no matter what he was up to.

Damn it, she really wanted to go to Eleri's house. She'd been thoroughly enjoying helping her friend transform what had been an ugly TV cabinet into something new and fresh. Besides, she didn't want to let Eleri down; both of them had been looking forward to it. She sent her a quick text to tell her she was running late, and as she did so anger shot through her.

Right, that's it. She'd had enough.

Jabbing violently at her phone again, she got through to Meryl. 'Have you heard from Henry?' she demanded, skipping the niceties.

There was a slight pause, then Meryl said, 'No. Why, is there something wrong?'

Yes, there bloody well is *something wrong,* Lottie thought viciously. It was so wrong, she didn't know where to start. 'Henry was supposed to be home so I can go out,' she said. 'He's late. *Again.*'

'If you give me ten minutes I'll come and sit with the children until he gets home. I'm sure there's nothing to worry about.'

Lottie blinked. She hadn't been worried. Should she have been? She was so het up she hadn't even considered the possibility that something might have happened to Henry. He spent an awful lot of time on the road, and occasionally when the weather forecast was bad or she heard of an accident while she was listening to the radio, she would pray he was OK.

But his safety hadn't once crossed her mind this evening. She'd been so busy imagining him up to all kinds with *that woman,* that she hadn't stopped to consider there might be something else wrong.

Feeling slightly chastened, she said in a more reasonable tone of voice, 'I've phoned him and texted him, but I think his phone is switched off.'

'He's probably driving,' his mother pointed out.

Lottie bit her lip. Henry usually answered because he had hands-free. Not every time, admittedly – it depended on the situation and where he was, but he generally did pick up his calls. Was his failure to answer this time because he couldn't, and not because he didn't want to?

Oh, God, now she felt dreadful. This niggling worm of worry that Meryl had injected into her stomach was growing into a twisted python of a thing, making her feel sick. How could she go and enjoy herself – although *enjoy* probably wasn't the right word considering the mood she was in – when Henry might have been involved in a car accident? How could she be so selfish?

Ashamed, she was about to say that it was fine and she wouldn't go out after all, when her phone vibrated.

'Hang on a sec, that might be him now. I've just had a text,' she said to Meryl.

It was indeed from Henry.

On way home, will be half an hour.

Lottie didn't believe what she was seeing. 'He's on his way back,' she said, flatly.

'Do you still want me to babysit? I'm just getting in my car.'

'Yes, please, if you don't mind. I don't want to let Eleri Jones down.'

'Of course not. I wasn't doing anything this evening, anyway.'

Lottie paced up and down while she waited for Meryl to arrive, and she was out of the door even before her mother-in-law had clambered out of her car.

Lottie hadn't made the slightest attempt to prepare the children for bed. That was supposed to have been Henry's job, so she said, 'Don't worry about the children. Henry can see to them when he gets in. Sabrina is in her room, and Robin and Morgan are watching a film. It's only got about twenty minutes to go, so there's no point in putting them to bed before that as they'll only howl. They might as well stay up until their dad comes home. After all, they haven't seen him all day.'

This last was said with some acerbity.

—

As Lottie stamped towards Eleri's house, she was almost incandescent with rage. Not only was he late, but he'd had her worrying he might have been involved in an accident when he'd been with another woman all along. *How dare he! How very dare he!*

'Are you OK, love?' Eleri asked, when she opened the door to Lottie.

'Men!' Lottie cried.

'Enough said. Come in. Glass of wine? You look as though you need it. That is, if you don't mind drinking and putting hinges on.'

For the first time that evening Lottie smiled. 'They might be a bit wonky,' she warned.

'What the hell. They can always be redone, can't they?'

Eleri led Lottie through to the garden and out to her summer house. In the centre of it sat the TV cabinet, resting on top of some old cardboard to protect the floor.

If Lottie hadn't known it used to be a TV cabinet, she never would have guessed. Bits of it had been taken off and were lying around in various stages of preparation. The main reason why she was there was to remove the shelf that the TV would have sat on, and take it back to her house where she would cut a small hole in it and insert a washing-up bowl. That was what Eleri planned to use as a pretend sink.

As Lottie stared at it, she thought she might have some small lengths of dowel that she could affix to the side of it to make it look like a draining board. It would only need little pieces, because the area wasn't a large one. The other side of the washing-up bowl would be where potential young cooks could pretend to chop vegetables and prepare food.

Lottie and Eleri carried on dismantling the TV stand so Lottie could get to the length of wood she needed. It was going to be reassembled in roughly the same manner, with the addition of a few shelves and some hooks, so Lottie carefully stacked each piece in order, so that she knew where they had to go when she came to reassemble it.

'You're doing a grand job on the sanding,' Lottie said, 'and I see you've done a couple of test colours. What are you going to go for?'

Eleri stood back, hands on hips. 'I quite like these ice cream shades,' she said. 'The pale blue, together with the mint green and the pink is very on trend.' She laughed. 'Listen to me, saying things like "on trend".'

'It's true, though. Think of the colours of the dressers and the appliances in *The Great British Bake Off*, and you're almost there. You could put some fairy lights across the top of it, or maybe some bunting?'

'Ooh, I like that idea. And a friend of mine has got a kiddies' bench and table she no longer uses. It's been in the garden for ages, but she's happy for me to have it. It will need a good sanding down and painting, and I was thinking of asking Gracie if she'd make some cushions to go on it. It would look like a proper little kitchen-diner then.'

'You've thought this through, haven't you?' Lottie said. 'If their parents don't mind, their children will be able to eat there, too. It could get a bit messy, though,' she added.

'That doesn't matter – as long as everyone has a good time and enjoys the food, that's all that counts,' Eleri said.

The pair of them admired their handiwork for a moment, sipping their wine. Lottie was careful not to drink too much, as she didn't want her mouth to run away with her when she got home. Despite outward appearances, she was still very annoyed, incredibly upset and almost in a state of disbelief. She still couldn't understand why he'd do this to her. Didn't he love her any more?

He couldn't, could he, if he was sleeping with someone else? It was just a pity she loved him with all her heart, because he had quite happily trampled all over hers.

Chapter 21

Henry

So much for hoping to find some oars and make amends to Lottie, Henry thought, after he had switched his phone on and saw the number of missed calls and the several texts from his wife, each one getting progressively shirtier. He had totally and utterly forgotten he was supposed to be looking after the children that evening. *Could this day get any worse?*

Oh, yes, it could, he realised, when he saw his mum's car in the drive. Lottie had gone out regardless of him not being home. He didn't blame her, but he wasn't in the mood for speaking to his mum this evening. He wasn't in the mood for speaking to anyone; not even Lottie, because after being so late she probably would have ignored him anyway.

'Hi, Mum,' he said, wearily, as he trudged into the house. Oh, Lord, the children were still up. He should have expected it, because he was supposed to have put them to bed. Lottie had probably been hanging on waiting for him to come home, and had then phoned his mother in desperation.

'Lottie hasn't long gone,' his mother said, cheerfully. 'The boys have just finished watching a film, and she told me not to bother to put them to bed, because you'd do it.'

I bet she did, Henry thought grumpily. He could do without this too, but it wasn't fair on the children if he took out his bad mood on them. They hadn't done anything wrong. Neither had Lottie, come to think of it. Nor his mother. He was the one to blame. Although it wasn't his fault he'd lost his job. Oh God, what a mess.

'Had a good day?' Meryl asked, her eyebrows raised as she looked at him.

'All right, I suppose,' he said. He probably wasn't fooling her, but right then he didn't care.

'Everything *is* all right, isn't it, Henry?' she asked.

Henry gave a start. 'Yes, why do you ask?'

'Nothing.' His mother's tone was offhand, but he knew her too well, so when she carried on saying, 'It's just that Lottie seems a bit out of sorts,' he knew he was in for a grilling.

'Mum, I'm tired, and I've got to get the kids to bed. Can we do this another time?'

'Do what?'

'Chat about Lottie.'

'So there *is* something wrong?'

'I didn't say that.'

'You didn't have to.'

'Mum, leave it, it's nothing.' Or it would be nothing if he could get himself another job, and fast. He didn't know what was up with Lottie, but he had so much on his plate at the moment he couldn't begin to work her out. No doubt she'd tell him eventually; she usually did. Besides, in the past when she'd been having a moment and he'd asked her what was wrong, her usual response had been, 'Nothing.' Yet she expected him to know anyway. What was he, a mind reader?

It might have been with undue haste that he steered his mother to the front door, but he didn't care about that, either. All he cared about was putting three children to bed, two of whom were getting quite fractious because they were overtired. Sabrina was up in her room, as usual, probably playing on some game or another. But at ten, she wasn't a baby any more, and he trusted her to get herself ready for bed when he told her she should.

The other two were a different matter. Robin protested all the way and Morgan, getting a second wind, gave Henry the runaround, charging up and down the landing and in and out of bedrooms, giggling like an idiot while wearing a pair of pants on his head. It wasn't his son's best look, but it did make Henry smile.

Eventually all three children were safely tucked up in bed, Morgan fast asleep, Robin getting there, and Sabrina reading. He stuck his head around her door. 'Are you all right, sweetie?'

She glanced up at him, her face illuminated by the bedside light, and he was struck by how gorgeous she was. Fresh-faced and clear-eyed, her cheeks still rounded yet with a hint of cheekbone underneath, she was the image of her mum. At that moment, he could almost imagine Lottie as she would have been at the same age. The child was far from being grown up, but he could see hints of the adult his daughter would soon become, in her face and mannerisms. It was fascinating, awe inspiring, and exciting all at the same time. Together, he and Lottie had made this new human being; three of them in fact, and watching them grow up was an absolute delight.

He sat on Sabrina's bed and she moved over to give him some room. 'What are you reading?' he asked.

'*The Witches* by Roald Dahl,' she said, closing the book slightly to show him the cover.

'Is it any good?'

'I suppose.'

'I remember when I used to read to you every night,' he said, wistfully.

Sabrina didn't look impressed. 'I was a baby, that's what you do with little ones. I can read all on my own now,' she told him, slightly sarcastically.

Henry ruffled her hair and she pulled a face. 'Get off,' she whined.

Abruptly, it struck him suddenly and with great force that his daughter's childhood was fast disappearing. She was racing headlong into being a teenager, and although he guessed he probably wouldn't lose her totally, he knew she would retreat from him. It was beginning already. It was only natural, but he didn't like it one bit. He wanted his little girl back, his little princess who would wrap her arms around him, kiss his cheeks, and tell him he was the best daddy in the world.

He couldn't remember the last time she'd done that.

Ignoring her frown, he leant across the bed and kissed her on the forehead. He was grateful she didn't wipe at the skin his lips had touched. But he had a feeling she wanted to.

Henry made a promise to himself that no matter what happened, he was going to make the most of spending as much time as possible with his family – the children especially. The last ten years had flown by and so would the next ten, and suddenly they'd be grown and gone, and he'd no longer be able to rock his children in his arms, or be covered in sloppy kisses and told 'I love you, Daddy' in a high, piping voice.

With tears in his eyes, he wandered back downstairs and slumped in front of the TV.

It was some time later when he heard Lottie return, and he sat up a bit straighter, feeling slightly stiff, both physically and emotionally. He had a feeling he'd be in for a bit of a battering for being so late and not being contactable, and he braced himself for the onslaught.

But as he'd surmised earlier, Lottie ignored him. She didn't even glance at him as she walked past the living room and into the kitchen. It was as though he didn't exist. He debated whether to go and speak to her, ultimately deciding it was best to let sleeping dogs lie. He could tell she was annoyed with him, but it would blow over. It always did. The best thing he could do was to keep his head down and wait it out. It shouldn't take too long; they very rarely fell out for more than a day or so.

He was about to sneak off up to bed when she stalked into the living room and stood in front of him, her hands on her hips. 'So, what's the excuse?' she demanded. 'You knew I was going out this evening.'

'Sorry, I was in a bit of a blank spot,' he lied, unconvincingly.

Lottie raised her eyebrows, her lips set in a thin line.

'I messaged you as soon as I could,' he assured her.

'Bullshit.'

'Look, I'm sorry, OK?' He held his hands out, palms up, in a gesture of supplication. 'You were still able to go out. My mum came round, didn't she?'

'Yes, but no thanks to you. It was just sheer luck she didn't have anything on this evening.'

'I said I'm sorry. Couldn't you have rearranged?'

She rolled her eyes. 'Why? So that you could be late again on another night instead?' she argued.

'Lottie, you have no idea what's going on,' he said, throwing caution to the wind.

'Tell me, then,' she demanded.

Henry reined himself in. With the mood she was in, he didn't want to confide in her. It would only make matters worse, and after the day he'd had he could do without the aggro. Not knowing what else to say, he fell silent.

He was dimly aware of Lottie shaking her head in disgust before storming out of the room.

Feeling suddenly very sad, he let her go.

–

Henry could hear Lottie moving about, getting ready for bed, but he stayed where he was until the house fell silent. Even then he was hesitant about being in the same room as her.

When he finally took himself upstairs, he saw he didn't have to be. Morgan's bedroom door was firmly shut and he guessed that was where his wife intended to spend the night. Filled with sadness, he shucked off his clothes before slipping into his side of the suddenly very empty double bed. It was one thing not wanting to start the conversation back up; it was quite another to have her not share his bed.

Not only had he lost his job, Henry felt he was in serious danger of losing his wife and his children, too.

For the first time since he was a child, Henry cried himself to sleep.

Chapter 22

Lottie

Lottie obsessively checked her Instagram account for what must have been the twentieth time in an hour. She was enjoying a cup of coffee in the kitchen before she had to pick the children up from school, while watching Morgan colour in (she used the term loosely) a line drawing of an elf, and hoping to get some interest for her post of the renovated door.

She let out a gasp when she saw she now had forty-three likes, and the number was climbing steadily. She had only posted it half an hour ago, and she was already pleased with the results. But more importantly, she'd also posted it on Etsy for sale!

She'd thought long and hard about doing this, scared someone might want to buy it then take one look at it and change their mind. But, as Delia told her yesterday, she would never know unless she posted it. Delia had also told her that she didn't realise how talented she was, which had made Lottie blush and feel rather uncomfortable. But even as she had brushed the comment away, she knew she'd done a decent job of transforming the door into a coat rack. It was practical yet unusual at the same time. In the right setting it would look stunning. It needed a rustic farmhouse-style property to set it off, but it wouldn't look

185

out of place in an industrial-style loft. It didn't look out of place in their own house, but they had enough furniture and enough hooks and shelves, and she didn't see the need for any more.

She almost wished she'd shown Henry the finished product but, to be honest, she couldn't be bothered. She was still smarting from the other evening, even though he'd made an 'effort' and had arrived home early yesterday.

She still couldn't get her head around the fact that he was more than likely having an affair. It didn't seem possible somehow, not her Henry. She wouldn't put him down as being the type. But then again, what *was* the unfaithful type? What she meant was, she'd thought he loved her too much to even look at another woman. And that was what pained her most – that he didn't.

Had he fallen out of love with her? He must have done, or he wouldn't treat her like this. When had he realised he didn't love her any more? Over the past day or so, she'd racked her brains but she couldn't identify any particular point. It must have been gradual; so gradual that she hadn't noticed. But she noticed it now, all right.

'Finished, Mummy,' Morgan declared, holding up the red and green scribble covering most of the elf and the rest of the paper.

'Well done! Shall I put this one on the fridge?'

He nodded enthusiastically, then rubbed his eyes and yawned. He'd been up since five thirty and Lottie had spent the biggest part of the morning in the park trying to wear him out and take his mind off the impending visit of a certain jolly man in a red suit. Lottie hadn't even put the tree up yet but Morgan was demanding they leave out a carrot, a mince pie and a glass of milk just in case Santa was early.

After school, Delia had promised to pop over with Mick and Tyrone, and Lottie was still in two minds about saying anything more to her friend about the state of her marriage. She was no further forward when it came to gathering concrete evidence, despite the circumstantial evidence mounting up against Henry. She didn't want to be one of those women who was constantly jealous; up until now she hadn't been in the slightest, but at this very minute she didn't particularly like herself. More importantly, she liked Henry even less.

She popped Morgan upstairs for a nap after she'd given him lunch, and figured she probably had about half an hour of peace, but for the first time in ages she didn't have something to work on, having finished the sledges she'd been making, and was at a bit of a loose end.

The problem with being at a loose end was that it gave one time to think, and she was totally fed up with thinking; all it did was wind her up and make her head spin. She was the type of person who liked to be busy; having time on her hands didn't suit her. She simply wasn't used to it, so she needed to find another project sharpish, if only to take her mind off Henry and the state of her marriage.

Picking up her phone, she logged into Freecycle. After Henry's disapproval when she'd brought the sledge home, even though it had only cost £5 and she'd made another two from wood she'd already salvaged (which was considerably cheaper than buying three plastic ones the next time it snowed), she was reluctant to spend money on anything to do with her hobby. She'd see what she could find online for nothing, though the area this particular group covered was quite extensive, and if she found anything she'd have to wait until she could get her hands on the car before she arranged to collect the item.

She was busy trawling through posts and having a good gander at the photos and wondering what she could do with things – the ideas sluggish and slow to come to her – when she received a notification.

Someone wanted to buy the door!

Except, it wasn't a door any longer, was it? She'd described it as an unusual coat rack and had posted several pictures. *And now someone wanted to buy it.*

Squeee!!

Lottie danced around in a circle, waving her hands in the air. Suddenly she sobered. What if, when they came to pick it up, they didn't like it? What if they thought it was rubbish? Oh, God, what was she going to do?

The potential buyer had provided their contact number and name, and asked how soon they could come round to view it. Lottie decided there was no time like the present; the sooner they came to see it, the sooner she'd know whether she should take it off the market, and never try to sell anything she'd made ever again.

It was with a mixture of excitement and trepidation that she spoke to the woman who had expressed an interest, and they arranged for her to pop around in an hour or so.

Goodness, this was moving far too fast for Lottie, and she didn't know what to make of it all. She'd only posted it this morning and it was just after lunch, and very shortly she might have made her first sale. Or not.

Lottie carried the door carefully out from the shed and into the hall, where she propped it up against the wall, then she waited impatiently for the lady, whose name was Jo, to arrive.

–

'Oh, it's even better in real life,' Jo said. 'What an absolutely marvellous idea; you're so clever to think of it. We've bought an old barn, and trying to furnish it with statement pieces isn't easy, but this will be ideal. All I need to go underneath is a little seat so I can sit on it to take my shoes on and off. You wouldn't happen to have anything like that, would you?'

'No, but I'll keep my eye out for you, if you like. What was it you were after?'

'I don't know – something made out of old pallets maybe? I like the rustic look, and I like a bit of history. I don't necessarily mean old, but something that's a talking point, which has a story behind it.'

Lottie grinned. 'Would you like to come upstairs and have a look at my son's boat?'

'I'm sorry, I thought you said *boat*.' Jo was looking quizzical.

'That's right, a boat.'

After Jo had gone – taking the revamped door with her, having paid the full asking price – Lottie was so ecstatic she could barely contain her excitement and her pleasure.

Without thinking, she reached for her phone and called Henry.

Chapter 23

Henry

When Henry saw his wife's number on the screen, he frowned. They had hardly spoken in nearly two days, and he wondered why she was ringing him, before guessing she probably wanted him to pick something up from the shop on the way home.

This was what his marriage had come to – two strangers passing in the night. They'd become more like lodgers than husband and wife. He still held out hope that as soon as he landed another job they'd put all this behind them. He'd give himself one more week, that was all, just one week, and if there was nothing on the horizon, he'd have to tell her.

'Hi, Lottie,' he said, with a certain degree of reticence. Her answering squeal made him wince, and he held the phone away from his ear before hastily putting it back again and praying to God there was nothing wrong. 'What's up?' he demanded, his heart in his mouth.

'I've sold the door!' Lottie cried.

Henry's mind went blank for a minute – what door? What was she talking about? Then he remembered, and his thumping heart gradually returned to a less alarming rhythm. 'Is that all?' he said, relieved that nothing was seriously wrong. In fact, it was good news.

There was silence on the other end for a second, then Lottie said, 'Thanks,' and suddenly the call ended.

Henry hadn't moved – he was in the car park of a service station on the A44 – so he didn't think it was the reception, but he'd been holding the device to his ear so tightly that he might very well have disconnected her with his face; it wouldn't be the first time. But when he tried ringing her back, it went to voicemail.

Silly Lottie – she was probably trying to call him. They must both be on the phone at the same time, trying to ring each other. He left it a minute before phoning her again, staring at the screen in anticipation. When she didn't answer, he guessed it *was* probably due to the phone reception, so he resumed his journey before trying again some time later.

It still went to answer phone.

That was strange; maybe she was out and about? There were some dead spots in Applewell so he'd speak to her when he got home.

There was no chance he would be late tonight, because he didn't have any clients booked in. The only thing he was required to do on this, his last day of employment at Baldwin Ltd, was to drive to head office and return anything that belonged to the company.

Having woken at the crack of dawn, he'd left early, Lottie still asleep (in the marital bed, thankfully) and the children not yet stirring, because he had wanted to get there and back in as short a time as possible. It was a six-hour round trip, with maybe an hour to hand everything over, so that meant seven hours before he was home again. He didn't have much to return, just a laptop and some paperwork, and that was about it. Come to think of it, an hour was probably too long – five minutes should do it.

But when he arrived, he realised that five minutes had been over-egging it. Two was more accurate. He'd gone to reception, where the woman behind the desk had been expecting him. She had a checklist which she used to diligently tick off every item as he handed it to her, then he was done. No 'thank you', no 'goodbye', no exit interview. Nothing. And that just about summed it up as far as he was concerned.

He didn't feel particularly different on the drive back, even though he was now officially unemployed. The only thing he felt was free, which was quite a peculiar feeling considering his future was most definitely uncertain and he was consumed with worry. And not just about his finances, either.

His most immediate worry was what he was going to do with himself next week with no work to go to. He could always tell Lottie he'd taken a few days off, but she might think it odd. He'd be better off going to the library in Aberystwyth.

He'd already scrutinised all the obvious job sites for his type of work, but maybe it was time he expanded his horizon. He'd done all the trawling he could, and applied for any and all sales jobs he'd found. Perhaps he should consider alternative lines of employment? At this point he'd do anything.

As he spotted a sign for Worcester, Henry decided to take a little detour. He'd been to the city several years ago, and he remembered the cathedral with the calm sweep of the River Severn beyond. He was hungry, and Worcester was as good a place as anywhere to grab a bite to eat. He'd been up so early that he'd not had breakfast and neither had he made any sandwiches to bring with him, so he decided to treat himself to a portion of chips. He'd been sorely tempted the other day at New Quay, but after the phone call from Sally Chisholm, his appetite had deserted him. Now, though, his mouth watered at the thought of piping hot chips liberally covered in vinegar, washed down with a can of something cold and fizzy.

He parked the car in a multistorey on the outskirts of the city centre and strolled down towards the river, soaking in the festive atmosphere. The streets were busy with shoppers and every window he passed was decorated with trees and gift ideas, fairy lights and baubles.

He thought about the present he'd bought for Lottie, which was hidden in the boot of his car, and wished he'd not given in to the impulse to buy it. As far as jewellery went (was an ornate hairpin classed as jewellery?) it hadn't been too expensive, but he could have done with not spending the money. He should have taken it back for a refund after he'd had the phone call from Sally Chisholm, but in the dismay of discovering he'd not got the job he'd forgotten he'd bought the damned thing in the first place. Maybe he'd return it the next time he was in the area?

After purchasing his rather early lunch – the chip shop had only just opened and he'd had to wait for the chips to finish frying – he found a bench and sat on it to eat his food, wolfing it down so fast he gave himself hiccups. The fizzy drink didn't help, but he gulped it thirstily, then deposited his rubbish in the nearest bin.

Wiping his greasy hands on a tissue, he automatically checked his phone. As it had been getting increasingly more silent over the course of the past week or so, he wasn't surprised to see he had no notifications, no messages and no missed calls.

With nothing to do and nowhere to go, and considering it was still relatively early in the day and far too soon to go home even with the two-and-a-half-hour drive it would take him to get back to Applewell, he decided he'd have a mooch around and explore the cathedral first because it was only a short walk from where he'd eaten his lunch, so he made his way towards it, the impressive tower easily visible from where he had been sitting.

Walking along the riverbank with a weak December sun on his face and the gurgle of the water in his ears was exceedingly pleasant. Rafts of swans and quite a few ducks bobbed up and down on the water, following him for a while, hoping he might have some food to throw for them. When it was clear he wasn't going to feed them, they veered off to look for better candidates.

Henry wasn't entirely sure whether he could get to the cathedral from the path running alongside the river, but then he saw a stone archway with steps leading up and realised he could. He paused for a moment to look at the inscriptions on the side of the wall indicating how far the river levels had risen when the Severn had flooded over the years. Many of the marks were above his head. Flooding didn't appear to have affected the cathedral, though; it was roughly eight hundred years old, he read, when he went inside and studied the information board near the enormous main doors, and it was still standing and appeared to be in good nick.

There was a soothing, peaceful atmosphere inside, and he took a seat on one of the long pews and gazed up at the magnificent stained-glass windows. He didn't think he'd been in a church since his wedding day, but he couldn't be 100 per cent certain. Surely some of his friends had got married after he and Lottie had tied the knot, but if they had, he couldn't bring it to mind.

Henry wasn't a religious man, but he did appreciate history, and he also appreciated the sense of reverence in which the walls of the building were steeped. It made him feel quite small in a way, to think of the thousands of people who had gone before him, walking the aisles, their footsteps polishing the large flagstones beneath his feet. There would be thousands more after him, and in some ways it made his own existence feel small and inconsequential, making him realise that his problems were tiny in the great scheme of things.

Feeling rather melancholy, he strolled through the town, dipping into some of the older parts of the city with its cobbled streets and Tudor buildings, and then, quite suddenly, as he trod his solitary and aimless path, he wondered what on earth he was doing.

At that very moment he wanted nothing more than to be at home with Lottie, wrapping his arms around her and holding her close. But he also knew that even if he was at home right then, the last thing she'd want to do was to be cuddled by him. There must be something he could do to put his marriage back on the right track, without admitting to her that he was a total failure. He had no doubt Lottie would understand and be supportive, and that she wouldn't blame him for losing his job, but he didn't want to see the worry in her eyes that he knew would be there.

He wondered if it had been his comment to Sally Chisholm about wanting to return to his own bed at night that had lost him the opportunity at Allinson's. He'd said it in a joking manner, but he hadn't been joking at all. He was a homebody and he didn't want to spend night after night on the road. But the way he felt right then, if Sally offered him the job today he'd jump at it despite any onerous travel. Everyone knew it was easier to find another job when you were already in one. He also wondered whether the scent of desperation he had undoubtedly exuded had also put her off.

Abruptly he came to a halt, and gazed around, wondering where he was. He'd been so lost in his thoughts that his feet had taken him out of the city centre proper and he wasn't quite sure where he was. Great – he was lost in a strange city and now he couldn't find his car.

'Excuse me,' he said to a middle-aged woman walking past. 'I seem to be lost. Could you point me in the right direction for the city centre?' If he could find his way back to the river, he could retrace his steps to the car park.

'Of course, my duck. Were you after any particular street or shop?'

'I want to get to the multistorey car park.'

'You're not too far away. If you turn back the way you came, go left and left again, you should see it.' She pointed down the road behind him.

'Thank you so much, I really appreciate your help.'

He followed her instructions until he got to the end of the road he was on, then he turned left onto another street and was reassured when he could see a blue and white parking sign ahead of him. Relieved, he hurried along the road, dodging around some scaffolding where a building was being renovated, his attention on the sign.

When he bumped straight into a large, yellow skip outside the building, having not concentrated on what was in front of his nose, it brought tears to his eyes. 'Ouch!'

He rubbed his hip where he'd caught it on the corner of the skip, and gave the container a foul glare, even though it was his own fault for not seeing it. How could he have missed it: it was bigger than his car and crammed full of rubbish. He eyed a battered chest of drawers which was perched precariously on the mound of rubble, and prayed it wasn't going to fall on him. The last thing he needed was to be buried underneath a pile of old wood.

Gingerly he walked around the skip until he reached the pavement, then trotted along it, heading resolutely for the car park. It was time he was back on the road and on his way home. Although Lottie hadn't told him she was going out again that evening, he didn't want to be too late home. He probably wasn't going to be much fun tonight – when was he ever these days? – but he felt a burning need to be in the bosom of his family. Even if his wife ignored him and his daughter thought he wasn't cool, at least his two boys would be delighted to see him.

Locating his car on the third floor of the car park, Henry made a conscious decision to spend more time with the children this weekend. It was ironic in a way – in theory he could spend the whole of next week with the kids, if it wasn't for the fact that he had to pretend to go to work.

Putting the distressing thought out of his mind, he circumnavigated the car park and popped out of an exit on the same street with the scaffolding.

He was about to drive on past when he stopped the car.

Thoughtfully, he got out, walked up to the skip and peered at the mound of detritus, his attention coming to rest on the chest of drawers. Surely Lottie could do something with it? It was quite big and would have originally had three drawers on the top, three drawers in the middle and two longer ones on the bottom. The two longer ones were still in place, three of the smaller drawers were also in position, but of the remaining three, one had fallen out and was half buried beneath pieces of broken plasterboard, and two appeared to be missing.

Henry glanced at the building, but it was boarded up and he couldn't see anyone working in it. He looked around, debating whether he should do what he was thinking of doing, before deciding he'd do it anyway.

Quickly, he pulled his car up in front of the skip and reversed as close as he could to it, then he opened the boot and folded down the back seats. Working as fast as he could, he picked up the drawers and stacked them into the footwells; then, with a final glance up and down the street to make sure nobody was about to shout at him, he reached up and dragged the chest of drawers towards him.

Crikey, it was heavier than he'd thought, but with a bit of wrangling and a lot of huffing and puffing and the odd swear word, he managed to slide it into the back of his car. It only just fitted, and he lowered the rear door with care.

When it was safely inside, he scuttled around to the driver's side, dived in and drove off quickly. He felt extremely guilty, even though he knew it was going to landfill. It had been put in the skip for good reason – nobody wanted it, nobody cared what happened to it – but he couldn't help feeling as though he'd stolen something.

He just hoped Lottie didn't mind him bringing home a battered old chest of drawers, and that she took his offering in the spirit it was intended. There was also the small hope in the back of his mind that when she did something extraordinary with it, she would be able to sell it, like she'd sold the door.

It was just a pity he was having to pretend he was in work next week, because he might have been able to help her. But even as the thought entered his head, an idea was taking shape. He wasn't quite sure where he was going with it yet, and it might come to nothing, but he knew exactly what he was going to do on Monday while he was pretending to be in work, and he discovered he was strangely excited about it.

Chapter 24

Lottie

What the hell had Henry been thinking of, bringing her a damaged chest of drawers, Lottie thought but didn't say, because Henry had reminded her of a hopeful puppy bringing her his favourite ball and expecting her to be pleased about it. She couldn't decide whether she was pleased or not; in one way she was, because she'd only just been lamenting not having anything to work on, but in another way she was still highly sceptical of his reasons. There was also the thought in the back of her mind that perhaps he was giving someone else the chocolates and flowers that should have been for her.

'Don't tell me you got this from John Porter's farm?' Lottie asked, walking around it, and wondering what on earth she was going to do with it.

'I got it out of a skip,' he said.

Lottie shot him a quick look, and he hastened to add, 'It wasn't from around here.'

Thank God for that! She'd hate to think that someone they knew might have seen him clambering about amongst other people's rubbish and taking things.

'I'm not sure what I'm supposed to do with it,' she said. 'It's not as though we need any additional furniture, although we may well do when the extension is built, but that's ages away yet and I don't have anywhere to store it.'

'I was thinking you could do what you did with the door,' Henry said.

Lottie resisted the urge to roll her eyes and sigh. 'It would take a great deal of work to turn this into a coat rack,' she pointed out.

'That's not what I meant. I was thinking you could turn it into something else; or do it up and sell it.'

'You've changed your tune,' Lottie said.

'I'm not sure I follow.'

Good grief, what was wrong with the man? His reaction when she had phoned him earlier to tell him she'd sold the door had been lukewarm at best. Which was why she'd hung up on him – she'd been incredibly upset. She still was. He hadn't even been interested enough to ask how much she'd sold it for, which was a bit rich considering he'd made such a fuss of her buying a five-pound sledge, and had also been reluctant to go out for a meal in the Busy Bumble, supposedly because of the cost. She would have thought he'd be delighted to know they had a few extra pennies in the coffers but, oh no, he hadn't been in the least bit curious.

'You couldn't have cared less when I told you about the door being sold,' she said, 'and now you're bringing me a chest of drawers and expecting me to perform miracles on it.'

'I *was* pleased, honest! It's just the line went dead before I was able to say anything.'

He took a step towards her and Lottie took a corresponding step backwards. He halted, with a puzzled and slightly hurt look on his face, and Lottie bit her lip. What if she'd got all this wrong? What if she was reading too much into things, like Delia said? Was she making a mountain out of a molehill?

Perhaps she might be, but her instincts were still telling her that something was dreadfully wrong. And Lottie knew damn well it wasn't her.

'I've got an idea what you can do with it…' he began.

Lottie was seriously tempted to tell him she had a good idea what she could do with it too, but Henry wouldn't like her suggestion and he might find it rather painful.

'Go on.' She sighed.

'I originally thought you could make some new drawers, and just have it as a chest of drawers again, but what would be the fun in that?' he said.

Lottie folded her arms. 'The wood would be different, but that probably wouldn't matter if I painted it. But just giving a piece of furniture a simple paint job is old hat.'

'I'm sure it isn't – not everyone is as clever as you,' he carried on.

Lottie pulled a face. He was behaving really weirdly, buttering her up and giving her compliments. 'What was your idea?'

'Could you make a seat out of it?'

Lottie was about to tell him to get lost, when something the lady who'd bought the door said popped into her head. Jo had wanted a simple seat underneath the coat rack. *Could* the chest of drawers become a seat?

Lottie was pretty sure it could. She'd have to take the top off of course, and remove all except for the two drawers at the bottom. In fact, they'd come in handy for popping gloves, umbrellas, hats and scarves in.

With most of the sides and the back exposed, she could reinforce the plank above the two drawers by reusing the wood from the top, and turn it into a seat. With a pair of new handles on the remaining drawers, and some plump cushions, it would look absolutely fabulous. It wouldn't take very long, either. The biggest issue she had was her lack of sewing skills, and she'd want the cushions to fit snugly on the seat. She knew where she could get some foam cut to size, but she wasn't all that good with a sewing machine. That she didn't own a sewing machine was another problem. But she knew a woman who did, and she wondered how much Gracie would charge, and hoped she'd be able to find some suitable fabric. She was thinking of something chintzy, something a bit cottagey but not over the top, in bright colours. She would paint the seat in the same colour as the coat rack, with complementary fabric, then she'd upload a photo and ping it off to Jo. If Jo didn't want it, Lottie would put it on Etsy and see what happened. After her sale today, Lottie was feeling a little more confident about her abilities.

Filled with excitement, she couldn't wait to start. Henry must have seen something in her face, because he smiled at her. 'You can envision it too, can't you?' he said.

'Oh, yes!' Lottie said. 'Don't just stand there, give me a hand getting it into the shed. Then you can cook tea, while I get started on it.'

To her surprise, Henry didn't murmur. He willingly helped her carry it into the shed, and then he left her to it.

–

Eager to begin, Lottie swiftly changed into her work clothes, which consisted of stuffing herself into a set of overalls and rolling the sleeves up. She was absolutely thrilled to have something to work on, and she was even more thrilled Henry had given her the idea of what to do with the chest of drawers.

This was what she really liked doing. Also, she had come to realise that she thoroughly enjoyed imparting her knowledge to Eleri – Lottie had gained a great deal of satisfaction from teaching her, which had come as a surprise. Obviously she taught her own children all manner of things, from telling the time with a proper analogue clock, to tying their shoelaces, although Robin still struggled with his and it would be a while yet before Morgan could do either of those things. She'd taught them loads of things over the years, and she'd enjoyed it, so it shouldn't have come as such a surprise to discover she'd loved showing Eleri how to transform the ugly old TV cabinet into something new.

But, as Henry shouted down the garden to tell her their evening meal was ready, she once again realised she had totally immersed herself in what she was doing, and hadn't once given Henry's (alleged) infidelity or her marriage a second thought. Which yet again made her question his motive for bringing these things home for her to work on.

Chapter 25

Henry

Bringing the chest of drawers home had been the right decision, Henry decided; Lottie had been in a much better mood when she came in from the shed yesterday evening, and he guessed it had probably helped that he'd cooked tea as well.

So he'd got up on Saturday morning in a much better frame of mind with regards to his home life – he ignored the work problem – and he vowed to make the most of the weekend. With his newfound enlightenment when it came to what was important in life, he wanted to do something fun with the kids today. Something that didn't involve spending any money, of course.

It looked like it was going to be a chilly and crisp December day he saw, when he peered out of the window. There was a layer of frost on the lawn and a robin was perched on the fence, proudly showing off its red breast.

He quickly got dressed and trotted downstairs. The two older children were eating breakfast and Lottie was trying to persuade Morgan that putting marmalade into his porridge wasn't a good idea when Henry appeared.

'How about we go and choose the Christmas tree today?' Lottie said, when she saw him. 'If we leave it too late, all the best ones will be gone. We can have hot chocolate and marshmallows in the little cafe there.'

'Yay!' Robin waved his spoon in the air and even Sabrina looked enthused. Morgan shouted 'Yay', too, but Henry suspected the little boy didn't know what was being suggested; he'd been a tad too young last year to fully understand what Christmas was about.

With a sinking feeling, Henry realised Lottie was suggesting a visit to the farm where they usually bought their tree from. And why wouldn't she? It had become a bit of a tradition, but he was reluctant to spend the money. However, the tree was an expense he was going to have to suck up if he wanted to avoid telling Lottie about his job situation – or lack of one. But hot chocolate for everyone would set them back the best part of twenty quid.

'I was thinking of going to the beach,' he said, improvising frantically. 'We could take a couple of flasks of hot chocolate with us, and some marshmallows. If we build a fire we could toast them on it, and maybe have some hot dogs, too?'

'I want to put up the tree,' Sabrina said. 'Mum, tell him.'

Lottie stared at him dubiously. 'It'll be freezing, and we'll still need to get a tree at some point.'

'How about we buy one from Pins to Elephants? I noticed Tony has got quite a few outside the shop this year, and we'll be supporting a local business.' As well as not making a twenty-mile round trip and using petrol he didn't want to use now he no longer had a company to claim the mileage from. 'What do you say kids? We can toast marshmallows on the beach and pick up a tree on the way home? Or would you prefer a couple of hours in the car?' Two hours was an exaggeration, but all's fair in love and saving money.

'Beach! Beach!' Robin was bouncing in his chair with excitement. 'Can I help you build a fire?'

'Me! Me! I wanna build a fire!' Morgan scrambled down from the table and raced to the front door.

'Are we allowed?' Lottie was looking doubtful.

'People camp there in the summer and build fires.'

'I'm not so sure…'

'It'll be fun,' Henry insisted. 'And why drive all the way to the Christmas tree farm when we can buy one from Tony and spend the rest of the day on the beach? The kids will only whine in the car – they always do. *Are we there yet?*' he cried in a high-pitched voice, laughing as he dodged a thump from his daughter.

Lottie nodded. 'OK. If you make the hot chocolate, and get the kids dressed – old clothes, mind – and make sure they've got their hats and gloves, I'll pop into the village for some rolls and marshmallows.'

Henry watched her grab her purse and make a dash for the door before any of the children realised where she was going. Sabrina wouldn't want to accompany her, but Robin and Morgan might. A trip to the shops, any shop, was usually an excuse to ask for sweets.

Once Lottie had left, Henry sent the children upstairs to get ready, giving Sabrina strict instructions that she was to supervise the boys and make sure they wore their warmest clothes. As he listened to them charging about overhead, he measured out enough milk to fill two large flasks and put the liquid in a pan to heat up. Then he grated some chocolate and added it to the milk, along with cocoa powder, a dash of vanilla extract and his secret

209

ingredient – maple syrup. Not much, but just enough to give the drink a touch of added sweetness.

After stirring continually for a few minutes, the mixture was good and hot, and he poured it into the pair of pre-warmed flasks and screwed the lids on tightly, but not before he'd added yet another secret ingredient to the flask meant for him and Lottie. Brandy. Yum.

By the time Lottie returned, Henry had made sure all the children were dressed and in the right clothes for the occasion, he'd unearthed the rucksack from under the stairs and had packed it with a change of clothes for each child – no doubt one or more of them would be certain to get wet. He'd also packed the flasks and a bottle of water, plus the ancient toasting forks from out of the shed, and he was just adding paper plates, plastic mugs, a bottle of ketchup and the all-important box of matches to the bag.

Lottie raised her eyebrows and smiled her approval, handing him a pack of sausages, some fresh bread rolls, and a large bag of squishy marshmallows.

Then they were on their way, Lottie holding Robin's hand and Henry carrying Morgan, with Sabrina trailing slightly behind as though she didn't want to be seen with her siblings. Or her parents, for that matter.

But when the family arrived at the cove, Sabrina was as excited as the other two, and they charged off down the beach, making patterns in the soft wet sand with their wellington boots.

Henry made sure to pick a spot well above the high tide mark, on dry fluffy sand, to pitch their camp. Immediately behind was a bank of pebbles, driftwood and dried seaweed, and he put the rucksack down and proceeded to gather everything needed to make a fire.

Lottie flopped down onto the blanket she'd been carrying and sighed.

'Are you OK?' he asked her, hoping she wasn't too disappointed at not going to the Christmas tree farm.

But then she smiled, and he realised his idea of coming to the beach was a good one.

Her eyes never leaving the children who were careening up and down the sand with great energy, she said, 'This should wear the little blighters out – much better than having them fidgeting and grizzling in the back of the car.'

Eventually, though, the youngsters ran out of steam and settled down to various tasks, involving sand art (Sabrina), building sandcastles (Robin), and kicking them over (Morgan). As usual Robin didn't mind having his sandcastles destroyed the minute he constructed them, and the three children played happily for a good long while despite the cold, their breath clouding above their heads.

Henry and Lottie snuggled into their coats in front of the fire, and watched their offspring play.

Every so often Henry glanced at Lottie, and he'd smile. His problems hadn't gone away, and they would still be there on Monday, probably ten times worse, but for now he was simply grateful he had his family around him and they were all happy and healthy.

He still didn't intend to tell Lottie just yet, but he would soon, and he had a feeling she would be OK with it. She looked so content right now, though, that he had no intention of disturbing her equilibrium until it was strictly necessary. If he could get away with not telling her until after Christmas, that's what he would do.

She seemed to have recovered from her disapproval of him, and Henry put that down to him making more of an effort. Although spending time with his family, seeing to the children and helping Lottie wasn't an effort, was it? He was thoroughly enjoying himself. With him in a better mood, no wonder his wife seemed more relaxed. They'd get over this, of course they would. They would come out of the other side, and when he looked back on it, Henry would think of it as nothing more than just a bump in the road.

Gradually the chill got to the youngsters and they gravitated back to their parents and the promise of a crackling fire and some food.

There was something special about eating outdoors. The hot dog sausages were charred on the outside and tasted all the better for it, the rolls were fresh and the whole thing was surprisingly tasty. Henry put away three all by himself. He'd brought some fruit too, knowing that Lottie liked to try to ensure the children had a healthy diet. He peeled a banana and fed half of it to Morgan, eating the other half himself, because Morgan couldn't manage a whole one. And once that was eaten, he helped the children spear their marshmallows and toast them, Lottie overseeing everything with an eagle eye. Henry knew he'd remember this day as long as he lived. With the sun sparkling on the water, the intense concentration on the faces of his children as they held the long metal forks over the flickering flames of the fire, the scent of burning wood, and the salty tang of the ocean filling his senses, the gentle lap of the waves on the sand in the background, he was happier than he'd been in a long time.

This was what life was all about, Henry concluded – not working himself to death, not trying to buy the biggest, or the best, or the newest; but enjoying the simple things in life – and trying not to burn your fingers or your mouth on the marshmallows.

After they'd eaten, the children wandered off to play for a little while longer, allowing him and Lottie a few more moments of precious peace, sitting together in companionable silence.

Lottie appeared to be lost in her thoughts. When she caught him staring at her, she gave him a small smile, but there was a hint of sadness in it and he wasn't quite sure what had caused it. But when he slung his arm around her, pulling her into him, she rested her head on his shoulder and he knew without a doubt there was nowhere else he wanted to be, and no one else he wanted to be with.

Chapter 26

Lottie

The sun was dipping low in the sky by the time they'd had enough of the beach, and Lottie was becoming increasingly chilled despite tearing up and down the sand in a madcap game of tag. With the sun waning, the cold intensified, so she rounded up the children while Henry packed everything back in the rucksack, and they made their slow way up the wooded valley towards the lights and warmth of home.

'Bye, bye,' Morgan said, waving at the beach from his perch on his father's shoulders.

'Are we still getting the Christmas tree?' Sabrina wanted to know, as the first houses came into sight.

'Of course we are! I think it's about time we put the tree up, what with it only being two weeks until the big man comes down the chimney,' Henry said.

Lottie lamented the sight of Sabrina's dubious expression. Her eldest child still believed in Father Christmas, but only barely. Lottie would be loath to place a bet this being the case next year, and she was filled with sadness at how fast the children were growing up. Making a pledge to have more days like today to forge memories as a family to sustain her and Henry in the years to come, she decided to make an event out of decorating the tree when they got home.

–

They were all gathered around the collection of fir trees propped up outside Pins to Elephants and trying to make a decision, when Lottie suddenly shrank back behind the nearest one. She'd spotted a familiar and rather unwelcome figure prancing towards her. Of all the people she had to meet today, when she was covered in sand, windswept, red-faced and smelling of woodsmoke, was the immaculately dressed and impeccably made-up Natalie Sharp. The woman was trotting along on impossibly high heels and bearing down on them like an out of control truck.

'Lottie, darling, are you thinking of buying a tree? I'm surprised you don't whittle your own out of an old door or something.'

Lottie scowled at her. 'You saw that, did you?'

'Your little Instagram post? What an *interesting* thing you did with it. Who'd have thought a door could have been made into a… what was it again? It wasn't clear from the photo.'

It had been very clear, and so had the description of it; Lottie had made sure of that. Natalie hadn't liked it, but then again, Lottie hadn't expected her to.

Henry was gazing curiously at the woman and Lottie sensed his confusion. No doubt he was aware of an under-current, but he wouldn't be able to identify what it was. On the surface Natalie appeared to be quite charming and complimentary, but Lottie saw right through her.

When Lottie failed to answer, Henry said, 'It was a coat rack, wasn't it? You sold it, didn't you?'

Lottie was surprised he remembered, thinking back to how unenthusiastic he'd seemed when she'd told him she'd sold it. She uttered a vague noise of agreement in the back of her throat, making sure her eyes were firmly on Morgan.

Natalie uttered a tinkling laugh. '*Really?* How odd. Still, people these days will buy anything if they think it's rustic or handmade. The cruder, the better.'

Henry was beaming proudly, as though Natalie had praised her, when Lottie knew the comment had been nothing but pure bitchiness.

'Lottie is so clever, isn't she?' Henry said, and Natalie gave him an incredulous look.

'I'd better be off,' she said. 'I want to see if the butcher has any foie gras, though I suspect not; it's a bit too exotic for our little village, but Callum loves it so.'

'Foie gras?' Henry pulled a face as soon as Natalie was out of earshot. 'Can't stand the stuff myself. Her husband is welcome to it.'

'Callum is her *son*.'

Henry's eyes widened and he jerked his head at Robin. 'There's hope for him yet, then. Maybe Robin will grow out of the chicken-nugget stage one day.' He frowned. 'I must say your friend doesn't look old enough to have a grown-up son.'

'She's not my friend; she's Callum's mum. He's in Robin's class.'

'No!' His head turned to look at Natalie, who was hotfooting it to the butcher's. 'Who feeds their six-year-old foie gras?'

Lottie refused to let the woman's sourness spoil her day. 'Have you seen a tree you like, kids?' she asked in a bright voice, ruffling her fingers through the branches of the tree she'd hoped to hide behind and releasing the heady scent of pine into the air. She breathed in deeply, and not merely to enjoy the smell. Natalie Sharp had got to her, and Lottie had only just managed to keep hold of her temper. The woman was insufferable.

'I like this, Mummy,' Morgan said, picking one which was far too tall for their living room.

'I don't think that will fit, buddy,' Henry said, bending down. 'How about this one? It's got more branches on the front than the back so it will sit in the alcove next to the chimney perfectly.'

The tree was eventually chosen after much debate, and they made their way home, Henry with the intention of returning to Pins to Elephants in the car to pick it up, leaving Lottie to nip up the attic to dig out the boxes of decorations.

Lottie decided that she'd put some Christmas songs on while they trimmed the tree, and make some mulled wine for later – more for the delicious aroma which would infuse the house rather than the alcoholic content, although that would be welcome, too. Once that was done, they'd light the wood burner, and settle down after tea to watch a festive film.

Debating what to cook, Lottie dug through the items in the fridge and freezer, before settling on a hearty lamb stew. She could prepare it in less than ten minutes with the help of a packet of frozen root vegetables, and it would carry on simmering while they got on with the important task of deciding which bauble should go where.

She'd only just popped the ladder back up and closed the hatch to the attic when Henry appeared in the hall, shuffling his way inside as he wrangled a rather tall tree through a rather cramped space. Despite choosing one of the smaller trees, it looked huge when it was upright, as Lottie held it steady while Henry filled the tub with soil and sand.

The children meanwhile were having a great time taking things out of the box and exclaiming over them, Lottie keeping a wary eye on Morgan to make sure he wasn't being too heavy handed.

'Sabrina, can you find the Christmas playlist on my phone?' she asked, letting go of the tree and praying it wouldn't keel over, and soon the cheery sounds of 'Jingle Bells' filled the air and everyone sang along. Except for Morgan, who simply shouted 'jingle bells' repeatedly because he didn't know the rest of the words.

'Something smells nice,' Henry said after a while, as he sniffed the air.

'I'm making lamb stew for tea,' she said.

'Perfect.'

Henry had hit the nail on the head. Today *had* been perfect. His idea of going to the beach and choosing a tree on the way back had been inspired, and with the whole family gathered around to decorate it, and festive tunes playing in the background, Lottie felt that Christmas had finally arrived.

Henry was no longer behaving oddly. Maybe she had been imagining it, or overreacting? Although she continued to have a suspicion that something had gone on with him, she began to relax and enjoy herself. Today had been magical, and the evening was shaping up to be just as lovely.

As Henry lifted Morgan so he could place the angel on the top of the tree, Lottie's heart filled with love and joy. With the room illuminated solely by the fairy lights on the tree and the romantic glow from the log burner, the haunting melody of 'Silent Night' filled the air.

Sabrina began to sing, her pure sweet voice trembling on the air, and one by one they all joined in.

This was what Christmas was all about – her family. She was so grateful for the love they shared that tears rolled slowly down her cheeks, and the gentle touch of Henry's lips as he kissed them away made her heart soar.

There was no way Henry could have been unfaithful to her. No way.

Chapter 27

Lottie

During the school holidays, when Lottie didn't have the routine of getting the children ready for school, weekends seemed to go much quicker than weekdays, and she'd barely blinked before it was Monday morning again and Henry had to leave for work. She waved him off, her emotions fluctuating between not wanting him to go, and needing some time away from him to think.

They'd had two lovely days together. His suggestion that they go to the beach had been so out of character lately, it had taken her by surprise, and she'd been left questioning herself. Had she been seeing things that simply weren't there? Putting two and two together and coming up with a number that was considerably larger?

Or he *had* been having an affair, and maybe it was over? Had Henry seen the error of his ways and ended it, and was now trying to make amends?

Lottie kept mulling it over and over until her thoughts were a jumbled mess and she didn't know what to believe any more.

All she could do from now on was to monitor how he behaved and see whether he carried on in the same manner. Since that furtive phone call there hadn't been any others, and his moodiness seemed to have receded;

he hadn't been late home since Wednesday when she'd asked his mother to step in, and—

Wednesday! Was that when he'd ended the affair? Or maybe the other woman had ended it? Something had definitely happened on that day, because he'd looked dreadful when she'd got back from Eleri's house: tired and with dark circles under his eyes, the rest of his face startlingly pale, and he'd looked upset. She'd been too angry to realise it at the time, but on reflection it was obvious. And then there were the things he'd brought her: the boat, the door, the chest of drawers. She'd read that some men, if they were being unfaithful, assuaged their guilt by giving their wives gifts. Perhaps he hadn't been bringing her things to keep her busy but because he was feeling guilty and he knew she'd appreciate an old boat more than a gold pendant. Besides, after the way he'd acted about her spending money on anything that wasn't essential, he could hardly splash out on a piece of jewellery for no apparent reason, could he, especially with Christmas less than two weeks away.

There she was again, making herself feel sick with all this second-guessing.

'Mummy, want to go to the beach,' Morgan told her, tugging on the hem of her jumper.

Robin looked hopeful, but Sabrina shouted 'No!' from the living room. It was a teacher-training day for all three children, and Lottie could seriously have done with them being in school because she wanted to try to find some time to work on the chest of drawers, which no longer looked like a chest of drawers but was in bits in the shed. She'd have to wear out her two youngest children somehow, so they'd be content to play quietly later. Or sleep.

'Not today, sweetie,' she replied. She couldn't face carting three children and everything they'd need the two miles it would take them to get there. Besides, they'd only visited it two days ago, and it was freezing outside. She'd take them to the park later – it was closer to home if they got too cold. 'I know! How about if we see if we can find some holly and pine cones instead?' she announced, the idea popping into her head. They could have a go at making a wreath for the front door and a decoration or two. They might even be able to pick some mistletoe if it wasn't too high up.

After an early lunch, the four of them made their way through the village, heading for the woodland on the hillside behind Applewell.

'Off somewhere nice?' Eleri asked, seeing Lottie walk past the cafe and rushing outside to speak to her.

'We're going to find some pine cones and holly to make a wreath,' Lottie said. She had her rucksack on her back which contained the usual tissues, first aid kit, spare hats and gloves (because no doubt one of them would lose something) and bags to carry their finds home in. The children were dressed in their oldest clothes as she knew they'd more than likely get covered in mud.

'I haven't done that for years,' Eleri said. 'Do you have to dash off or can you spare some time to pop in and have a look at my kiddies' corner?'

'You've finished it?'

'Not quite, but it's coming along.'

'Can we, Mum?' Sabrina looked hopeful. She hadn't been as keen as the other two when Lottie had announced they were pine-cone hunting, although Lottie knew her daughter would enjoy making the decorations later.

'Just for five minutes,' Lottie warned, 'but we're not staying for drinks or cake.'

Sabrina cocked her head to one side and studied her mother. 'You can have my pocket money, if you don't have enough money to pay.'

'Pardon?' Lottie's brow knitted.

'I heard you and Daddy talking. If you haven't got any money, you can have mine. My piggy box is full.'

Lottie draped her arm around her daughter and pulled her close, sudden tears pricking the back of her eyes. 'Thank you, sweetie, but we don't need your money.'

Damn it, now look at what Henry's done. His miserly ways had got Sabrina thinking they were destitute and couldn't afford a glass of cordial and a cookie in the local cafe. This was becoming ridiculous. The extension wasn't worth all this scrimping and saving. It wasn't as though they desperately needed it; it would be nice, and it would give the family more space, but it wasn't essential. They had a perfectly good house as it was.

Lottie was aware of Eleri staring at her oddly, so she straightened up, lifted her chin and said, 'Do you know what, I think we *will* have something while we're here.'

Bugger the cost. It was all well and good not having a holiday, and saving money by doing things that didn't cost anything, but she also wanted to be able to treat the children now and again, without having to worry about it. She wasn't buying them an expensive computer game – this was a drink and a cake. Surely Henry couldn't begrudge her that? And if he did, sod him.

After complimenting Eleri on the kiddies' corner, Lottie took a seat nearby so she could keep an eye on Robin and Morgan, who were busily making pretend food in it, and ordered all three children a drink and a cookie. She treated herself to a coffee and a slice of cake, and as she waited for Eleri to bring their order over, she admired the woman's handiwork. Eleri had done a fabulous job of repurposing the TV cabinet.

'So many people have commented on it,' Eleri said, popping three glasses of strawberry cordial on the table and seeing the direction of Lottie's gaze. 'I've told everyone it used to be something else in a previous life. I'm thinking of putting up a picture of what it looked like before. You won't believe the number of people who've asked me how I did it. I tell them it's all down to you.' She gave Lottie a thoughtful look. 'Quite a lot of folk have said they've got stuff they want to give a new lease of life to but don't know where to start.'

'You've seen the number of hours that goes into it,' Lottie began, but Eleri cut her off with a shake of her head and a grin.

'That's not what I meant. I was talking about showing people how to do it themselves, not doing it *for* them. You could run a workshop and people would pay you to attend.'

Lottie pulled a face. 'I'm not sure about that...'

'Have a think. There's definitely a call for it. Upcycling is on the up.' Eleri chuckled at her own joke.

It was a novel idea, and it was lovely of Eleri to have thought of it, but it simply wasn't doable. Not only did Lottie not know the first thing about running a workshop (showing Eleri how to do something was entirely different to sharing her craft with a load of strangers), but she didn't have anywhere to run a workshop. She could hardly do it in her shed.

She had to admit, though, that she'd enjoyed teaching Eleri the various techniques she used, and seeing the finished result had given her the same buzz she got from transforming something herself.

Oh, well, she'd just carry on doing what she was doing, and sell the odd piece or two for the fun of it. Which reminded her – she needed to upload the 'before' photo she'd taken of the chest of drawers on Instagram. And when she'd finished renovating it, she'd give Jo a call, and see if she was interested.

The door had been surprisingly profitable despite Natalie's acerbic comments, and Lottie was thoroughly enjoying repurposing the old pieces. Which brought her full circle to Henry, and the reason he was finding things for her to work on. Would he bring her something else today? Or didn't he need to any more…?

Chapter 28

Henry

In Henry's opinion, Aberystwyth was the logical place to go when pretending to be at work and hoping your wife didn't find out you were living a lie. It was far enough away so the likelihood of him being spotted by anyone from Applewell was slim, yet near enough so he didn't have to waste any more money on petrol than was absolutely necessary.

It also had a decent library, where he could stay all day in the warm. He didn't fancy wandering the streets when it was so cold outside.

He was early and the library hadn't opened yet, so he'd taken himself off to the seafront and watched the world go by for an hour or so, shivering on a bench. He could have done with leaving home later, but he was nearly always on the road by seven thirty, eight at the latest, and it was important he didn't deviate from routine, otherwise Lottie might smell a rat. He'd been sorely tempted to stay at home today, and tell Lottie he'd taken a day off. They'd had such a lovely weekend, and with the kids' school being closed because of a teacher-training day they could have done something nice together – but he didn't want to arouse Lottie's suspicions now the pair of them were back on an even keel.

By lunchtime, he'd done a fair amount of trawling the internet – and not just the job sites, either. He'd spent the first hour applying for anything he thought he had even the slightest chance of being considered for, but it had been the remaining couple of hours that had excited him.

Firstly, he'd set up an account with something called Freecycle. He'd recalled Lottie mentioning it as a place where community-minded people gave away items for free. From what he could gather, some of it was stuff that could easily be taken to a charity shop, but others were things no shop would accept, and would probably end up in landfill otherwise.

Henry found one or two items on Freecycle which might be good contenders for what he had in mind, but the downside was that he had to put in a request to their owners and hope one or the other of them would choose him to be the recipient of their unwanted possessions.

It was no way to do business.

Business. That was an interesting word... Henry knew he hadn't thought his idea through properly, but he wanted a few things in place before he shared it with Lottie. And even if they were able to get his idea off the ground, he'd still have to have a decent-paying job to fall back on.

There was also the issue of how long it took Lottie to turn something old and derelict into something new and useable. He wasn't sure of the length of time exactly, but he knew it was a good few days when all the separate hours she spent on a piece were added together.

Which didn't bode well for his idea.

Relying on Freecycle as a source of things to renovate was a bit hit and miss. Boot sales might be a better bet, but paying for something to work on would eat into any profits – and that was the same for charity shops. Delving into skips was even more of a challenge than Freecycle, because it would depend on him wandering the streets of various towns and villages and hoping he'd spot one which had something worthwhile in it – a long shot at best. He'd been lucky to find the chest of drawers in the one in Worcester.

As he mulled the problem over, it suddenly came to him that there was one place where lots of discarded items could be found – the household waste recycling centre.

Henry slapped a hand to his forehead. Why hadn't he thought of it before? It was genius! There'd be an endless supply of broken and damaged items no one wanted. He might have to hang around, waiting for suitable things to come in, but he could do that. OK, maybe not once he had a job, but he had plenty of time on his hands at the moment, and if he could build up a stock of things for him and Lottie to work on…

His wife had far greater skill and expertise than he, but Henry was sure she could teach him how to sand and paint – they'd make a great team. He could do most of the grunt work, leaving her free to work her magic – which would be a better use of her time. It would also hark back to the early days of their marriage when they wandered around boot sales together, picking up bargains to furnish their new home with. Those had been such enjoyable times.

Excitement surging through him, Henry decided to leave the library and head for the nearest civic amenity site, as it was called. First though, he'd have a celebratory sandwich and coffee on the seafront.

–

Sitting on a bench overlooking North Beach, Henry took out his flask and foil-wrapped lunch from his bag and as he ate, he mulled over his idea, wondering if Lottie would think he'd lost his marbles, or if she'd get on board with it. It wasn't as though he was planning on doing this rather than working (although the thought had occurred to him), but all businesses started small and he and Lottie didn't have to sink their life savings into the venture, or anything as drastic. The whole idea, as he saw it, was to renovate things at a minimum cost. No investment needed – apart from their time, which, he conceded, was a bit of a drawback. He hadn't forgotten his insight about what was important in life – his family – and he intended to spend as much time with the children as he could while they still wanted their old dad around.

Henry packed the remains of his lunch away and hurried back to his car to warm up, eager to see what the local amenity site had to offer.

The household waste reclamation centre lay on the outskirts of the town, on a large industrial estate. It took a bit of finding, but when he eventually drove in through the gates, excitement coiled in his stomach. Aside from the massive containers for metal, garden waste and card-board, there was one for wood, and he didn't even have to get out of his car to see that there might be a few suitable pieces in there.

He found somewhere to pull over which wasn't going to impede anyone with a boot full of rubbish to dispose of, and looked around for an attendant, spotting an older fellow in a Hi-Vis jacket and wearing several layers of clothes underneath it.

'Excuse me, I know this might be a bit of an odd question, but would I be allowed to take something from there?' Henry gestured to the container, wondering how he'd get into it and, more importantly, how he'd get out again.

'We're used to odd questions,' the man replied. 'Have you thrown something away by mistake?'

'Er, not exactly. My wife upcycles old furniture, and I wondered—'

'No, mate, sorry,' the man interrupted, shaking his head. 'It's not allowed due to Health and Safety. It used to be that anyone could take anything, but they stopped that years ago.'

Henry didn't need to ask who 'they' were – he took it to mean the local council – and his spirits fell. 'That's a shame.'

'You're telling me! You wouldn't believe the stuff people chuck out. It's criminal, that's what it is. I've seen perfectly good fridges, cookers, hat stands, wheelbarrows – you name it, people skip it.'

Henry nodded. 'That's why my wife upcycles things. She doesn't believe in throwing things out when they can be repurposed or mended. The problem is, it's hard to get hold of items she can work on, without paying too much.'

The man rubbed his chin. 'I'd like to help, but I don't see how I can. I can't let you dibble about and take what you want – they'd have my guts for garters. I daren't put anything to one side for you, either, as it's against the rules to let anyone take anything. It's a pity we don't have one of them tip shops, like they've got in Swansea.'

'A what now?'

'A tip shop – a place where you can buy stuff that's too good to be skipped. Operatives like me sort through everything that's brought in and set aside anything decent.

You can get stuff from there as cheap as chips, so I've heard.'

Henry said, 'But you still have to pay for it, right?'

'You don't often get something for nothing,' the man pointed out. 'It might be your best bet.'

Maybe, but Swansea was too far away to make it viable, Henry realised, his heart sinking. Oh, well, it was a good idea while it lasted. He hadn't been entirely sure where he'd been going with it anyway – it wasn't as though he could make a career out of rescuing bits of old furniture and handing them over to Lottie for her to do her thing. He'd still have to have a day job.

Henry was beginning to question his sanity. Was he so desperate to move into a different line of work, or had it been a pipe dream that had taken him away from reality for a few hours?

A bit of both, if he was honest.

He was about to thank the man for his time and leave when he said, 'I don't suppose there are any jobs going here, are there?'

The man's eyes widened and he pursed his lips. 'Now you come to mention it… Fancy a brew?'

–

The pay wasn't bad, according to Alan (the man in the Hi-Vis jacket) but it wasn't the most exciting job in the world and it meant being outside in all weathers. At the moment the pair of them were sitting in a Portacabin with a heater on full blast and a hot cup of tea in their hands.

Trying to sell feed to farmers and smallholders isn't exciting, either, Henry thought, and although he spent a considerable amount of time in his car travelling from one client to another, the farmer's 'office' was very often a draughty barn or a field. He'd been known to have to stand in the pouring rain, holding a shouted conversation with a bloke who was trying to persuade a load of stroppy cattle to go where they didn't want to go, while filling in a soggy order form that he'd had to dry out on the dashboard of his car later. Nope, Henry's job hadn't been all glitter and glamour, either.

'Then there's the general public,' Alan told him. 'You can get some right angsty blighters. I've nearly come to blows a couple of times. They don't listen, and when they do, they don't want to do what you tell them.'

Henry chuckled as Alan told him a few tales as they drank their tea and shared a packet of Hobnobs. There were three other operatives on duty besides Alan, and he'd asked one of the others to take over supervision of the site before he'd shown Henry into the little Portacabin for a quick cuppa.

'Of course, you'll have to apply through the proper channels,' Alan advised. 'The job is on the council website. Have you done this sort of thing before?'

Henry shook his head.

'Pity, they'll want a bit of experience. If you don't mind me asking, what do you do?'

It pained him to say it, but Henry might as well be honest. 'I'm unemployed. Got made redundant, Friday just gone.'

'Sorry to hear that. What did you do?'

'Agricultural feed salesman.'

'This'll be a bit of a comedown for you, then? If you was to get it, that is.'

'Not really.' Henry took a slurp of the strong tea and tried not to shudder. 'A job's a job, and I think this is a pretty worthwhile one.'

'What? Helping people dump their rubbish?'

'It's better they do it here, than on the side of the road,' Henry pointed out.

'That's true enough; I can't stand fly-tippers. They should be shot, the lot of them.'

Henry smiled at the man's no-nonsense, straight-talking outlook on life. 'I still don't like the idea of so much being thrown away, though. I assume the wood and the metal are reused?'

'Aye, the metal is sorted and melted down, the wood is pulped and turned into woodchip.'

'That's a shame,' Henry said, eyeing a pallet and wondering what could be done with it. It was a perfectly good pallet and it seemed wasteful to simply pulp it. Think of all the resources that had gone into creating it in the first place.

'Right, I'd best get back to work,' Alan said, getting to his feet.

Henry stood. 'Thanks for the chat and the heads-up on the job. I'll go online today and apply for it.'

'You can put me down as a reference, if you like. That should go some way to helping you.'

Henry was astounded. 'Thank you, that's very generous, but you don't know anything about me.'

'I don't need to. I know a rum 'un when I meet one, and you ain't it. Here…' Alan scribbled his details on a scrap of paper and handed it to Henry. 'Good luck, and let me know how you get on.'

Henry drove straight back to the library, feeling better about things than he had for days. He wasn't out of the woods yet, but things might be starting to look up.

His euphoria didn't last, though. He applied for the job and only met the cut-off date for applications by the skin of his teeth, and by the time he arrived home he'd talked himself down. He'd been so carried away at the prospect of getting a job at the council tip he hadn't thought it through properly. The wage was less than Alan had told him – Henry guessed Alan was the more senior guy on the site and was probably paid accordingly. Plus, the salary the job was advertised at was on a sliding scale, with the employee starting on the bottom point and increasing every year until the post-holder reached the maximum after five years.

It was only slightly more than his basic wage at Baldwin.

Still, any wage was more than he was on now, and he had to admit that some months the commission he earned was rather sparse, and had been getting less year on year as more clients had ordered online, thus cutting out the need for salesmen.

The only high point in the day was arranging to collect one of the items he'd requested on Freecycle on the way home. Taking a coffee table home for Lottie was probably the only constructive thing he'd do today.

Chapter 29

Lottie

The small woodland not far from Lottie's house was vastly different during the winter, to the rest of the year. A place that had previously rang with birdsong was now mostly silent; only the wind sighing through the bare branches overhead disturbing the deep peace.

That, and Lottie's children, because the boys, especially, thought the whole world needed to hear them as they raced around, kicking through the damp, fallen leaves and screaming at the tops of their voices. She pitied any small animals that lived there, as the noise was quite phenomenal.

A squirrel chattered overhead, his indignation clear, and Lottie sent him a silent apology.

Sabrina, at least, was relatively calm as she walked by her mother's side, but it didn't last long as the lure of damp leaves and muddy puddles won through her studied disdain.

Glad they were letting off steam, Lottie waited until the children began to tire – it took a while in Robin's case – before she attempted to gather them up to search for anything that could be used to make wreaths and garlands.

'Is this one okay, Mum?' Sabrina asked, holding up a large pine cone. It was the perfect shape and size.

'Boys, look what Sabrina's found. Do you think you can find ones like this?' She took it from her daughter and placed it carefully in one of the bags she'd brought along. 'Shall we leave the boys to find more cones and you can give me a hand picking some ivy? Remember the carol, "The Holly and the Ivy"? Why do you think those two plants are mentioned at this time of year?'

'Because they're Christmas plants?'

'They're Christmas plants for a reason,' Lottie told her. 'It's because they're evergreen, which means they don't lose their leaves in the winter. In olden days, it was thought of as a sign that spring would come again.'

Sabrina looked interested, so Lottie went on to share some other nuggets of Christmassy information with her as they searched for long strands of ivy which could be woven into a wreath. As they worked, Lottie kept an eye on the other two, praising them for their patience as they rooted around beneath the trees.

Eventually they had a fair collection of cones, ivy, small fir tree branches and holly – Lottie hadn't let them help with snipping twigs off that because of the thorns.

'I'll make us all some hot chocolate when we get back,' Lottie promised, picking up the bags of assorted foliage. There was a decent haul and she was sure the children could make some great decorations from it.

'Like Daddy makes it?' Robin asked hopefully, and suddenly Lottie was filled with a pang. It would have been nice if Henry could have been with them today. He would have loved messing about in the woods, and she found herself missing him.

Part of her still wanted to know what had been going on with him these past weeks, but an even larger part of her realised no good would come of knowing. Because once she knew, she wouldn't be able to *unknow*. The knowledge would sour things between them, maybe to the point where their relationship would never recover.

Lottie realised she was prepared to put everything behind her for the sake of their family and the love she had for Henry, because there was no doubt in her mind that she loved her husband as much now as she'd ever done. It would be a shame to throw it away and turn the children's lives upside down for what had probably been an aberration. As long as nothing like it ever happened again – and she still wasn't entirely convinced anything *had* happened in the first place – she could brush the whole thing under the carpet. That wasn't to say she wouldn't keep her eyes peeled in the future, but she'd happily put this in the past.

Sitting at the kitchen table surrounded by her children, safety scissors, pots of glue and glitter, Lottie was content. She and Henry had reconnected, they had Christmas to look forward to, and she was determined to make it their best one yet.

Until, that is, Henry arrived home early again. It wasn't being early that bothered her – it was the dilapidated coffee table he'd brought with him.

'Look what I've got!' he announced, shuffling into the kitchen, his face obscured by the piece of furniture he was carrying.

Abruptly, Lottie's doubts and fears resurfaced, and the thoughts she'd previously had about him bringing her things leapt into her head, claiming centre stage.

'I'll take it out to the shed, shall I?' he continued. 'Or do you want to have a look at it first?'

Lottie was still clearing up the glitter – the stuff got simply everywhere – so she used that as an excuse. 'I'll take a look at it later, if you don't mind.'

She straightened up and watched him sidle out through the back door. Did she honestly believe he had an ulterior motive for bringing her things? Was she really so conniving and cunning? And where was he getting all this stuff from, anyway?

Maybe he'd got bitten by the reusing bug since John Porter had given him the old boat, and he was now on the lookout for things he could scavenge. That's what Delia would probably say, if Lottie asked her.

Henry came back into the kitchen, blowing on his hands. 'It's freezing out there. I wouldn't be surprised if it snows soon.' He shrugged out of his coat and looked at Lottie. 'I couldn't help noticing you've made a couple of sledges.'

'I repaired the one I bought, and used the template to make another two. The kids will have one each if it does happen to snow.' She paused. 'Where did you get the coffee table?'

'Oh, er, I found it in a lay-by near Borth.'

She could tell he was lying as he had a shifty look on his face, but why would he lie about where he'd got it from? Who would leave a coffee table in a lay-by, anyway?

How strange.

So much for her vow to put her suspicions behind her. How could she, when he was behaving like this?

'What did you get up to today?' Henry asked, and she was sorely tempted to ask him the same question, and she would have done if she hadn't been so scared of his answer.

'We went to the woods and collected some fir cones and holly to make decorations,' she said. 'You ought to see the state the kids got into. Morgan was covered from head to toe in mud.' Lottie tried to sound as normal as possible, and she was fairly sure she'd succeeded. Now wasn't the time to confront him; she wanted to wait until she had some concrete proof first. 'Before we went, we called into Eleri's cafe,' Lottie added, slightly defiantly.

'And?'

'We all had drinks and some cake.'

She was expecting Henry to be cross, and she might not have told him at all if it hadn't been for the children, one of whom would surely blurt it out.

'That's nice. I wish I could have joined you.'

Yeah, I bet, she thought sarcastically, and sorrow swept over her. If her suspicions were correct, how was she supposed to deal with it? What was she supposed to do? How would she carry on without her soulmate in her life?

It would be so much easier if she didn't love him so very deeply...

Chapter 30

Lottie

Lottie delved into a large box of curtains and began rifling through them. She wouldn't be sure what she was looking for until she found it, and nor was she sure she'd find any suitable fabric, anyway. Most of the curtains in Under-Cover were too lightweight, or the wrong colour.

'Are you looking for anything in particular?' Catrin called. She was behind the counter, writing out sales tags and attaching them to the last batch of clothing the charity had been given, humming along to an upbeat Christmas tune on the radio.

'I'm turning a chest of drawers into a seat, and I need some fabric for the cushions,' Lottie said, checking that Morgan wasn't making a nuisance of himself.

Thankfully the other two were back in school today, so she only had her littlest to worry about. She planned on taking him to the park on the way back as a reward for being a good boy while she rooted around in the charity shop.

'I saw the photo you put on Instagram. You've got your work cut out to make that old chest of drawers into a seat. If you don't find anything there' – Catrin nodded at the box – 'Gracie might have something. Are you planning on making the cushions yourself?'

'Crikey! Not a chance. If I did, the seams would come apart as soon as anyone sat on them. I'm going to ask Gracie if she'll do them.'

'I saw your Henry yesterday,' Catrin said, as Lottie continued her rummaging.

Lottie noticed her slipping a Freddo bar into Morgan's hand, and she turned a blind eye. 'Oh? Where was that?' she asked.

'I was visiting my sister in Tregaron, and he was in the village. I waved, but I don't think he saw me.'

'He gets about all over the place,' Lottie said. 'I never know where he is from one day to the next.' *Or who he's with, apparently...*

She straightened up, suddenly losing interest in fabric as her thoughts took her in a direction she didn't want to go. 'I expect he wanted to supplement his sandwiches,' she added. Or did his mistress live in Tregaron? The village was close enough to Applewell, but not *too* close.

'He might have been, but when I saw him, he was going into a house down the road from my sister.'

He was what? 'Do you know whose?' Lottie asked, keeping her expression and her tone as neutral as possible.

'No idea,' Catrin said, cheerfully.

Lottie felt anything but cheerful. She felt like giving her husband a good shake. What was he doing going into a house in Tregaron?

She tried not to jump to conclusions. Whoever lived in the house might also own a smallholding, or a riding stable, or a pig farm, for all Lottie knew. Tregaron was extremely rural, with only a handful of houses and not much else. The house Henry had entered might well be on the outskirts of the small village and have a farm attached to it.

But her instincts wouldn't let it lie, especially since he'd told her he'd found the coffee table in a lay-by near Borth.

Borth was nowhere near Tregaron. It wasn't even in the same direction. Which made her wonder if he was trying to put her off the scent.

Other women whose husbands were cheating on them got gifts of flowers, or chocolates, or even jewellery. What did she get? A grubby, ring-marked coffee table that had seen better days.

She'd looked up the signs that your man was having an affair on the internet and Henry ticked nearly every box, apart from the one where men who were cheating tended to want to have more sex with their wives.

Lottie recalled him turning her down, but then she also recalled their passion earlier in the month. He'd not been as ardent and as loving as that for a long time, so the jury was still out on whether he ticked that particular box or not.

But however many boxes he did or didn't tick, she was convinced her husband was up to no good, and she was determined to find out what it was. And when she did, when she knew for certain, it would be the end of their marriage.

It saddened her beyond belief that it had come to this, but she was furious, too. How dare Henry throw away everything they had and everything they'd worked so hard for because of a bit on the side?

Lottie didn't feel she could take any more. For the last month or so, she'd been on tenterhooks because of Henry. And now this, just when she'd thought their marriage was back on track.

Absently, she picked up an odd curtain, feeling the thickness of the fabric between her fingers, and tried not to cry. She was exhausted, emotionally rather than phys-ically, the not-knowing draining her until she felt empty and hollow. She couldn't carry on like this; tonight she'd ask him outright. No doubt he'd lie to her (again) but maybe, just maybe, he'd tell her the truth. The timing might be crap with Christmas only a week away, but she had to know one way or the other.

She might have been able to forgive him – she'd been prepared to do precisely that yesterday in the woods – but only because she believed the affair was over.

He might not be having an affair she conceded (yeah, right – what other explanation could there possibly be?) but if he wasn't, he was still lying about something and that something was tearing their marriage apart.

They'd never had secrets from each other, or not to her knowledge at least. Not until now.

Even if he didn't have another woman, would she ever be able to trust him again?

Chapter 31

Henry

On the way home from his second day of pretending to go to work, Henry had noticed he'd had a message about the other item on Freecycle he'd expressed an interest in, from a lady called Crystal, who had said it was his if he wanted it.

He had pulled over and replied to it, thinking that he might as well fetch the baby piano for Lottie, even if his daft idea regarding what she could turn it into had been exactly that – a daft idea.

> Thanks. I appreciate it. Where are you and when can I collect? Henry Hargreaves.

At least he hadn't been late home this evening. In fact, he'd been a little earlier than usual, but for some reason Lottie hadn't seemed too pleased to see him. In fact, when he'd leant towards her to give her a kiss, she'd turned her head at the last moment and the kiss landed on her cheek instead. He hoped it had been unintentional, but he suspected not. His wife was being rather off with him again, and he had no idea why. They'd had a great weekend, and yesterday evening had been pretty good too, after he'd arrived home from 'work', although she hadn't been as enthusiastic about the coffee table as he'd hoped. He'd collected it from a house in Tregaron and he'd been rather pleased with it. Maybe she was tired after three full-on days with the kids, and he guessed she had probably been making up for lost time by working in the shed today while Morgan napped.

'Why don't I cook tonight, and you can get on with doing something else?' he suggested.

'Thanks. I'd like to spend an hour in the shed and do some more work on the chest of drawers.'

He smiled ruefully; surely that should be his line? His mates were only too happy to escape to their sheds, garages and gardens. In the Hargreaves family, it was the other way around. 'How's it going?'

'Why don't you see for yourself?'

He was right – she was trying to juggle the kids and her hobby, and he probably wasn't helping by bringing her more things to upcycle.

When he stepped inside the shed, he scanned the assorted pieces of wood propped up in various stages of being painted, and tried to make out which bit went where. It looked a mess but he assumed Lottie knew what she was doing. She usually did.

'I've left the bottom two drawers as is,' she said, 'and I'm going to use the top of it and cut it down to make a seat to go on top of the drawers. The back and the sides can stay as they are, or maybe I'll cut them down a little bit; I haven't decided yet. Then when I put it all back together, I'm going to use a couple of pieces of foam I've ordered, and ask Gracie to cover them, to make cushions for the seat and back.'

'Wow, you don't hang about, do you?' Henry said. 'I'll keep a lookout for anything else I can find.'

He couldn't quite decipher the look she gave him, but before he could try to interpret it, she said, 'I might already have a buyer for this. The woman who bought the coat rack said she was looking for a seat to go underneath it. I'm hoping this will do nicely.'

'I'm sure it will,' Henry said. 'But even if it doesn't, I have every faith in you. You'll sell it sooner or later. And my bet is on sooner.'

She ran a hand lovingly down one of the sides which hadn't yet been painted but had been sanded down. 'How was your day?'

Henry perched on the edge of the worktop, one Lottie had made out of pallets, and he thought of the pallet he'd seen in the recycling centre. It was a pity he couldn't tell her what he'd really been up to. Shuffling uncomfortably, he eased his phone out of his back pocket and put it on the worktop. There, that was better.

'The usual,' he said. 'Clients and stuff. How about you?' He was quite happy to stay in the shed for a while chatting to his wife, but he couldn't stay too long because he'd have to go inside soon to check on the children; although no doubt Sabrina would come and find them if Morgan was doing something he shouldn't. And if Lottie asked too many questions about work, he could always use the kids as an excuse to cut the conversation short.

'Morgan and I went to the park, and before that I called into UnderCover.' She picked up a piece of wood and turned it over in her hands. 'I had a chat to Catrin.' She gave him a look from underneath her lashes as though she expected him to say something.

'That's nice. How is she?' he asked politely. He didn't know Catrin all that well but she seemed pleasant enough.

'Did you know she has a sister?'

'Yeah, I went to school with her.'

'She lives in—'

'Mum! Sabrina painted my face. Look!' Robin charged in, his expression indignant underneath all the face paint.

'Come on, young man. Let's leave your mum to it.' Henry put his hand on Robin's shoulder and guided him back to the kitchen, where he found Sabrina with her paints, her tongue protruding slightly as she worked. Morgan looked like a cross between a tiger and a Klingon.

Henry tried not to laugh as he kissed the top of the little boy's head, avoiding the paint, and wondered what to cook for tea.

He found some chicken breasts in the fridge and a couple of jars of curry sauce in the cupboard. With rice, and a few poppadoms, it would make a quick and tasty meal. It would only take about half an hour, so he decided to wait a while, because he knew when he called Lottie in to eat she probably wouldn't go back out again, and he wanted to give her some time to herself to play in her shed.

'Dad, can I paint your face?' Sabrina asked, and Henry sighed. Having make-up and such like smeared over his face wasn't his idea of fun.

'OK, but I don't want to look silly,' he said.

'Why, who's going to see you?'

'Your mum. She'll laugh at me.'

'She won't care,' Sabrina said, and Henry was taken aback. His daughter was probably right – Lottie wouldn't care that much, if at all. She seemed to be caring less and less lately, despite the weekend, and once again he knew it was all his own fault and he had no one else to blame, but that didn't help.

Resigned, he sat at the kitchen table and gave his daughter a free hand. Did it matter how silly he looked? Sabrina was having fun, and that was all that mattered.

After she'd finished, he was forced to examine himself in the mirror, and was unsurprised to see that he had flowers dotted all over his face – she'd stuck sequins and sparkly bits on him, too. He looked an absolute plonker, but it had made his daughter happy and that's what was important.

'Right, you lot, I'd better start cooking tea. We're having chicken curry – OK, guys?'

There was some murmured assent, which gave Henry hope that they'd eat at least some of it, so he put the TV on for them for half an hour so they could wind down before they ate. Sabrina had her nose in a book, but he left the other two quietly watching cartoons while he set about preparing their meal.

When it was nearly ready, he shouted to Sabrina, 'Can you tell Mum that I'm just about to dish up? She's in the shed.'

There was silence for a moment, then Sabrina stamped past him out to the garden. But when she came back in, her mother wasn't behind her and Sabrina had a very peculiar expression on her face.

'What's up, sweetie? Is everything all right?' he asked.

'Mummy says she's got something in her eye.'

'Does she need any help?' He didn't want to stop what he was doing because it would either go cold, or if he left it simmering it might spoil.

Sabrina shrugged. 'I think she's been crying.'

'You do? Why?'

'Because she's sniffing and her eyes are red. Her face has gone blotchy too, like mine does when I've been crying.'

'No, I meant why has she been crying?'

Another shrug. 'I don't know.'

Henry was about to abandon his task when Lottie walked in. She didn't look at him; instead she went into the downstairs loo, and he could hear her washing her hands. When she came back out and took a seat at the table, he thought Sabrina may have been right, and Lottie had indeed been crying.

'Is everything all right?' he asked.

'Never better,' Lottie said, but she still didn't look at him, and he could have sworn she'd spoken through clenched teeth.

'I've made chicken curry.'

'Fine,' she said, but when he put her food down in front of her, she didn't eat a great deal. Instead, she pushed it around the plate.

'Sabrina's been painting my face,' he said, trying to make conversation. Since when had talking to his wife become so difficult? 'See?'

'Lovely,' Lottie said, but her attention remained on the meal she wasn't eating.

Henry stared at her with concern. She looked upset about something and he wondered what it could be. She hadn't been herself since he'd come home this evening; or should he say, she was acting the same way as she'd acted before the weekend. But he'd thought all that was behind them now that he wasn't being such a grumpy arse. Maybe she'd had something more on her mind than his moodiness, and he couldn't help feeling a little panicked over the swiftly growing distance between them.

Knowing now wasn't the time to ask – not in front of the children – he shelved it for later, when they were alone.

'Mum,' Sabrina whined. 'You haven't even looked at it.'

'What? Sorry, love.' Lottie looked at him; or rather, she stared in his direction but her eyes didn't meet his. What *was* going on with her?

He was none the wiser as he was clearing up after their meal, while Lottie was getting Morgan ready for bed. He'd given the countertops a final wipe over and had hung the dishcloth over the tap and she still hadn't come back down.

'I'll be up in a sec to bath Robin,' he called up the stairs. He'd just quickly check his emails and messages, then he'd wrestle Robin into the bath. That child had a major aversion to soap and water.

Now, where was his phone…?

Henry glanced around the kitchen, but he couldn't see it. Puffing his cheeks out, he tried to think where he'd seen it last, and then he remembered – he'd taken it out of his pocket when he'd sat on the workbench in the shed. It was probably still there, unless Lottie had moved it. Knowing her, though, she'd been so wrapped up in what she'd been doing she most likely hadn't noticed it.

He found it exactly where he hoped it would be, and he touched his finger to the screen to unlock it. Immediately his attention was drawn to a message.

> Give me a call? Crystal

There was a phone number underneath. So he did.

'Good afternoon, the Star Hotel?' a female voice answered.

'Hi, is that Crystal? This is Henry Hargreaves. You messaged me about the piano?'

'Oh, hi.'

'Where are you?'

'Danyravon.'

The next village, so not too far. 'When is a good time for you?'

'Would you like to fetch it now? The sooner it's gone the better.'

'Sorry, I can't tonight. How about tomorrow, during the day?'

They arranged a time and Henry reached for Lottie's scribble pad, flipped over onto a fresh page and wrote down Crystal's address.

'I've got to warn you, it's in poor condition and it's not got any innards,' she said.

'That's OK, Crystal, I'll see you tomor—' He broke off abruptly, almost jumping out of his skin on seeing Lottie standing in the doorway, her arms crossed. '—tomorrow,' he finished. 'Bye.' He slipped his phone into his pocket and tore off the sheet of paper with Crystal's address on and put that in his pocket, too.

Lottie shook her head slowly, her face inscrutable.

'I can't help it if customers ring me,' he said, feeling defensive. She turned smartly on her heel and he called after her, 'I said I'd bath Robin and I will.' She needn't have come looking for him.

'Don't bother,' she threw over her shoulder, and Henry frowned.

Had the weekend been nothing more than a mere brief upward blip in the generally downward slope their marriage appeared to be on?

Damn and blast, he had to get to the bottom of what was up with Lottie, but right now didn't seem like the best time. He'd give it a day or so and see if her mood improved. He knew he was being a coward, but he was scared of asking her just in case he didn't like what he heard.

Because what if she told him she didn't love him any more? What would he do then?

Chapter 32

Lottie

Even though Lottie had gathered herself together enough to go inside the house and try to eat the meal Henry had prepared, all she could see was the message on his phone. The words swum in front of her eyes, seared on her brain. So that was the woman's name – *Crystal*. Lottie had expected something classier, but then again, how classy could a husband-stealing hussy be?

When Lottie had noticed purely by luck (or bad luck – she had yet to decide) the incoming message on Henry's phone, she'd been in shock, not sure what she had read. She remembered snarling as the message faded and the screen went dark, and she'd desperately snatched up his mobile and swiped at it, tears welling up and threatening to spill over.

'Four fat snakes!' she'd hissed when she remembered it was password protected, and she didn't have the faintest idea what his password was.

With jerky, stabbing movements, she had tried a few of the more obvious ones, such as his date of birth, a mish-mash of the children's names, their wedding anniversary. The last had found her barking out a bitter laugh. As if he'd use that!

She'd imagined chopping his finger off to use his fingerprint before she had been forced to concede defeat as she'd heard her daughter's quick footsteps outside, and had swiftly dashed her tears away with the back of her hand so Sabrina wouldn't see.

How she'd managed to sit through dinner without screaming at him or throwing something at him she honestly didn't know, and she'd escaped upstairs as soon as she possibly could, leaving her lying, cheating, pathetic excuse for a husband to clear up on his own.

When he yelled that he'd be up in a minute to bath Robin, it took all her willpower not to break down and sob. Would this be the last time he'd bath their son? Was he planning on leaving her, on leaving his children? Oh, God, what would she do? How would she cope? She and Henry were a team, they'd had each other's backs; they loved each other, damn it!

Or so Lottie had thought.

From where she was standing or rather, sitting – she'd slumped onto the floor at the side of Morgan's bed, her hands clenched into fists as she willed herself not to cry – she might still love him, but he clearly didn't love her any more.

What had happened to make him fall out of love with her? Had there been a defining moment that she hadn't noticed? Was he in love with this 'Crystal' woman, or was it simply a fling? Did it matter *what* it was? Cheating was cheating, regardless of the emotions – or otherwise – of the cheater. His motives were irrelevant. That he'd done it at all, was.

Lottie couldn't imagine her life without Henry in it. She didn't want to. It was unthinkable.

Yet, she *had* to think about it, for her own sanity and for the sake of her children.

There was no way she'd be able to sweep this under the carpet now, to turn a blind eye and pretend it hadn't happened. She had finally accepted that even if she tried to carry on for the sake of the kids, the knowledge would rot her from the inside out, tainting every aspect of her life. Besides, her children deserved better than that, from her and from Henry. They could stay together for them, but she'd be so unhappy that her misery would be bound to rub off on them.

And what if he did it again?

Lottie let out a low moan as a terrible thought leapt into her mind. *What if he'd done it before?*

Was Henry a serial adulterer? He was on the road so much that she had no clue where he was, or who he was meeting. He could have been unfaithful to her for years, with any number of women.

Oh, God…

'Mummy, Daddy said he'd bath me.' Robin appeared in Morgan's room, and Morgan sat up, wide awake.

'I want Daddy to read me a story,' Morgan said.

'I've just read you one,' Lottie told him.

'You didn't.' He shook his little head firmly, forcing Lottie to wrack her brains. *Had* she read him a story? She couldn't remember.

'Where *is* Daddy?' Robin asked. 'Has he gone out again?'

'Isn't he in the kitchen?'

'No.'

'In the living room?'

'No.'

'Right, I'll go and find him. Robin, you stay here with Morgan and see if you can help him choose a story.'

Lottie got stiffly to her feet, her heart a leaden lump in her chest. If Henry had gone out without telling her, she'd—

Do nothing, that's what she'd do. There was no way she'd confront him tonight, not in front of the children. Their happiness was paramount and if she could spare them from their father's fickleness for a while longer, she would.

She shot down the stairs, taking them two at a time, and thundered into the kitchen, glancing through the open door of the living room as she dashed past. Sabrina didn't look up. Robin was right, his father wasn't in the house.

Lottie was about to find her phone to call him, when she noticed that the shed door was open. Knowing she'd most certainly not left it like that, she guessed that's where he was. He was fetching his phone. But surely he should have come back in by now? She hadn't moved it; she'd dropped it back onto the workbench, feeling somehow soiled after touching it, and that's where she'd left it.

With her heart in her mouth, Lottie opened the kitchen door and quietly made her way down the path to the shed. She had a fairly good idea what he was doing – he would be messaging his bit on the side, safely out of sight, thinking he was being clever.

She'd show him.

But it was worse than she'd feared. He wasn't just texting the tart, he was *speaking* to her.

'Sorry, I can't tonight. How about tomorrow, during the day?' He paused, then said, 'Two o'clock, great.' He reached for her notepad, scribbled something on it, then added: 'That's OK, Crystal, I'll see you tomor—'

He broke off abruptly when he saw her, and guilt flashed across his face. The expression was only there for a second, but she noticed it. And she also noticed the way he hurriedly tore off the sheet of paper he'd written on and put it in his pocket. Lottie would give her right arm to know what was on it – it was clearly something he didn't want her to see.

She shook her head, unable to speak, scared of what might come out of her mouth if she allowed herself to say anything. So she left him to it, and went back inside.

The hardest thing she'd ever done in her life was to act normally for the rest of the evening. She'd confront him, but she needed more proof, irrefutable proof that her lying, conniving, low-life husband couldn't wriggle out of.

The question was, how was she going to get it?

And how was she going to carry on without him once she had?

–

Lottie had been in bed for at least an hour, her thoughts a whirling, jumbled mess of pain and desolation, when she had a lightbulb moment. She'd looked through Henry's pockets earlier, searching for the piece of paper, but hadn't been able to find it (which made her even more suspicious) and she had finally gone to bed – Morgan's bed. She'd been lying there, listening to her son's soft snuffles and getting kicked every now and again as he wriggled and squirmed in his sleep, agonising over what she should do. How to proceed? She needed to be proactive, not reactive. If she wanted proof, she'd have to get some: moodiness, lying about where he'd been and secret phone calls weren't going to be enough. She didn't want to give him the chance to offer a rational explanation that would make her doubt herself, not when she knew in her heart that something was very wrong.

Lottie would never have described her husband as manipulative or duplicitous, but what could she think? She clearly didn't know Henry, that was for sure. If someone had asked her even as little as a couple of months ago whether she'd thought Henry would ever cheat on her, she would have given them short shrift.

But not now.

There had been something nagging at her subconscious all evening and when the lightbulb moment came, she sat up so quickly she almost woke Morgan.

'Shh,' she crooned, smoothing his forehead, and she waited until he'd settled back down before creeping out of bed and going downstairs.

Theirs was an old house, with creaks and groans abundant, but Lottie knew her home like the back of her hand, and she diligently avoided each noisy stair and breathed in as she squeezed through the half-open door into the living room, knowing full well that it squeaked at the smallest movement. After quickly finding what she wanted, she grabbed her phone from off the coffee table.

Going outside was just as fraught, as the back door tended to shut with a *thunk* unless you held on to it, and she winced as it clicked shut. Once outside, though, she was on safer ground, as her and Henry's bedroom (was it to be hers alone before too long?) was at the front of the house.

Breathing more easily, she unlocked the padlock securing the shed as quietly as she could and slipped inside. She was tempted to turn the light on, but she didn't, just in case. Instead, she used her phone to provide some illumination, and hoped it would be sufficient.

Her notepad was still on the bench and didn't look as if it had been moved. Propping her phone against a pot of paint, she drew the pad towards her, crouching down so she was at eye level with it, and scrutinised it closely.

Just as she'd hoped, there were faint indentations in what appeared to be a pristine sheet of paper. If she'd have turned on the shed light, she probably wouldn't have seen them, but in the oblique light from her phone, she could just about make out the marks.

Clutching the red crayon she'd appropriated from the children's art and craft box firmly in her hand, and holding her breath, Lottie turned it lengthways and stroked it gently across the paper.

Like magic, the barely there writing began to appear, and when the words were finally revealed, Lottie realised she had what she needed.

An address.

–

'You want to do *what* now?' Delia asked the following day, the disbelief in her voice unmistakable.

'Follow him. I know where he's going to be and when.'

'That's not exactly following, is it, and are you sure you know what you're doing?'

'If you mean, "Am I sure I want to find out what he's been up to", then yes.' Lottie was speaking quietly because the children were hanging around her this morning, as if they knew something was going on. Sabrina and Robin were usually good at entertaining themselves, and Morgan more often than not joined in because his siblings were much more fun than his mother. But not today. They'd been somewhat subdued during breakfast and she'd hardly managed to escape one or the other of them for longer than a few seconds, not even to go for a wee.

'Is this where I come in?' Delia asked.

'Please.'

'I'm not too keen on sneaking around after Henry.'

Lottie was appalled. 'I wouldn't dream of asking you to do that! I'd hoped you'd be able to mind Morgan for a couple of hours, and pick the others up from school.'

Delia's sigh of relief wafted over the airwaves. 'You don't have a car,' she pointed out. 'And you're not insured to drive mine.' Her friend clearly wasn't keen on Lottie's idea. Lottie herself didn't know whether she was keen on it, either. But she had to know for certain – she *had* to!

'I don't need to use your car. I've made other arrangements.'

'Like what?'

'Donald Mousel.'

'You've asked Donald to help you find out whether your husband is having an affair?'

'I didn't put it quite like that,' Lottie replied. 'I asked if he could take me to Danyravon at one o'clock today.'

'What do you intend to do? Wait in his taxi until Henry shows up at this woman's address? And then what?'

'I'm not that stupid. If I wait in the taxi, Donald will guess what's going on and it'll be all over Applewell by teatime.'

'Sooner, knowing Donald. His heart is in the right place, but he's a bit of an old busybody and he loves nothing better than a good gossip. Remember when George Nightingale got it into his head to run away to Liverpool?'

Despite her misery, Lottie uttered a small chuckle. George, ashamed that people knew he was a hoarder, had planned on leaving Applewell because he thought everyone had been talking about him. Donald's taxi had been his transport of choice and Donald had been instrumental in making George see that no one cared about his hoarding – the only thing they cared about was George himself.

'I'll ask him to drop me off a couple of streets away, and I'll wait for Henry to show up.' Wait was too nice a word – she was going to lurk. Thankfully the Star Hotel – Lottie shuddered at the thought of what Henry intended to do inside its walls – was in the middle of the small village, overlooking the tiny harbour, so she wouldn't look out of place sitting on a wall or a bench and admiring the view. All she'd have to do was to make sure Henry didn't see her before she saw him. Lottie had checked out the hotel on the internet, and she'd even done a virtual walk past it. She was surprised that a small establishment like the Star Hotel rented rooms by the hour, but maybe business was slow. Besides, if the other occasions when Henry had been late were any indication, he would be in there for a damned sight longer than an hour.

Lottie clenched her jaw to hold back the tears. Now was not the time for breaking down – there'd be plenty of opportunities to do so over the days, weeks and months to come. What she needed to do now was to stay strong and hold her nerve. Which wasn't going to be easy, and goodness knows what she'd do when he arrived at the hotel. Would she barge in and kick in the door to their room, to find him and his floozie in a compromising position? Or would she skulk away, her tail between her legs, and sob on a bench next to a litter bin?

Whatever happened, however she dealt with it, one thing was certain – after today, her life would never be the same again.

Chapter 33

Henry

Danyravon was one of those seaside places that had sprung up in days gone by because of its tiny inlet of sheltered water. Originally it had probably been a fishing village, but now it relied on tourism for its existence. There were several B&Bs, one or two pretty shops selling assorted gifts, a cafe, a Chinese takeaway and one proper hotel which was called the Star.

Henry rarely visited Danyravon as there wasn't much demand for animal feedstuffs amongst its tiny population, but there was a riding school nearby that he was familiar with, and several farms on its outskirts.

The Star was right on the seafront. From the outside it looked less like a hotel and more like someone's house, with net curtains at the windows and a chipped and faded gnome on the step. A 'Vacancies' sign hung from plastic suction grips in the bay window, and when he rang the doorbell, an old-fashioned ding-dong sounded from deep inside.

'It's open,' a female voice called, so Henry pushed the door open and went inside.

Immediately in front of him was another door, this one already open, the olive-green tiled walls and floor of the porch leading into a wide hallway with a set of stairs carpeted in a garish blue, green and red pattern, and adorned with a hideous flowery paper on the walls. A chandelier hung from a ceiling that was Artexed to within an inch of its life.

When he spotted a short, rotund, middle-aged woman with blue hair, wearing an apron with the body of a naked man on the front (the picture's modesty was preserved by a fig leaf) and wielding a feather duster, Henry wondered if he had the right address.

'Uh, s-sorry, I was looking for a lady called Crystal,' he stammered.

'You've found her. Henry, I presume? Come in.' She gestured for him to move closer. 'What do you think?' Her arm shot out to encompass the hall.

'Very nice,' he said, not meaning it in the slightest.

'Don't lie – it's hideous. We've just bought the place and it needs some serious work. Talk about being stuck in the last century. If this doesn't bring back awful memories of seventies guest house landladies, I don't know what will.' She lowered her voice. 'We even found a stash of nylon sheets in the back of the airing cupboard. Remember them?'

Henry couldn't say that he did; he had no idea what she was talking about.

'Never mind. Let's show you the piano, and if you see anything else you can take off my hands, feel free. We've moved everything we want to get rid of into the family suite at the front. It's jam-packed, even though we've shifted loads already. You're not in the market for a nineteenth-hand mattress, are you? I wouldn't call it second-hand because it's older than Methuselah, judging by the sag of it. And don't get me started on the stains.'

Henry looked at her in horror. 'Er, no, thanks. Just the piano.' Although if there was anything else that wasn't saggy or stained, he might be interested.

'Follow me,' Crystal instructed.

Henry was pleased to see that her rear was encased in a pair of leggings and a long T-shirt, with no hint of the naked male backside that he'd been secretly dreading. 'Why the apron?' he asked, as they came to the first-floor landing.

'A friend gave it to me as a joke but it's come in rather handy, and as I won't be able to wear it when I'm serving breakfasts I thought I'd get my use out of it while we're doing the renovations. And it makes Mrs Griffiths next door frown when she sees me in the garden with it on, so that's a bonus.'

Henry decided he liked Crystal.

She stopped, a hand on an ancient doorknob with a keyhole beneath it. 'Here we are. Brace yourself, it's not pretty. The smell is interesting too – mothballs and boiled cabbage is the best way I can describe it, although why a bedroom should smell of cabbage is beyond me.'

Crystal flung open the door with a flourish.

Henry sucked in a breath. Crumbs, it was like looking inside a crammed-full junk shop. Was that a standard lamp with a pink tasselled shade? And that dressing table with the age-spotted mirror was simply enormous. He guessed the wood might be mahogany, but he wasn't sure. It was dark and imposing, and a serious piece of furniture.

Crystal saw the direction of his gaze. 'I've got someone coming to look at that later,' she said. 'I was tempted to hire a skip and bin the whole lot, but surely someone, somewhere, must have a use for this stuff. A few bits are almost antique. The piano is over there, by the window.

It's only a small one, and the legs come off, and it doesn't weigh half as much as it should because, as I said, the innards are missing. We found it in the second-floor bath-room.' She giggled. 'I didn't like to ask what it was doing in there.' She pointed to a picture balanced on top of what Henry thought might be a commode. 'I don't suppose you'd like a framed print of a flamenco dancer, would you? It was all the rage when I was growing up – my mother had one just like it.'

Henry looked at it. To be fair, it had a certain charm, but the woman's swirling dress was so near the flames of the campfire he was worried it might catch fire.

'Didn't think so,' Crystal sighed. 'Maybe if it was mounted and had a different frame?' She barked out a loud laugh. 'Who am I kidding? I'll have to persuade the charity shop to take it, but they've had so much off me lately that they cringe when they see me coming. It's only a little shop...'

'Have you tried the one in Applewell?' Henry suggested helpfully. 'They might be interested, and I know a lady who'd probably take any sheets or curtains you don't want.' He was eyeing the dusty, sun-striped, crushed-velvet monstrosities in a most alarming shade of mustard that hung at the bay window. The colour might have been called gold at one point, but it now looked more like baby poo. He pulled one of them across a fraction to check, and grimaced. Yep, baby poo. 'This room has got the most gorgeous view,' he said, gazing out at the tiny harbour with its narrow strip of beach to the side of it. 'It's peaceful, too.'

'That's what we're hoping to achieve – a peaceful, tranquil retreat,' Crystal said. 'Sort of Zen-chic, if there is such a thing.'

Henry could see how that would work. Danyravon was a far cry from the bright lights of Aberystwyth, and the Star would make an ideal hotel in which to spend a relaxing holiday. Eventually.

Crikey, a woman sitting on a bench down there didn't half look like Lottie. She'd been turned around on it, staring inland rather than out to sea, but she'd swivelled back to face the harbour before he'd managed to get a proper look.

Thinking about his wife made Henry recall the reason he was there, but now that he'd seen inside the Star, there was one thing he had to ask before he got down to business. 'Are you taking bookings while you renovate?' He couldn't imagine anyone wanting to stay here in its current condition.

'Good lord, no!' Crystal looked appalled at the idea.

'I only mentioned it because the sign in the window said "Vacancies".'

'Bugger. I must take that down. Right, do you need a hand getting the piano out, or can you manage?'

'I can manage,' Henry said, and Crystal left him to drag it out by himself, after telling him to give her a shout when he needed help getting it down the stairs.

He'd taken the legs off it, and was just about to manoeuvre it through the door while wondering if it would fit in the car or whether he'd wasted both his time and Crystal's, when he heard Crystal yell, 'Oi, what do you think you're doing?'

'Looking for my husband,' a woman who sounded exactly like Lottie yelled, followed by the noise of a door crashing open.

And just as he was thinking that his wife was so much on his mind at the moment that he was seeing and hearing her at every turn, a woman who most definitely *was* his wife shoved open the door to the bedroom he was in, barging straight into the piano and knocking him backwards.

'*Lottie?*' he gasped, winded.

'Caught you!' Lottie cried, then froze. Her eyes darted around the room, before coming to a halt on him.

'What the hell?' he demanded, pushing himself away from the wardrobe he'd fallen back on, and rubbing his shoulder.

'Oh, sh—sugar. You're not… I mean, I thought… Oh, *Henry.*'

'Do you know this woman?' Crystal appeared in the doorway brandishing her feather duster like she meant business.

'She's my wife,' Henry said, weakly. He put a hand out to steady himself. What the hell was going on? 'Lottie, what are you doing here?'

'I could ask you the same thing!'

'I was collecting this.' He pointed to the piano. 'For you,' he added, in case she didn't understand.

'What about Crystal?' Lottie was wearing a horrified expression.

'What about me?' Crystal asked.

Lottie whirled around. '*You're* Crystal?' She turned back to Henry and her face drained of colour. 'Oh.'

'What's going on, Lottie?' This was surreal. Henry was starting to wonder if there was a hidden camera, that this was some kind of a weird wind-up, and his shocked face would be broadcast on a TV show in the not-too-distant future.

Lottie slumped against the wall. 'I thought… you were acting… I'm still not sure I… Shit.'

'What's going on, love? Are you having some kind of a breakdown? Should I call an ambulance?' Crystal's tone was sympathetic.

'I'm fine,' Lottie said, but Henry could tell she wasn't.

'How did you get here? Are you following me or something? And why are you asking about Crystal?' He gawped at her, trying to find a logical explanation, but failing.

'Donald's taxi.' She looked so miserable his heart went out to her. No matter what was going on, she was his wife and he loved her unconditionally. Seeing her so distressed upset him greatly.

'Are you in some kind of trouble?' he asked.

'No, but I thought you were,' she replied, in a small voice.

'Look, if everything's okay, do you mind if I get on? I've got a meeting with my architect in half an hour.' Crystal was backing away, her expression wary.

'Of course not. I'll just…' Henry gestured at the piano.

'I'd… um… better leave,' Lottie said.

'Is Donald waiting for you?' Henry's thoughts immediately went to how much a taxi ride to Danyravon and back, plus waiting time, would cost. It seemed to be the only thought he could effectively grasp right now. Everything else was a swirl of dreamlike and outlandish images.

'No. I'll have to give him a call to fetch me.'

'The car's outside.' Henry fished in his pocket for his keys and tossed them to her. Lottie caught them instinctively. 'I'll take you home, but first I need to load this in the boot. And Lottie? We need to talk.'

He waited for her footsteps to fade on the stairs before he resumed his grappling with the piano. He'd meant it when he'd told her they needed to talk. It was about time he told her his side of the story regarding the redundancy and his jobless state, because she'd patently discovered his secret – and was unmistakably not happy about it.

Chapter 34

Lottie

Seated in the car, Lottie had never felt so humiliated in all her life. It even exceeded the time when her waters had broken in the middle of a school concert, and she'd overheard some parents telling their children she'd wet herself rather than them having to explain the more gruesome details of having a baby to their offspring.

Ok, so she'd got it wrong big time today, but she was still convinced Henry was cheating on her. And now she'd totally blown her chances of finding out for sure. He'd be ultra-careful from now on, and she knew he was already being careful because she hadn't found any evidence so far. Crystal didn't count, but that failed to explain why he'd been so secretive about meeting her.

And if Crystal wasn't the name of the woman he was seeing, what was? Who was the woman with the sharp blonde haircut and the sharp navy suit? For Lottie, the desire to discover the truth was eating away at her so deeply it hurt. How much longer could she go on not knowing but suspecting? Look at the mess she'd made of things today. She'd made a right idiot of herself, and goodness knows what that poor woman in the Star Hotel must think of her.

Lottie had been all set to use any means possible to find out what Henry was getting up to and who he was getting up to it with; but when she'd seen him standing so blatantly in the window of what was undoubtedly a first-floor bedroom and then drawing the curtain, she'd seen red.

She couldn't remember leaping up from the bench and charging across the road, and neither did she have particularly good recall of barging in through the hotel's door and thundering up the stairs. She did, however, remember pushing open the first bedroom door she came to with some considerable force and being shouted at by a woman who she'd ignored, before trying the next door along the landing.

What she'd seen, compared to what she'd expected to see, had taken her several seconds to make sense of, and even then she wasn't sure she'd been successful in deciphering the image before her. Her fully clothed husband had been in a room chock-full of old furniture. There wasn't a naked woman, or any other kind of woman for that matter, in it, and the anticipated bed of iniquity proved to be several grubby mattresses propped up against a wall.

Humiliated and embarrassed didn't begin to describe it, and when she'd discovered that Crystal was a middle-aged, dumpy woman with blue hair, Lottie's mortification had been complete.

Henry's shocked expression would be seared on her eyelids forever, and the woman believing that she must be having a breakdown sent shudders of shame through her.

Thankfully, Henry had spared Lottie from having to phone Donald Mousel to ask him to come to get her: if he saw the state she was in…

Because she *was* in a state, and not just because her attempt at catching Henry in the act had so spectacularly backfired. The reason was more to do with Henry's parting shot – that they needed to talk.

Dear God, he was going to tell her he was in love with someone else. She simply knew it. And no matter how convinced she'd been that he was unfaithful, she wasn't ready for such a life-changing confession.

For some reason, if she'd caught him in bed with his lover, her indignation and outrage might have kept her going. But to have a cold-blooded discussion after she'd made an incredible fool of herself was unbearable.

She desperately needed some ammunition, and soon, to bolster her dwindling fury, but there was none to be had. Or rather, none that she could get her hands on, his phone being about his person and locked, and there being nothing incriminating in any of his pockets or in his wallet. The only place she hadn't scoured was the car, but he'd be daft if he'd left anything in here because she frequently drove it on the weekend to go to the supermarket or—

Lottie sat up straight and her eyes widened. There was one place she hadn't thought to look, and that was in his briefcase. Come to think of it, the battered old case normally lived at the bottom of the stairs where he had a habit of leaving it, but she couldn't remember moving it since last week. In fact, she couldn't remember seeing it at all lately. Which meant he probably hadn't brought it into the house, which also meant he might have something in there he didn't want her to see.

It was a long shot, she realised, but the long shot was sitting innocently on the back seat of the car.

Lottie made full use of the opportunity.

Expecting the briefcase to be heavier than it was, she reached into the back, grabbed hold of it and hauled it towards her, nearly knocking herself in the face with it.

When she looked inside, she saw the reason – no laptop. There was very little in it at all, in fact, apart from some letters and some bits of paper.

She took everything out and began examining them.

What she saw made her gasp in shock.

There was a P45 and a letter giving notice of redundancy. Both documents had Henry's name on them, and the letter was dated over a month ago and gave a last day of employment as the Friday just gone.

Lottie flopped back in her seat, her mind spinning and her pulse hammering.

This couldn't possibly be right.

She checked again.

It *was* right; she hadn't misread anything. Henry had been made redundant, and was now unemployed.

Two thoughts shot into her mind, and she wasn't sure which one she was the most upset about – that he hadn't told her such momentous news, or that he'd lied to her about going to work these past few days.

–

Lottie sat in the passenger seat of their car, staring rigidly ahead, as Henry opened the boot, put the back seats down and, with Crystal's help, loaded the small piano into it.

She didn't think he'd noticed that his briefcase was on her lap, its contents in full view, until he climbed into the driver's seat and glanced across at her. She was conscious of his eyes on her face, but she didn't trust herself to look at him. Relief at him not having an affair warred with hurt that he hadn't confided in her. Was she so much of a harridan that he felt he couldn't tell her he'd lost his job? What did that say about the state of their marriage (she deliberately ignored that her thinking he was unfaithful said just as much)? And how did he think he'd have been able to keep it from her?

'I'm sorry,' he said, his voice breaking as he stared at the letter. 'I didn't mean you to find out like this.'

'When were you going to tell me?'

'When I'd got another job. I didn't want to let you down.'

Lottie shook her head in disbelief. 'You do realise I thought you were having an affair?'

'A *what*?' He actually laughed, and Lottie wanted to sock him one, despite her abhorrence of violence. 'That's ridiculous!' he cried.

'As ridiculous as you not telling me you've been made redundant, then pretending to go to work?'

Henry sobered immediately. 'I suppose not.' He drew in a sharp breath and let it out slowly. 'Is that why you followed me?'

'I didn't follow you. I overheard you arranging a time and I saw the address. I got here before you did.'

'You've been going through my pockets?'

Lottie bit her lip. 'I used the crayon trick.'

'The what—? Look, never mind.' His expression was stricken and his eyes were wild. 'I'd never be unfaithful – I love you more than life itself.'

'And I love you too, which was why I had to know.'

'I can't believe you thought I was having an affair with Crystal. She's old enough to be my mother.'

'I didn't know that, did I? I thought she was the woman I saw you with in Builth Wells.'

'You followed me to *Builth Wells*?'

'No, Delia took me and Morgan to the Winter Fayre at Penygraig Castle and I saw you go into a cafe with a blonde woman as we were driving past.' Lottie's gaze sharpened. 'Who is she?'

'Someone I hoped would give me a job. It didn't pan out.' He rubbed his hands across his face and she only just heard his muffled, 'I've let you down. I'm a rubbish husband.'

'Did you lose your job on purpose?'

'Of course not!'

'Then you didn't let me down, and you most definitely aren't rubbish! These things happen, and it's unfortunate it's happened to us, but we'll get through it as long as we're honest with each other. We're a team, and never forget that, you daft man.' She blew out an exasperated breath, her emotions in a tail spin, the overriding one being relief, funnily enough. Redundancy they could overcome: adultery not so much.

She'd have to take time to process this new development, but before she did, there were more important things to concern herself with. 'Right, what are you doing about getting another job, and how can I help? It's probably about time I went back to work, so I'll start applying for jobs, too.'

'But I wouldn't want you to work, and not because I want you chained to the kitchen sink, but because it'll cost a fortune in childcare and the children still need you to be there for them.'

Aw, Henry was so sweet. She was still mad with him for making her think the worst, and was even more cross that she'd had to go to such lengths to discover the truth, especially since he'd have had to have told her eventually, but she could see his actions were coming from a good place.

'We've got some savings behind us, so we're not destitute,' she said, feeling guilty that she'd taken such great delight in telling him she'd visited the cafe. What she'd spent in there could have bought them their food shopping for a day.

'But what about the extension? I know you've set your heart on it—'

He looked so upset, she wanted to cry. 'Stuff the extension, it isn't important. If we never get it done, it doesn't matter! What's important is that we're all together, we're healthy and we love each other.'

Lottie leant across the gap between the seats and pulled her husband into her embrace, feeling ridiculously happy and light-hearted considering Henry was out of work. She'd meant what she said, and she was just about to give him the best kiss of his life when his phone rang.

'I'd better get that,' he said. 'It might be about a job.'

It was, Lottie deduced by the expression on her husband's face, and when the call ended Henry had a sparkle in his eyes that she hadn't seen for a while.

'I *am* a rubbish husband,' he declared with a smile. 'At least, I hope I will be,' and he proceeded to tell her all about the interview he'd just been invited to, and the man who'd made it happen.

Chapter 35

Henry

This time Henry didn't need to sneak his best suit out of the wardrobe and into the car, and neither did he have to change in the toilets of a roadside cafe. This time Henry had a kiss from his wife, who wished him luck before he set off.

He and Lottie had had an in-depth discussion regarding the pros and cons of taking the job with the council, and the pair of them had jointly arrived at the decision that he should accept should he be offered it.

The one thing that stuck in his mind was Lottie's ambivalence about the extension.

'I'm not bothered,' she'd said. 'These past few weeks has made me appreciate what's important in life, and having more room in the house so everyone can better avoid each other isn't one of them. We are a family and we should enjoy spending time in each other's company. When you get another job, I suggest we blow some of our savings on a decent family holiday – nothing exotic, but somewhere we can all enjoy.'

'Good idea,' he'd said, but he still felt a little sad that Lottie wouldn't have the large family room with the new kitchen that she yearned for. She was right, though – what was the point of scrimping and saving for goodness knows how long, when what they should be doing was living life right now. And by that, he didn't mean splashing the cash around; what he'd meant was not working all hours God sent in order to buy something unnecessary.

Henry angled the car's rear-view mirror and checked that his tie was straight (it was) and that he didn't have a dribble of toothpaste on his chin (he didn't). He thought he might be overdressed, but having never been to an interview for a household waste operative before, he hadn't been certain what to wear, so he'd fallen back on his suit, and hoped he didn't look too smart.

'Come in. Mr Hargreaves, isn't it? It's a pleasure to meet you. My name is Hazel Dean and I'm the HR officer. This is Gareth Warner and he's in charge of waste management.'

Henry shook hands with them both and sat down, feeling extremely nervous, but he was pleasantly surprised when neither of the interviewers asked him a great deal about any previous experience in household reclamation sites, because it was clear from his application form that he didn't have any.

After they'd run through the usual spiel of asking him to tell them about his working life to date, and him attempting to stress that he had many transferable skills and wasn't averse to hard work, the more challenging questions began.

'Why do you want this role?' Ms Dean asked him.

Ah, now, he could have a stab at answering that, having anticipated the question and prepared an answer. He spoke eloquently (he thought) on needing to conserve the earth's resources and not simply send things to landfill. He'd done his research and could even quote facts and figure, ending up with, 'I want to become part of the solution, not the problem.'

Ms Dean and Mr Warner were nodding in agreement.

'You certainly have the commitment,' Mr Warner said. 'Is there anything you want to add in support of your application?'

'Actually, there is, but I'm not sure whether it will support my application or whether you'll think I'm being presumptuous.'

'Go on.'

Henry took a deep breath and said, 'My wife is extremely active in reducing, reusing and recycling in terms of upcycling and repurposing items of furniture, and since seeing the incredible work she does, I think the council needs to have one of those tip shops, where discarded yet perfectly functional items can be bought by people who can find a use for them. The society we live in is a throwaway one, and it's criminal that so many things are being discarded when they still have a great deal of life left in them. When you consider all the resources that go into manufacturing the things in the first place…' He trailed off, self-conscious, realising he'd overstepped the mark and was doing himself no favours in trying to convince these people that he was right for the job. If anything, he was talking himself out of one by saying that fewer people should visit their local waste centres.

'Thank you, Mr Hargreaves,' the HR manager said, getting to her feet. 'That was… enlightening. We'll be in touch soon to let you know whether you've been successful, as we have other candidates to see.'

Of course they did – he wasn't naive enough to think he was the only one.

Not feeling at all hopeful, he stood up and shook hands.

Downhearted, he made his way to the reception area and was in the process of signing out and handing his visitor's badge back, when he heard his name being called.

'Mr Hargreaves?'

Thinking he'd forgotten something, he patted his pockets to check for his keys, his phone and his wallet and was relieved to discover all three were still about his person.

'Mr Hargreaves? Can you pop back into the meeting room again? We'd like to have a quick word.' Ms Dean was smiling.

Oh, my God, they were going to offer him the job!

Henry could barely contain his excitement as he followed the HR officer back to the room where his interview had been conducted, and took the seat he'd sat in a few moments ago.

'Let me be frank,' Mr Warner said. 'You're not the right fit for the job.'

Henry's heart sank to his feet so fast he thought he might pass out. How cruel to call him back before they'd even finished interviewing their full quota of candidates. He must have unimpressed them so spectacularly that they didn't need to deliberate about his application. Oh, well, at least he knew and wouldn't be on tenterhooks all over Christmas waiting for a phone call or a letter.

'However, we think you're perfect for something else. This role is brand new and hasn't even been advertised yet, but it's a project we've been considering for a while,' the man said.

'Oh?'

'How do you feel about managing your very own tip shop? There is a council-owned building directly behind the reclamation site that has recently been vacated by the Parks and Highways Department which would be perfect. It would be your responsibility to source goods from the skips, and prepare them for sale. What do you say?'

What could Henry say? 'Yes, please!'

'As you so rightly pointed out, far too much is going to landfill, and anything that isn't has to be reprocessed. All monies earned from the project will go towards other council-run initiatives, so it's a win-win situation. Of course, there still will be plenty of things that have to be recycled, such as cardboard, scrap metal, wood...'

'Including broken furniture?'

'Well, yes, obviously. We can't be trying to sell tables with missing legs.' Mr Warner chuckled and shot Ms Dean a look.

'Ah,' Henry said. 'I've got an idea about that...'

–

Henry picked up the bottle of reasonably expensive wine he'd bought on the way home, and poured himself and Lottie a glass. 'Here's to us and our future.' They were celebrating him having got the job by enjoying a child-free night at home. Bliss!

They clinked glasses and Lottie took a sip. 'Mmm, this is nice. Crisp but not too snappy.'

'You just made up the snappy part' he said. 'I'm sure wine aficionados wouldn't call anything "snappy".'

'You'd be surprised – they use all kinds of words to describe fermented grape juice.'

'Not those ones, obviously. Stop behaving like a heathen and eat your meal.' Henry grinned at her, opening his mouth when she speared a prawn with her fork and held it out to him. 'That's delicious,' he said, after chewing slowly and swallowing the morsel.

He gazed into her eyes, and she gazed back. Heat began to build inside him and he cupped her face, leant across the table and kissed her, gently at first but then with rapidly growing desire.

Food forgotten, Henry took Lottie by the hand and led her upstairs. And afterwards, when he held her in his arms, her breath soft and warm on his chest, his heart was filled with joy, and he whispered, 'I love you, Mrs Hargreaves.'

'I love you too, rubbish man. Now, are you going to keep talking or are you going to show me just how much you love me?'

'Again?'

'*Oh, yes!*'

Chapter 36

Lottie

Lottie crept downstairs, careful to avoid the creak on the third step and the seventh, hooked a coat off the rack near the front door and stuffed her bare feet into a pair of wellies. She hadn't expected to give the children this particular gift on Christmas Day, but when she'd been drawn to her bedroom window by the oddly coloured light outside, and she'd realised what was responsible for it, she'd been unable to go back to bed.

Despite not having gone to sleep until well after midnight – her late night had been more to do with her husband making love to her than the pair of them tiptoeing around placing stockings under the tree – and anticipating Morgan's leap from the land of Nod before the cockerel crowed, she was surprisingly wide awake and ready for the day.

As she eased open the door to the garden and stepped outside, her foot sank into a good six inches of snow and she turned her face up to the heavens. Huge fat flakes were falling softly, and it was so quiet she imagined she could hear each one land. The world lay under a white fleecy layer of excitement, and she smiled as she thought of her children's faces when they saw that not only had Santa been, but that it had snowed in the night.

What a wonderful thing it was to be a child, she mused, as she fetched the sledges from the shed ready to prop them in the hall for the children to see as soon as they raced headlong down the stairs. Their joy and amazement would be a delight to watch.

But first they would have to get through the present opening, her insistence they eat anything other than chocolate for breakfast, and then the fight to get them dressed in warm clothing, before they dashed outside to play in the snow.

The day beckoned, but Lottie took a few precious moments to revel in the stillness of the early morning. Magical – that was the best way to describe it, and she offered up a silent prayer of thanks. She had so much to be thankful for: Henry, for his support and misguided thoughtfulness; their gloriously wonderful children who made her smile every single day; Henry's new job and the opportunities it gave both of them… But most of all she was thankful for the love they shared. And she had no doubt that Henry loved her as much as she loved him.

Quietly, she brought the sledges in one by one, but it wasn't until she'd leant the last one against the wall near the front door that she realised Henry was watching her from the living room.

He had a glass of orange juice in one hand and a small, gift-wrapped box in the other. 'Buck's fizz,' he said, after handing her the glass and laughing at her shocked expression when she tasted the alcohol in it.

'What are you doing up?' she asked, her eyes on the present. Was it for her? She hoped so.

'I thought we could have a minute to ourselves before the mayhem starts,' he said. 'This is for you. Open it,' he urged.

Lottie took it and carefully eased the string from around the wrapping paper, revealing a pretty box that looked as though it might contain jewellery.

Feeling apprehensive – didn't Henry know her enough by now to realise she didn't do jewellery? – she eased the top of the box off and lifted the tissue paper to reveal the most gorgeous hairpin she'd ever seen.

'It's for your hair, instead of a pencil,' Henry said. 'And it's made from stuff found on the beach. That's what they call sea glass.' He pointed to the tiny beads surrounding a smooth flat stone.

Henry did know her well enough, after all.

'It's perfect,' she whispered, and she took it out of the box, twisted her hair into a bun on the crown of her head and slid the hairpin into it.

Lottie kissed him, and they stood for a while, arms wrapped around each other, until a noise from upstairs indicated the children were stirring.

'Quick, open yours,' she said, going over to the tree and rooting around underneath. She handed him an oddly shaped package.

Henry said, on seeing the wooden mug, 'Did you make this yourself?'

'Of course.'

He traced the engraving of the five figures she'd carved into it – two adults and three children. 'I love it. I love *you*,' he said, and he was about to kiss her again when shrieks shattered the peace and the thunder of three pairs of feet overhead made him smile.

Lottie's heart filled with love, and tears welled in her eyes as she watched him with their children. It was all she'd ever wanted, for them to be a happy family. It looked like wishes sometimes did come true.

Epilogue

Lottie

The huge workshop had a tendency to echo when there was only Lottie in it, but today the space rang with the sounds of chatter and laughter, and the rasp and bang of tools. The air was redolent with the tang of paint and sawdust, and there was a vibrancy that was missing when she was in there on her own. Although she prized the quiet times when she could mend broken things and bring other items back to new life, it was the sessions where she helped others upcycle their own unwanted objects that she loved the best.

'How are you getting on, Jo?' she asked, gazing assessingly at what appeared to be a jumbled mess of assorted pieces of pallets, but which she knew would eventually be transformed into a substantial garden chair that would withstand the weather and look even lovelier when adorned with fat, padded cushions.

'Fine, I think. I've sketched out what I think should go where, but I'm not sure how I'm going to angle the back. I want a slight recline on it, otherwise I'll be sitting bolt upright.'

Lottie and Jo discussed how she could achieve that, and Lottie rubbed the woman on the arm as she made to move off. 'You're doing a fantastic job,' she enthused.

'I'm so glad you told me about these workshops. Although I simply adore the coat rack and that lovely seat I bought off you, there's nothing like making things with your own fair hands, is there?'

'I agree – and the more people who have the skills, the knowledge and the enthusiasm to make do with what they've got, the better.' She looked up as the door opened, expecting to see Henry, who was located in the tip shop next door.

At Henry's suggestion, the tip shop had been named Your Turn – as in 'your turn to own an item previously owned by someone else' – but the person hovering hesitantly was someone who Lottie would never, in a month of Sundays, have expected to see.

Cautiously, she walked over to Natalie Sharp, forcing a smile on her face. 'Can I help you?' she asked, wondering if it was just pure nosiness that had brought the woman here.

'You might be able to.' Natalie's eyes cut away to the various people beavering away on their projects. There were seven of them taking part in the session today. 'I'd like you to repair my son's bed.'

'What's wrong with it?'

'I don't know what he's been doing to it, but it's suddenly gone rather rickety.'

'Are you referring to the fire engine bed? The one you bought from Nighty Night?'

Natalie nodded. 'Can you repair it, or not?'

'No, sorry, I can't. But *you* can.'

'What do you mean you can't? I thought that's what you did.'

'I teach others to repair and renovate their own things,' Lottie said calmly. 'I can teach you, too, if you want.'

'I don't think so. I'll have to buy Callum another one.' Natalie lifted her nose and looked down it, but she made no move to leave.

'You could have asked me this yesterday when you saw me at school,' Lottie said. 'So why are you really here?'

Natalie looked away.

'Were you just being nosy?' Lottie persisted, a small, teasing grin on her face.

'Might have been. Everyone's talking about it.' She waved a dismissive arm around the workshop.

By 'everyone' Lottie assumed Natalie meant the other mums at the school gates, and maybe one or two other residents of Applewell.

'Is Callum's bed really in need of repair?' Lottie asked, still unsure whether to be amused or cross.

A nod.

'I tell you what, why don't I pop round later and take a look? I'm not going to mend it for you, but I'll show you how you can fix it yourself.'

'I'm no good with a screwdriver and whatnot,' Natalie objected.

'It's lucky you probably won't have to use a whatnot then, isn't it? And I'll give you a quick lesson in how to use a screwdriver.'

Natalie narrowed her eyes at her. 'How much will you charge?'

'Not as much as having to fork out for a new bed.' Lottie sighed. 'You can have this on the house. I'd prefer to see you fix the darned thing than scrap it. Too much of that goes on already, without me adding to the problem.'

'That's very kind of you,' Natalie said. 'Actually, now I come to think about it – would it be possible to do something with it to make it look more like a boat?'

Lottie bit her lip to avoid laughing out loud. Dear God, she had a pretty good idea why Callum's bed had suddenly become rickety. 'It might be possible, but you'll have to learn how to do it yourself. Now, why don't you take a gander at what these lovely people are doing? You never know, you might be bitten by the renovating bug yourself.'

Henry

'What did Natalie decide to do, in the end?' Henry asked, as he and Lottie lay in bed later that evening, enjoying a post-lovemaking snuggle and chatting about their day.

'She said she'd think about it. I can't see her rolling her sleeves up and wielding a hacksaw, no matter how much money it saves her in the long run. Callum, on the other hand, is a budding carpenter – when I popped around earlier, there was nothing wrong with his bed except for a mysterious loosening of quite a few of the nuts and bolts. Then Robin told me that Callum had confided in him that he was going to have a boat for a bed, too. You've got to admire the kid's ingenuity.'

They lay there in silence for a while, Henry's arm around her, feeling the weight of Lottie's leg across his, and marvelling at his luck that this wonderful, talented, multi-layered woman was his wife.

He'd never felt so happy and contented. He'd found a job he loved (he never would have guessed he'd be so passionate about other people's unwanted possessions); he was able to spend more time with his family; and Lottie was flourishing in her new role as a tutor. She had also been approached by the local secondary school to give a talk on reusing and upcycling. Who'd have known that

Lottie's make do and mend philosophy would become so popular?

'Have I told you recently how proud I am of you?' he asked, nuzzling her hair. 'Or how much I love you?'

'Nope. Not since last night.'

'Then I need to tell you again,' he murmured.

'Why don't you show me instead?' his gorgeous wife suggested, and he was more than happy to oblige.

Henry Hargreaves, he said silently to himself, *you are the luckiest man in the world!*

Acknowledgements

Authors often thank a whole bunch of people first and foremost who have helped them get a book off the ground, before thanking those who are truly important – the readers. I want to do it the other way around, so my heartfelt thanks go to my wonderful readers, because without you I wouldn't write. Stories are meant to be read (or listened to) and that's the only thing I've ever wanted in my writing career – to take someone away from the real world for a few hours and transport them to somewhere magical. So, thank you for reading my stories and allowing me to carry on writing.

Thanks go to others, too: Emily Bedford, for her editorial skills in bringing out the best in the story; Belinda Jones for polishing my rough words and making them gleam; the pixies and elves at Canelo for everything they do behind the scenes and for the lovely cover.

I mustn't forget my family, either: my husband's unstinting support and providing me with endless and very welcome cups of tea; my mother for reading everything I write; my daughter just for being there. And my dog, who is my constant companion as I slave over a hot computer, and insists I take a break now and again to take her for a walk.